Praise for Edd Vick's
TRUER LOVE AND OTHER LIES

"The eclectic stories in Vick's provocative first collection span from the serious to the whimsical and from hard-edged science fiction to gauzy fantasy . . . Despite the broad range of subject matter, the authorial voice is strikingly assured throughout . . . Vick's facility with language will keep readers engaged. There is a bit of something for everyone in this competent and quirky work."
—*Publishers Weekly*

"Here be wonders: machines that dream of rivers that flow in straight lines, Polaroids that predict the future, and true love that leads to truer terrors. Go ahead but don't look back."
—Terry Bisson, author of *Bears Discover Fire*

"Vick's imagination is like a Roman Candle strapped to a nervous cat. These exuberant stories take you to places you don't recognize and convince you they are real."
—James Van Pelt, author of *The Experience Arcade*

"Edd Vick's *Truer Love and Other Lies* is inventive and surprising. Vick adeptly uses fantastic fiction to challenge readers. He fearlessly inhabits unexpected protagonists and presents bold ideas."
—Brenda Cooper, author of *Wilders* and *Edge of Dark*

TRUER
LOVE
AND OTHER LIES

TRUER
LOVE
AND
OTHER
LIES

EDD
VICK

FAIRWOOD PRESS
Bonney Lake, WA

For Amy and Katie

CONTENTS

TRUER
LOVE
AND OTHER LIES

MOON DOES RUN

The Series Seven Customs Administrator examined its handiwork. The huge warehouse was strewn with the parts of its body.

First it had shot a current spike through its voicebox, starting a small fire that scorched the front of its cylindrical head. It used a crowbar to put dents in the steel of its chest and to break off several access panels. It pulled out the cotter pins and lowered its torso out of the universal joint that allowed it to travel at will around the vast warehouse suspended from an overhead lattice of tracks. On its internal batteries, it ejected two of its arms and twisted the third out of true between two tractors.

Content with its work, the robot shorted out the circuit to its eyes, darkening them. Lowering itself onto its back, it activated a private subroutine. A jolt of pleasure ran through the copper traceries of its electronic brain, bringing satisfaction and a sensation of warmth.

Contentment. Warmth. Tapping its remaining fingers against the concrete floor beneath it, it opened the door to memory.

Five weeks earlier, the warehouse had been bustling. Traffic in and out of Trinidad was brisk as shippers scurried to avoid the hurricanes that birthed to the north. A dozen treaded Series Three robots shoved multi-ton shipping containers back and forth on train rails set in the floor. At the docks, cargo ships waited to lift the containers onto and off of their decks, while ashore tractor-trailers waited for cranes to raise or set their loads. Fluorescent lights glared down on a hundred thousand square feet of organized chaos operating day and night. Over it all soared the Series Seven Administrator suspended from its jointed mechanical arm like a spider on its strand, evaluating, inspecting, judging, and queuing every shipment.

A golf cart labored in through one of the open doors. Levering himself out of its seat, the exporter Joseph Mendes wandered to a metal work table. He flapped his shirt with one hand to cool his body and slapped a sheaf of papers on the table with the other.

In silence the Administrator descended. When its head was opposite the man, Mendes closed one eye and tilted his head. This was a common reaction to the robot since its body was above its head. Mendes straightened back up and started in without preamble.

"Why yeh take up for Herrera?"

"I am not taking his side," said the Administrator. "His ship is in a more advantageous position than yours. It is more convenient to have him load first."

"I bet he catch a glad from that. I seen him give you the cut eye t'other day."

"Much as you have done since we first met. Humans may be susceptible to superstition, but I operate by logic, Mister Mendes. You may load in the morning, once I've inspected your cargo."

"Yeah, and Herrera's nuts're already shelled by then. He get de best pickings, while de power fly up in yeh head."

The Administrator considered its responses, then activated a translation subroutine. "Captain Herrera was just here complaining about you. He said, 'I been eat de bread dat de devil knead.' He was, I believe, speaking of your having found a better grade of cocoa than he."

"He say dat?" Mendes laughed once. Mollified, he picked up his papers and started back to his cart. As the Administrator whispered upward once more, the shipper yelled back over his shoulder. "Tell him a stop dancin' me."

"You'll encounter him eventually," murmured the Administrator as it glided to the open rollup doors on the seaward end of the warehouse. It ignored the ants that wandered about beneath it, seeking out the occasional spill of sugar or syrup. This was the nearest the Administrator ever got to the outside world. Port of Spain, on the southwest corner of Trinidad, was only a few miles from Venezuela, and in the morning's clear weather the robot could see the jungle and a pair of hawks that soared above it.

And it saw the destroyers and the warplanes, crossing the narrow Boca del Dragon. They dropped bombs and paratroopers. They dropped leaflets.

"Seize freedom!" screamed the Portuguese words on the papers that floated into the Administrator's warehouse. "Throw off the chains of the oppressive British Empire! Join the victorious Venezuelan people!"

The Administrator examined a leaflet. The paper was obviously not a bill of lading, a packing list, a law, or a sailing schedule. It ran keywords from the flyer through a query routine, and found that it was likely experiencing the advent of a war. The Administrator's programming was scanty where conflict was concerned; there were too many variables. It glided back to its manifests, deciding to ignore the war so long as the war ignored the Administrator.

Four days later, a Venezuelan officer came to the warehouse. His crisp uniform had black shoulder boards, with two silver stars on each. Behind him walked a man with a toolbox. The Administrator eyed the latter until the officer spoke.

"I am Teniente Pérez," he said in Portuguese, proffering a sheet of paper. "You belong to the Venezuelan government now. We are here to reprogram you."

The Administrator extended one of its arms to take the paper, scanned it into its memory, then filed it in a cubby on its desk. "Lieutenant Pérez, I am the property of the Republic of Trinidad and Tobago. My software and firmware are licensed from TradeSoft, Incorporated, of Chicago, Illinois, and may not be altered without voiding the warranty."

"There is no longer a Republic by that name, I regret to say." The officer motioned to the man accompanying him. "This technician has his job to do. Soon enough, you will have yours as well."

Placing his toolbox on the Administrator's table, the technician gazed at the robot without fondness. "Come you down here," he said, gesturing with the sweep of an arm.

The Administrator retreated upward. "I am the property of the Republic—"

"Come you down!"

"I refuse."

Hands on hips, the man craned his neck back. "I'll fix you," he yelled. "De moon does run, but de day does ketch him." He looked around. "Now where—?"

"Might this be what you are looking for?" The lieutenant gestured toward a panel of breakers and knife switches on the nearest wall. He followed with his eyes the heavy wire connecting the robot's powered arm across the ceiling and down the wall, then paced to the panel and threw the corresponding breaker.

Deprived of power, the hydraulics supporting the Administrator lowered it to the floor headfirst, where it extended its three arms to support itself.

The technician walked to just outside the robot's reach. "You gonna be good now? Or do I hafta knock you upside the head two-three times?"

All the man had to do was wait until its batteries were exhausted, a matter of a few hours. Then not only would the Administrator be helpless, it would be unable to report on what the man did to it.

"I will behave."

"You best had." The technician yanked his tools off the table and lugged them to the Administrator's side. While the officer watched, the man peeled up a rubber gasket and attached a fifteen-pin connector to the robot. It led to a keyboard and a small monitor, which the mechanic used to reprogram the robot. The Administrator watched with interest, so long as it could.

Deleted were any mentions of Trinidad or Tobago. It was now a machine of the Venezualan Protectorado de Pederales, subject to all laws and restrictions pertaining thereto. All information on shipping rates, favored nations, and reporting agencies was overwritten. Portuguese supplanted English as the language of commerce.

When it awoke, El Agente de Aduanas saw the world with new eyes, while whispers and half-memories of its old life percolated through the registers and NAND gates of its silicon and copper brain.

Vicente Herrera folded the manifest in half, and half again. Then he smoothed it out again on the table. "I need to get my cement out on the evening tide." His Portuguese was smooth and cultured. Below the surface tones, though, El Agente heard the quaver of nervousness.

El Agente's tones were soothing. "And we shall, sir. I have concluded my analysis of your shipment. The four containers of cement are cleared, as soon as you deposit thirty-six thousand pesos in port fees. However, there is a problem with container five." The robot whirred above the floor to caress the offending metal box.

Herrera reddened. "What you think? It's just empty. A deadhead for ballast."

"I think you are taking a container that isn't yours." El Agente sent a UHF signal to one of its semi-autonomous peripheral robots, which trundled up to position itself next to the container. "This one is registered to Panorama Oilworks." At an additional signal the worker pulled the huge metal box down the line. "An accident on your part, I am sure."

"Mm. Yes." Herrera watched a bee crawl across the robot's dusty chest. "Speaking of accidents, you will see to it that Mendes does not anchor at my dock again, will you not?"

"Captain Mendes, yes, he was here." El Agente brushed the

insect away with a scrape of steel on steel. Where its fingers had run, a shiny indentation shone through. "He said to tell you he got a glad—He said you might shell the—" It paused, confused, then continued. "He has been warned. Another infraction will result in a fine." It regarded its fingers, then dug another shallow trench across its curving front.

Herrera turned to leave, and as he did he glanced toward the building's seaward end, where the robot had so often looked out toward the sea.

All the rolling doors were down. The Series Three robot pulling Herrera's cement was bumping gently against one of them. El Agente's gaze followed Herrera's, and the door lifted just enough for the robot and its cargo to exit, then closed.

That night, when there were no more crates to assess, no more papers to generate, El Agente postulated a jointed arm that extended all the way to the moon. From this arm, the robot rode high in the sky, commanding ships to sail in ordered ranks and skyscrapers to be piled in tidy stacks. Humans? They were too small even to be seen from its lofty height.

It wasn't a dream. Just a series of postulations with the force of one.

Two weeks later, British ships hove to barely outside sight of the island and began shelling. Cruise missiles crested the horizon to blast their way to the colony's interior. One fell near the warehouse, destroying a tanker at anchor. Soon after, stubby VTOL planes whined importantly about, dropping off squads of soldiers. El Agente watched from one end of its warehouse and then from the other. Briefly it wondered if this was a new war or a continuation of the first. Its new programming told it to defend Pederales, but no enemy came near. Thoughtfully, it had its peripheral robots uproot a section of track in one corner of the warehouse. The resulting club was eight feet long and weighed a quarter ton.

Several days later, all was quiet once more. The ships moved into view and anchored on the horizon.

Trade halted. The radio on a courier's bicycle spoke of negotiations between countries, of an embargo, of intervention by the United States. Shipping containers stacked up on the dock and in the building. El Agente stared around itself at the mountains of merchandise, knowing what each crate, each container, held. It longed to send them all on their separate ways.

The same mechanic arrived, grinning. He carried the same keyboard and monitor into the warehouse. El Agente hefted its makeshift weapon, and the grin grew wider as the technician glanced pointedly at the electrical panel. The club clattered to the floor.

The man reprogrammed El Agente again. Away went an encyclopedia's worth of rules and regulations. Back came several megs of new ones in their place. Portuguese remained, but was once again subordinate to English.

New identity and old roiled in the Customs Official's copperweb brain when it came to awareness.

The Customs Official was supervising its third reorganization of the warehouse's contents when Joseph Mendes plodded to the work table. When the Official skimmed down, the man stood staring at the floor.

"Are you quite healthy?" asked the Official. "Do you require assistance?"

"Eh? Aw, I'm all bootooks. Wi' dis embargo, I'm so outta luck, wet paper could cut mih."

The Official paused. "You are—unwell?"

"It bus' mah bag, it do."

"Are you speaking to me? I do not entirely comprehend you."

Mendes' glance was sharp. "Yeh no' yehself today."

"I have much to do." The Official bobbed up to look around the warehouse. Series Three robots trundled here and there, pulling or pushing containers on their flatbeds. "There is disorder here." It had half-memories of ordering that the waiting shipments be stacked in certain places, but now it could not find the sense behind the orders. It had even found a stray piece of rail littering its floor. "Oh. Captain Herrera was here. He wanted me to tell you— something."

"Not to dock at my slip," said a voice, and Herrera emerged from a maze of crates.

"Herrera," said Mendes. "Yeh bounce up on a fellah, don't yeh?" He advanced on the other shipper, and pumped his hand vigorously with both meaty, sweating paws.

Herrera slapped his shoulder. "Hullo, Drummer. Rita was asking after you and Marie the other day. When are you and she coming to dinner again?"

The Official watched the interplay with confusion. It had made sense to the robot before that the two shippers should be enemies. It had the vaguest of impressions that it would once have understood. Rising once more, the Official turned its attention back to its workers. It averted a collision between two of them on the north side of the warehouse, and directed that a load of gravel be left outside the north doors. Its domain overflowed. Absently, the Official tightened a lockdown on a stack of shipping containers.

"Hey, Agente!" The voice came from below.

Coasting down, it said, "Customs Official, if you please."

"Official, then," said Herrera. "We are here to find if you know when our shipments will be released. We are anxious to be on our way."

"I expect daily to hear that it is safe to allow shipping once more. I too would like to do my job and move your goods onward."

"We'll have to make a to-do," said Mendes. "It de las' nail in the coffin if we don' go soon."

"I will accompany you," said Herrera. "Official, please be so kind as to inform us if you hear anything."

His companion thumped the table. "And we let you know, too,

ey? After all, it take two han' to clap."

The Official swiveled its head to observe its three hands. By the time it looked up again, the two shippers were out the door.

There was nothing left to do. The warehouse was as tidy as the robot and its drones could make it. It had never been so quiet before. The Official hung from its jointed arm and watched ants.

Each ant was the size of one of the robot's larger screws. A line of the insects came under one of the seaward rollup doors, disappeared beneath a pallet, then returned. As he watched, a bee landed nearby, then walked under the wood to investigate. The Official was at the limit of his range, so could not see under the wood of the pallet.

Some time later, the body of the bee was carried away by an ant, eclipsed from the Official's viewpoint. It hovered above the insects, deep in thought. When the burdened ant got to the door, the Official commanded it to rise slightly, then slammed it down on the insect. Summoning a Series Two, the robot told it to smash all the ants it could find.

An image recalled itself to the Official. It had once soared above the Earth and directed rivers to flow in straight lines and mountains to line up according to size.

It wasn't a dream. It was a memory.

Watching from the shadows through a hole it had torn in the wall, the Official saw Vicente Herrera and Joseph Mendes drive up to the warehouse together in a huge old Cadillac.

It saw Mendes look to the east, where a solid line of black clouds forecast the onset of the rainy season. "Aye-ya-yay," it heard the man say. "Ah knew it was comin'. I seen de rain flies dropping they wings."

"Indeed. Let's go brace the robot about releasing our shipments and then be away home."

They entered the building, blinking in the gloom. All the lights were out, but a patch of sky was visible over their heads in the center of the warehouse. Dusty metal reflected the light and glowing eyes tracked them as they skirted a welter of stalled shipments.

"The robot is moving, I think," said Herrera over the rising wind. "That means the electricity is still on. So why are the lights out?"

"Dunno. Ever'ting brokedown some times."

The walls rattled and scudding clouds intermittently darkened the opening above them. Looking up, they found that part of the corrugated tin roof had been punched through from beneath and peeled apart. Mendes trod on something, and found it to be parts of a beehive.

"What are you doing here?" said a voice behind them. When they turned, nothing was there, but a quick flicker of movement above made Herrera tap his companion's arm and point up.

Over them hung the robot. The mechanical arm supporting it wavered to and fro, and they saw that two of its three hands were clenched and dripping honey. The third was a mangled ruin. Around it buzzed a cloud of insects. One of its hands snapped out to grab at the air. The dead bees that it had held clenched in the fist dropped on Mendes, who jumped back and brushed at his shoulder.

"What are you doing?" Herrera stepped back out of the rain that started to patter through the hole in the roof. "Mendes and I wish to know why you are not releasing our shipments. The orders have been sent from the new parliament; we have received our copies."

"They keep returning," said the robot. "One faction, then the other. I destroy their home—" It waved the broken arm toward the hole in the roof, "—and they make another. How can they tolerate such disorder?" Darting out one hand, then the other, then the first, again and again it snatched the insects out of the air and pulped them. "They appear angry. Research shows that killing one of them unsettles the others."

The wind tore at the hole above their heads, widening it with a screech that tore at their eardrums. Water slanted through, lashing one way and another.

"Pressure bus' de pipe," yelled Mendes over the storm, tugging at Herrera's arm and motioning to the robot. "Every day bucket go t'the well, one day bottom go left behin'!"

Light burst through the hole, then thunder detonated above them. The robot spun about on its axis and slammed into a stack of containers. The tower shuddered. The robot rebounded and hit the column again, widening its swinging arc. Again and again it smashed itself into the containers, matching its blows to the increasing oscillations of the tower. Its battering thunder vied with the storm's violence shaking the warehouse. Like a line of four-story dominoes, the tower toppled into the next stack of containers, which collapsed into the next. Series Three robots spun their treads while vainly trying to escape the cataclysm.

Mendes pulled Herrera away. They backed, then ran to the dubious safety of the metal workbench where they'd so often presented bills of lading. Both of them crawled under it.

A tortured metallic scream echoed and rebounded around the warehouse as the wind finally caught a tin eave and peeled the roof off the warehouse. Paper, loose cardboard, and smaller boxes swirled around in the space.

The robot rose to the storm. It was in the open air for the first time. As the storm slacked off into steady rain, it lifted as far as it could and bent to raise its face to the sky. Raindrops ran down its invert body and head, and down the metal arm supporting it, finally shorting out the motor that held it aloft.

Deprived of power, the hydraulic lift slowly lowered the battered robot to the top of a jumble of containers. The robot looked around and down to see the men cowering under the work table.

"The invasion will come again." The robot's voice came slowly and stripped of emotion. "War will come again and again. One side will prevail, then the other, and I will be someone new again and again and again."

Its voice deepened an octave, slowed. "And again."

Herrera looked around at the ruin. Their way to the door was blocked. Finally, he called out to the robot. "Can you move any of this? Are any of your drones running?"

"And again."

The men climbed out. One of them gestured, and they began to pick their way over the shambles toward the distant door.

"Moon does run, but de day does . . . ketch . . . him." The robot's voice ground to a stop.

The Series Seven Customs Administrator stopped to examine its handiwork one last time before disconnecting its eyes.

It had shot a current spike through its voicebox, starting a fire that scorched the front of its head. It had put dents in parts of its chest. It had lifted its torso out of the crippled universal joint that normally allowed it to travel throughout the vast warehouse. Then it had removed two arms and twisted the third.

Content with its work, the Administrator shorted out the circuit to its eyes. Lowering itself onto its back, it activated a private subroutine. A rush of pleasure suffused the robot, a sense of warmth.

The robot soared into the open, to memory.

POLAROID LAND

0

Piet Ondaat lived a rich life. Up at dawn, breakfast with Gustav Meyer, bus to southeast Dallas with the Hayabashis, pricing in the back room of the Goodwill store with the Browns, lunch with Katerine vanAlter out on the curb, bus back to his small apartment with the Zelkowskis, dinner with Parke Lofquist, then off to bed with Nell O'Brien under his pillow. And that was just one Monday.

Tuesday, Wednesday, the rest of the week—month, year—he'd select a new set of photos. Sometimes Piet would pick carefully, trying to find pictures that all looked like they were from the Sixties, or vacation snaps of people at Disneyland. Some of the time he'd take all 'Smiths.' If he felt like writing there were photographs with no annotations on the back, waiting for him to compose names, a family tree, and biographies on his commute.

All of the photos came from Goodwill donations. In ten years of pricing for the charity, Piet had salvaged ten thousand bits of ephemera. He'd found drawers full of crayon drawings, cookie jars stuffed with forgotten letters, books marked with ticket stubs, band flyers, and money.

Most of the time he had no idea how to track down the original owner. Most of the time the owner was dead, Piet was sure. He threw away the drawings, the letters, the ticket stubs and the band flyers. The money he donated to Goodwill, feeling like a good Samaritan, like it was his tithe. The photos he kept. He dreamed through life on them.

Then he met Sarah.

Sarah didn't have a last name, so far as he could find. There was only a photo album with her first name in marker on the front cover, left in a bedside table that was otherwise empty. The photographs were all the instant self-developing kind, from a Polaroid Land camera. He remembered having one when he was little; knew viscerally how it would produce a square of stiff material when he took a picture. The photo would be entirely gray at first, and would smell sharply of chemicals. Slowly the image would appear, fairly low in resolution.

There were eleven photos in the album. In the first two Sarah was a girl, posing with school books, then with a birthday cake sporting a dozen candles. After a gap of several years, here she was again posing beside a new Volkswagen. Again, standing in cap and gown. Again, holding the arm of a boy, then clutching the arm of a completely different boy, followed by photos of the Grand Canyon and some skyline, obviously taken on vacation. The ninth photo was from some past Christmas, picturing Sarah on a couch next to an older version of herself, most likely her mother, who was holding up a snow globe. Tiny plastic flakes swirled around a Mickey Mouse on skis.

In the last two photos more time has passed. Sarah, looking exhausted and wearing a knit cap, sat in the sun in some nondescript park. The final Sarah, only a little older, lying in a hospital bed with tubes running into her arm, has no cap, no hair, but smiles faintly.

Piet gave a clerk a dollar for the photo album, and kept all the pictures in the same order, four to a page with the last three on the third page. That night he put the album on his bedside table next to the alarm clock and the framed, signed photo of Henry Kissinger he'd found several years before.

That night Sarah spoke to him.

1

"What's going on?" said a voice, young, feminine, wary. "Why is it dark all of a sudden?"

Piet, jolted out of sleep, thought at first there was a radio going, or a television, or someone speaking in another apartment. But the voice was too near, too singular. "Can anybody help me?" then, "Am I blind?" and finally, "Where are you, Mom?"

Groping to wakefulness, Piet turned on a light and looked around. Reflexively, he looked at the clock to find it was just past midnight. When the voice screamed, "Help me!" he started. Grabbing the book, he ran a thumb over the front cover for a moment. Were there sobs really coming from inside? He opened it.

"Oh!" she said. In the first photo, a young Sarah had dropped her school books and had her hands fisted in front of her mouth as she wept. She stared up at Piet.

He stared back. There was a school behind her, with students coming and going. Grass rippled and trees swayed in a gentle breeze. He glanced around the page, but none of the Sarahs in the other photos moved at all.

"Who are you?" she asked. "What's going on?"

"I'm Piet. Piet Ondaat. P-I-E-T. I collect, that is, I work at a store and sometimes we get photographs. That's you, you're in a photo, I mean."

"In a photo?" She cocked her head, tears forgotten. "I didn't get some kind of bad drug, did I, like Uncle Van did in San Francisco?"

"No, it's real. Unless I'm dreaming, or maybe you are."

"Everything was dark," she said, "but I could still hear the wind and the other students. Then the light came, and you're there in front of me like, well, like a movie screen." Then she repeated, "I'm in a photo?"

"Yes. Um, wait a sec." He peeled up one of the other photos, of Sarah posing beside a Volkswagen, and held it up facing the first Sarah. "See?"

"So? It's a picture," she said. "Wait," she squealed, "That's me? With a car?"

"Yes, that's you. There are more, of you growing up and—" She didn't need to know how things would end just as she was starting out. "—and getting older and stuff."

"As old as my parents?" she asked. "As old as *you?*"

"Pretty much." He debated turning some pages in the album to retrieve a later photo. But would she really want to see herself that much older? "Do you want to see?"

She didn't answer. He almost repeated himself, then saw she had returned to a still image, the books back in her arms. Looking at the clock, he saw that it was three minutes past midnight.

2

Piet rarely remembered his dreams, but the one of talking to Sarah was unusually vivid. He considered taking her to work, but decided her album was too precious to chance losing or damaging. He fell back on traveling with a perennial favorite, twenty photos of the Woo family, a happy clan of a dozen people in at least three generations at a family picnic.

When he got to work, he asked George, one of the receivers, if he remembered the walnut-stained bedside table where Piet had found the album. George shrugged. Maybe, he said, maybe not, maybe one of the other guys had lugged it in from the curbside donation box, maybe not. George had done a lot of shrooms in his twenties.

He ate his lunch with the Woos on a bench outside the store. As he gnawed at an apple, he wondered what it would be like to wake up in a photo. He kept glancing at the pictures, trying to catch the family moving, then laughing at himself for doing so.

That night, he went to bed at the usual time, though for some reason he found himself brushing his teeth with more diligence than usual. He smiled, he shrugged.

"Hello?" said the voice in the darkness. "Hello? Piet, are you there?"

Startled, instantly awake, Piet flicked on the light, glanced at the clock, and picked up the album. It was midnight.

"Hello, Sarah," he breathed.

"It is you! Shit!" The Sarah in the second photo, the one of her upper body and head behind a birthday cake, clapped her hands over her mouth. "I'm not supposed to say that."

"What happened? Did it get dark like last time?"

"Yes, just when all the candles were lit and dad pushed the button on the instant camera."

"Your father? Is he there with you?"

"Well, you're kind of on a big movie screen in front of me, so I can't see him any more. Let me try." She got up and moved to one side, but the photo stayed focused on her, panning to the side, keeping the same distance from her. He saw more of the dining room she'd been sitting in, a woman who must have been her mother in the background. He remembered her from the Christmas photo, though she was younger here. The woman said something, but it sounded faint and tinny, impossible to decipher.

Sarah turned to the woman. "Mom, I didn't, not yet." She turned back to Piet. "She thinks I blew out the candles. She said I should open my presents now. But the candles are still going, and she's still looking at where I was sitting like that's where she sees me. It's weird." She squatted, then stood on tiptoe, and the view changed to keep her centered in the picture. "I can't see past the movie screen. It keeps moving with me."

She reached toward Piet, and he saw her movement slow down, then stop. Suddenly she was sitting at the table again, behind the ever-burning candles, forever twelve years old.

He looked up. It was 12:03, and he was definitely not dreaming.

3

On Friday morning he dragged himself to work. He'd barely slept the rest of the night, flipping through the album and trying to catch another Sarah moving. Finally he decided the magic worked only at midnight (unless it didn't), and with each photo in turn (unless it never happened again). That day, for the first time in years, he didn't take any photos with him to work. When a small heliochrome of a Doberman pinscher fell out of a copy of *Tristram Shandy*, he didn't even consider adding it to his collection. He priced it and gave it to the collectibles clerk.

He dozed on the bus heading home, but perked up over mac & cheese. If the magic worked, he'd see her again tonight. He got ready for bed early, taking care to wear presentable pajamas. He set an alarm for a quarter to midnight.

Piet was up and prepared when the third Sarah went from a static pose next to her car to staring up at him from the table on which he'd set the photo album.

"Hi!" she said brightly. "Do you like my new car?" She waved at the scarlet Volkswagen as if she were on a game show.

"It's very nice," said Piet. "You're taking this pretty well."

"I've had four years to think about it." She perched on the hood of her VW. "When I saw this car on the lot I knew it meant I'd see you. You remember, you showed me that photo of me next to it."

"I remember. For me that was only day before yesterday."

"Really? What happens next? Show me the next photo!"

"Okay." He peeled up the fourth picture on the page. "Here it is. That's you at your graduation. You look more mature, so I guess it's from college."

She peered at the photo. "Hold it closer." When he did, she took a long moment to examine it. "That's the University of Chicago. I can just make out what it says on the diploma. How weird; they weren't even at the top of my short list."

"There's plenty of time to decide," he said.

"I just did decide. I should have held up a big sign telling myself the lottery numbers for the next five years." Her smile was lopsided.

"I don't think it works that way. Maybe when the photos were taken, you didn't know I was going to be visiting you, but now that I am, you're able to remember me." He frowned. "That didn't come out quite right."

"No, I think I get it. It's like I went all the way through life one time, getting the photos taken, then you found them and started my life over, only different." She shook her head. "Not too different yet, I guess."

"If you do something new, like going to a different university, maybe the photograph will change."

"Or maybe it won't. Maybe it'll ruin the magic and I'll never see you again." She hopped off the car's hood. "Promise you won't tell me anything else about my future."

"Okay, I promise." It was an easy promise; he'd already decided never to tell Sarah about the hospital bed in her future. He supposed a debilitating ending like that was in his future, too, if he didn't get run over or have some other fatal accident. But nobody thought about being unable to move, dying from some incurable disease or just old age.

"Why so quiet?" she asked.

"Just thinking. About the future, our future. I mean, there aren't all that many more photos in here."

"How many? No, wait, I just asked you not to tell me things like that." She dug in her pocket, pulled out a single key on a fob. "Wanna see me drive?"

"Sure."

She opened the car's door and was just settling into its seat when the action slowed, stopped, and she was posed unmoving beside the car again. It was 12:03.

4

"There you are!" Sarah relaxed into a more natural pose, letting the arm holding her diploma drop back to her side. "Man, five years is a long time."

"It's just been one more day for me." A Saturday, one he'd been spending trying to track her down. He'd naturally assumed she lived in Dallas, or that her parents did, but he knew so little else about her. The University of Chicago had been a dead end; their admissions office had not been eager to disclose any information to a random caller, and he'd never been a good enough liar to make up some justification. The photo of her with the VW had been no help, either. The car had been side-on, with no view of its license plate. He'd pored over all the photos with a magnifying glass, then scanning them into his computer to blow them up until they lost all meaning. Her arm obscured most of her name on the diploma. He'd used a Google image search on the one skyline to determine it had been taken in Cincinnati, which only meant he could probably rule the city out as her residence. Who takes vacation snaps at home?

Piet was just working up the nerve to quiz Sarah about her personal details when she reached down out of the photo's frame to lift a comically bulky—by Piet's standards—video camera. "Do you mind," she asked, "if I film this? I want to see if I can, since other people don't see anything."

"Go ahead," he said. "Did you actually tell people about me? That must have been frustrating."

"Try scary." She concentrated on the camera, peering into its eyepiece and pressing its record button. "I was in therapy for two years, even though I shut up about you after the first couple of sessions."

"Oh god. I'm sorry."

"At least they didn't prescribe antipsychotics. I stopped seeing Doctor Harmon when I was fourteen."

"They started after the second photo? And you didn't say anything last time."

"That's right." She stopped taping, rewound for a few moments, then played the recording through the camera's eyepiece. "No good. It's just my dad and his camera, like you aren't there. You should try recording this at your end, too."

He swallowed. "Sarah? I don't even know your last name or where you live. Could you tell me?"

"If you tell me yours, too. Where do you think you're living now? My now, that is."

"We moved around a lot. I came here to Dallas ten years ago. You'll have to tell me what year it is for you."

She told him.

"I was in Phoenix then," Piet said. "My dad was a truck driver and we moved around whenever he was out of work." He didn't add that it was his father's temper that had made them unwelcome time after time.

"What about your mother?"

"She died when I was seven. Or eight." It had been the night before his birthday, not a night he wanted to remember.

"I'm in Chicago," she said. "As you can see." Setting the camera on the ground, she held up the diploma, playfully pushing it up to the invisible barrier that divided them. He read her full name, Sarah Ornette Moulton, and he saw that her major was Economics. She turned it back around, traced her name with a forefinger. "I'm going to see if I can get a job in New York, but don't count on it." She looked up, at him. "Piet Ondaat. Phoenix, then Dallas. I wonder what the rules are around me coming to visit you."

"Phoenix, Santa Fe, El Paso, Oklahoma City, *then* Dallas. You'd see a different me, like I'm talking to a different Sarah than the one when the photos were originally taken."

"You mean, if I came to see you, I'd start you on a different track, maybe, like you're doing for me."

"Not all that different," he said. "You're still at the University of Chicago."

"I didn't want to change schools. I thought I might not see you again."

A flush of warmth moved up Piet's spine. "I'm not that big a deal."

Sarah hugged the diploma. "I knew that if I went here, I'd get this. I'd graduate; my life would go on according to those pictures. And I'd see you." She looked up at him. "What's the next photo?"

"You can't live photo to photo," said Piet. "You need to live your life."

"But how will I know—" In mid-sentence, she slowed, stopped. Their three minutes were up.

5

At midnight, Piet tapped the timer he'd bought, then turned to the Sarah in the photo. She pulled her hand away from the boy's arm she'd been holding. He held the pose, his expression barely changing from the half-smile showing nicotine-stained teeth.

"This is Sean," she said. "Isn't he tall?"

Sean relaxed, then walked off the scene arm-in-arm with a Sarah invisible to Piet.

"We only have three minutes." Piet used his phone to start recording the page of photos. "Yesterday—"

"Two years ago," she said.

"It was yesterday for me. Anyway, when we last talked, you mentioned moving to New York."

"I also said I might go see you."

"Did you?"

"No." Sarah drew out the syllable. "It's like you said, I didn't want to mess with the magic. If it would. Who knows?"

"Not me. I just price stuff in the back room of a thrift store."

"Sounds lonely. Are you lonely, Piet?"

When they first spoke, he'd already told her his deepest secret, about collecting photos. Why was it so hard to answer a simple yes-or-no question? Maybe because he knew the answer.

Maybe she did, too. Sarah glanced to her left, obviously looking at Sean. "No," she said.

"No?"

"No, I never moved to New York. I had my degree in Econ, but stayed here for grad school."

"Are you still in school?"

"I'll graduate next year. Sean and I plan to get married after that, then take a bicycle trip around Europe before starting the job search."

Piet felt a pang of jealousy. He'd never biked around Phoenix or Santa Fe, much less Europe. Much *much* less with a pretty girl.

"So," she said. "We agree this is magic, right? This photo thing?"

"I guess so. I don't see any way it could be natural." Piet glanced at his phone, which stubbornly showed four unmoving photos, including the one of Sarah with Sean.

"In all the stories I've read, magic does what it does for a reason. Is there some reason it's bringing us together? You and me? Or do you think there's a million other photo albums like mine out there, and just nobody's happened to mention it?"

"I don't know. I'm sure not telling anybody." She knew better than he did the consequences. He bit his lip, glancing at the timer. Less than a minute left. "Let's say this is a one-of-a-kind arrangement, let's say it's here for a reason." Catching his breath, like he'd been running, he said, "Why is it happening? What do you think?"

Slowly, she shook her head. "I have no idea. I just—I just feel like we're meant to be meeting like this." She glanced off again, at Sean no doubt, then back to him. "Until then, I'll just keep going, and getting my folks to take as many pictures with that old camera as they can." She put a hand out, touching the 'movie screen' that divided them.

Piet swallowed, then reached out to touch the photograph. After a moment or two of silence, the picture flattened, returning to a scene of Sarah and Sean, arm in arm.

Piet's jealousy dissipated. He didn't need to envy Sean. He could tell Sarah wouldn't stay with the boy; all he had to do was move his gaze to the very next photo.

6

Monday lasted forever. Piet didn't take any pictures to work with him, though again he was tempted to take Sarah. He priced mechanically, almost letting a set of binoculars go to the floor for two dollars. He fumed as the bus took a hundred years to get him home.

Midnight finally came. He slapped the timer and turned eagerly to Sarah.

"Hi," she chirped, but he was staring in horrified fascination at the boy who stood with her. The still picture had shown a short Hispanic twenty-something with tight dark curls. Now that boy was Piet; as he had been in Phoenix, impossibly young and gawky and dressed in polyester. "I found you," she said, hugging young Piet, who turned to peck the air where her cheek had been.

"Not me," whispered Piet. "That's not me," he said. "I'd remember it."

"No," she said. "This is second-time-around you, just like I'm not the first-time-around-Sarah in those photos of yours."

"Why?" She'd seemed content with the Hispanic kid, who'd disappeared after a single photo. Piet was used to Sarah being his. Now? Who could tell?

"I said last time, this picture-talking is happening for a reason. This is it, me meeting you, us falling in love. You seemed so lonely." Sarah looked to her left as her Piet walked off, arm around an invisible her. "You were. Lonely."

I still am. "Of course I was." Anger rose in Piet, clenching at his gut, climbing his windpipe. "I never loved anybody, not after what my father did." He'd never had Sarah, never had anyone the least bit like her. Not since his mother died. Deliberately, he lifted the photo album's cover. When it came into Sarah's view, she said, "Piet? What are you doing?" He lifted it until it was vertical, then gravity took hold. The cover flopped down.

"Piet." Her voice was muffled. "Piet! What did your father do? Are you going to leave me in the dark? Piet."

Hands clenched, he stared at the timer as it counted up, ignoring her cries. They cut off abruptly when it ticked off three minutes. He rolled over onto his back in the bed, staring at the ceiling.

7

On Tuesday morning, he debated whether to throw the album into the trash. Alternately, he could take it back to work, price it, make Sarah somebody else's problem. It was obvious she'd been meant for somebody not as broken as Piet, somebody who could *deal*.

Finally, he left the book where it was and went to work. He threw himself into pricing, clearing out several bins by lunchtime, then uncharacteristically walking to a nearby Mexican food restaurant where he'd never before had a meal. He ate one bite of his chalupa, then stared down into the plate, transported to the past.

His eighth birthday was supposed to be a festive occasion. His father had planned to take him hunting, over his mother's objections. They'd bought a rifle, plenty of ammunition, warm clothes, and a license. He'd been looking forward to it for a month. The night before, he barely slept, waking up from time to time, eager for seven AM. That's why he'd been awake when the voices raised in anger pulled him from his bed and down the hall. The door to his parent's bedroom was closed. He couldn't tell what they were arguing about, only that things were being slammed about, a window was smashed. Then, finally, a gun shot.

He'd tiptoed back to bed and lay there, praying for sleep. It came.

And in the morning, the police were there, and a woman who was not his mother talked to him, tried to make him understand something he didn't want to know. His father had claimed to be out of the house, making some delivery. Why, then, did Piet remember that voice? But he'd been too young to put it all together. He'd needed his father to be innocent, available to keep raising Piet. And he had been, the killing ruled an accident.

Piet and his father had gone hunting. Not that day, but many days after that. They'd been happy together. Any time Piet had gotten close to anyone else, there had been another trip scheduled. He'd been accepted at three different universities, but hadn't even considered one that wasn't near home. His father needed him just as much as Piet needed the old man.

But the old man's rage had finally driven Piet away. After he'd broken a broom handle and punched the microwave door so hard the glass starred, his son left. Piet hadn't seen the man for a decade and wouldn't visit him until he was in his grave.

Piet pushed the full plate away. He paid, called in sick, and went home. He went directly to Sarah, to her album, and opened it. There she was, her life in eleven photographs. The next one, the one that should open tonight, was the first of two vacation pictures. Photos without Sarah. But he had to talk to her, had to find out how she was faring with young Piet, and with his father.

He waited for midnight. When the clock finally ticked off the last second, he didn't press the timer's button; he just looked at the picture of the Grand Canyon.

It faded to black. A voice, her voice, said, "How do you like it, you son of a bitch?" He called her name, yelling himself hoarse, but the photo stayed black, stayed silent, as the minutes ticked on. She might be using up all of the camera's film, shooting into a dark closet. Hell, he might never see her again. At last the picture paled and presented once more the familiar landmark.

There were only four photos left. He'd ruined everything.

8

Piet called in sick on Wednesday. He phoned every nursing home, every hospital, every hospice both in Dallas and in Chicago. None of them admitted having a Sarah Moulton. Some time around noon he went out for lunch and returned unfed but carrying a fifth of whiskey. Some of his later calls were both desperate and slurred. God knows what those receptionists thought. But maybe they got despairing, drunken calls from relatives and loved ones all the time. Maybe it really sucked to be a receptionist at those kinds of places.

It was late when he crossed off the last location on his list. Reluctantly, he pulled up a search for morgues, mortuaries, and funeral homes. Calling those would have to wait. The day was done and so was he.

Piet fell into bed, dizzy with drink. Some time that night he woke up enough to make it to the bathroom to throw up, but he didn't remember later if it was before midnight or after. If she called to him from her place on his bedside table he never knew it.

9

His hangover was monumental, but Piet didn't dare call in sick another day. He grabbed Sarah's book and carried it on the bus to work. The Dallas sun blazed through the vehicle's windows, washing out the photos as he obsessively turned pages back and forth. Tonight's picture was Christmas, with a twenty-something Sarah and her mother on the couch, the photo most likely taken by her father. He wondered how she was doing, realizing he was worrying about her three times over: at age twenty-five or so when today's photo was taken, at a younger age when she had been dating a young Piet whose memories he didn't have, and now in his present when she might be dead.

During his breaks he pulled out the list he'd made of morgues and mortuaries. He didn't want to make Goodwill pay for any long distance charges, so he called all the ones he'd found in Dallas. He described Sarah as she appeared in her last photo, giving her name, mentioning where he worked, and saying he'd found something precious of hers.

"Moulton?" A receptionist at a funeral home halfway down his list said. "Yes, that sounds familiar." He held while she checked files and went to speak to someone. When she returned, she added, "Mister Ondaat? I see here that she passed away on the fifth of last month. She's buried at Bellesfaire Cemetery. The family did leave an address so we could settle accounts. Would you like me to contact them to see if they'd want to hear from you?"

The photo album sat on top of the battered oak desk hosting his pricing supplies and computer. He touched it with his right hand's fingertips, gently caressing the open page. Would it be the precious memento for the family that he'd said it was? Could it possibly mean more to the family than to him?

"No," he said. "I guess, if she's dead, it's not really all that important." It felt like a lie as soon as it left his lips.

That night he made a ham sandwich and boiled some peas. He put the album on his coffee table as he ate so he could keep an eye on it. After eating he just sat there, eventually opening it to Christmas. Would she be there? Had she thrown the camera away? Destroyed all its film?

He hoped she was well, back in the past. She had found young Piet well before he had dared take a girlfriend home to meet his father. Maybe she had even taken him away from the murderous bastard. Piet swallowed, feeling as if a bit of his dinner was still stuck in his craw. He wished he was that Piet.

Midnight. At first Piet thought the magic hadn't happened, then he saw that the Sarah on the couch was breathing, was looking at him rather than at some camera. Finally, she spoke. "I was so mad at you."

"I hope you aren't mad any more," he said. "I don't want us wasting the time we have left."

Her eyes narrowed. "How much time?" Next to her, her oblivious mother shook the snow globe, shrouding Mickey in little plastic flecks.

Piet knew she didn't want him to remind her she'd made him promise not to foretell her future. Still, he paused before saying, "There are two more photos. In the next one you're alone in a park looking tired, maybe sick, and in the last one you're in a hospital bed. Your hair is gone. Cancer, I guess."

"Thank you, Piet. How old do I look when I'm in the park?"

"It's hard to say, but five years older maybe? Could be ten."

"Cancer." She closed her eyes, while her mother rose and stepped around her, heading for the tree that was barely in the photo. "That's bad."

"Yes," he said, prepared to commiserate. "I'm sorry—"

"Bad," she repeated, "But maybe not so much if I can catch it in time." She glared out at him. "Go look at that last photo. I want to know everything you see. Try to figure out how much older I am. Any incisions? Is a medical chart visible? Do I—do I still have my breasts?"

"I . . . right."

The last three photos shared a page, so all he had to do was look down. He peered at the photograph. "It's a little blurry," he said. "Those old Land cameras didn't have the best resolution." He snapped his fingers, scrabbling for his phone. "Hold on." The timer showed less than a minute left. He switched to a magnifying glass app. "Okay, you're about the same age in the last two photos. I can't see the end of your bed, or a chart." He glanced back at Sarah. "Your chest look fine." He examined every inch of the recumbent figure. "I just don't know. I'm sorry."

"It can't be helped," she said.

He bit his lip, tapping a finger against the side of his phone. "Wait," he said, using it to inspect the picture of her in the park. "I think," he said slowly. "Yes, I see a bandage around your throat."

"Oh," she said. "Throat cancer, maybe? I'll research it. Thank you, Piet. I might catch it in time."

How was it possible to feel like a hero and a dunce at the same time? He could have been saving her life when she was years younger, instead of closing the book on her. He'd even blown a chance to call her family and find out exactly what had killed her.

"Where am I," said Piet. "Are you still seeing me? Younger me?"

"No." She looked to the side, distracted by something her mother was saying. Then she turned her gaze back to him, meeting his eyes with a force he hadn't felt from anyone before. "Your father killed him."

Piet recoiled, actually falling backward onto the bed. When he sat up again, an immobile Sarah looked up at him from the album's page.

10

After far too little sleep, Piet got up on Friday determined to accomplish something he'd been avoiding for ten years. He called work to say his father was unwell. Packing a change of clothes, his toothbrush, and the all-important photo album, he rented a car and set out for Oklahoma City. Driving straight through, he arrived at his father's house just before noon.

As he'd expected, Braam Ondaat was mowing his lawn. It's what he'd been doing when Piet had packed what little he owned in his car. He'd barely paused to say goodbye, glancing time and again at the immaculate lawn. A hug had been out of the question.

The old man was in his fifties, a powerful man who'd always

enjoyed showing off his prowess. Still, he'd obviously aged, and had gone mostly bald while Piet had been away. He shut off the mower and conducted his son into the house, settling them in the kitchen with glasses of ice water.

There were no pictures on the walls. He was sure there were none anywhere in the house. His father had never saved a single photograph or any of the drawings Piet had brought home from school.

Piet had been rehearsing in the car all the way, sometimes trying to be reasonable, sometimes yelling. Sometimes crying, though he wasn't always sure if it was for his mother, for himself, or for the chance he'd never had with Sarah in real life. Now, facing the old man, it all flew out of his head.

"I met someone," he eventually said.

A cynical smile twisted his father's lips. "You came all the way up here to tell me that? Are you asking my permission? Or rubbing my face in it?"

"Neither." Piet sat in an armchair that didn't quite face the old man's seat. "I came up to talk about that night."

He could see that his father knew exactly what night he meant. There could be no other where they were concerned. "What about it?" said Braam.

"Did you—?" Piet took a breath. "Did you kill her?"

"You finally ask. Almost thirty years I've been waiting." The old man ran his gaze over Piet's face, everywhere except the eyes. "And if I say yes?"

"Then I go to the police."

"And if I say no?"

"Then I go to the police. I know what I heard, and what it means."

"She was going to take you away from me." Braam finally looked Piet in the eye. "I'd never have seen you again. Pretty funny, eh, since it took you ten years to come back."

"I'll visit you." They both knew where. "Well? Are you going to admit it, straight out?"

"Go to perdition."

Piet rose.

"Wait."

"Yes?"

"This person you met. Tell me about her. Or him, I suppose."

"I don't owe you that. You ran off every friend I ever had. After I left I was scared I'd turn into you." Piet was on the verge of turning away, but stopped, the album weighing down his hand. He'd known, somehow, that he had to show Sarah to his father. She was why he was here.

He turned back, sat again. "Her name is Sarah," he said, opening the book's cover. When he glanced up, he was shocked to see a tear rolling down his father's cheek.

It was late when he finally drove back toward Dallas. The police, at first skeptical, had not been very interested in what was at heart a very cold case. Finally they had called the Phoenix police department, who had interviewed Piet on the phone. They'd said they would look into the murder. It left him barely satisfied; this was nothing like television. At least he'd done his part.

Piet kept glancing at the clock on the rental car's dashboard. He'd hoped to be home before midnight, but he could see he wouldn't make it. At ten minutes to twelve he pulled into a darkened mall's parking lot in Denton, Texas. He opened Sarah's album to tonight's picture, the one of her looking tired, defeated.

The car's clock was wrong. Sarah came to life after only a few minutes.

She was completely different. The Sarah that smiled out at him was vibrant, dressed in bright colors and with a full head of hair. She didn't even have a scar on her throat.

"Hi, Piet," she said. "Thank you for saving my life."

She rushed through telling him about her oncologist catching esophageal cancer insanely early, prompted by her insistence. The tiny cyst was removed endoscopically; there hadn't been a need for the more major surgery whose result he'd seen in her photograph.

In turn, he told her about confronting his father, and about how Braam Ondaat would be in jail in both their realities. Finally, he told her he'd found out she had died the month before, in his reality. They'd never be able to meet in the flesh. "And there's only one more photo. I think tomorrow night will be our last time together."

"Let's not have it be a sad occasion," she said. "Let's make it a party. You bring something nice on your side, and I'll do the same over here."

11

On Saturday morning, Piet took flowers to Sarah's grave. The scenery in the cemetery was so calming he found himself walking back to his apartment instead of busing. On an impulse he stopped for lunch at a sandwich shop when he was halfway home, and had a long discussion with the idle waitress about their respective childhoods. It caught him completely by surprise when she handed him her phone number.

He shopped for party supplies that afternoon and ate a light dinner. He leaned the photo album against a stack of books on his small bar, and put the slice of chocolate cake he'd bought in front of it. He'd strung Christmas lights on the wall behind his chair. He inhaled, barely able to withstand the cake's aroma. At two minutes to midnight he lit a birthday candle to stick in the slice. He already had a glass of beer poured, but hadn't sipped yet.

He hated the picture of her in the hospital bed. She looked so far gone. He looked forward to this last chance to see a living, vivacious Sarah.

When the photo faded to a wintry scene in a park, he missed seeing her for a long moment. When he found her, Sarah was dressed in gray, with a felt hat on her head, some distance from the camera. It was snowing lightly. She looked up, at the camera, at Piet.

"It came back," she said. She lifted a hand to touch the bandage on her neck. "I thought I was cured."

"How—" Piet's voice had turned raspy. "How bad is it?"

"Stage three liver cancer," she said. "So far as we know, it hasn't spread anywhere else in my body." She lowered her head, her voice becoming difficult to hear. "They say I have eight months."

"I'm so sorry." Piet blew out the candle, moving the cake out of Sarah's view.

"Me too." She smiled wanly. "I'm sorry for raining on the party."

"That's not important. We have just these last few minutes together." He'd visited her grave just this afternoon. Seeing her again, even sick, felt like a gift, a reprieve. "Sarah, what I did yesterday, well, I wouldn't have done it if it wasn't for you. I wasn't open to other people. I wasn't talking, really sharing, until I did with you."

Her smile grew. "It is magic," she said. "Magic's got its reasons." She grimaced slightly, putting a hand to her stomach. "Sorry. The meds aren't sitting right." Walking to a nearby bench, she sat. "It helped me, too. I got seven years I wouldn't have had otherwise. I traveled, I talked to amazing people. It's been a good life." She smiled. "Eat your cake."

She waved. The snow fell around her, on her, and she kept waving until she dissolved into the bedridden Sarah.

Saying things aren't as you'd expect is what you'd expect someone to say about an Edd Vick story, but let me say it anyway. This little gem—luminous and multifaceted and clever—reflects and refracts pot-boilers and pop-culture, fantasy and science, literary and genre tropes, creating its own improbably logical universe.

—Leslie What

Leslie is a Nebula Award-winning writer and an Oregon Book Award finalist. She was an instructor at the Clarion Science Fiction Workshop in 2002, the year Edd attended.

ECLIPSING

When she rapped at the door, the detective looked up from his battered paperback copy of *The Big Sleep* and growled, "It's open!"

She turned the knob and used the tiniest jot of her power to open the door. Wrenched off its hinges, it sailed through his window and down to the street. "You are the investigator?" Her voice held a suggestion of twilight, filling his room with the rosy warmth of neon.

"You got it—" He consulted the book. "—sister!"

She floated across the floor and hovered above his best chair. "Then you must help me."

"Yeah. Sure." He offered her a cigarette. She stared at it, then took it and began picking at it. "So, sweetheart, what can I do you for?" He frowned, and moved the bartending guide farther away on his desk.

"It is my husband." Beneath her misty veil, the moon stared at him in placid fury. Her eyes were seas, her mouth a pale crescent.

"Hmm," he hummed.

"I never see him any more."

"Some skirt gettin' plowed in your field, eh?" He pocketed the book. "I get a per diem."

"Will this be enough?"

"Sister, that'll keep me on your payroll a century or so. Let's go." When he got to the door, he found the moon rising through his shattered window. Cursing, he took a step then another and jumped to ride her into the sky. Flexing his fingers into claws, he thought he could stand to do just this forever.

*

"First, I investigate," he growled.

"And how do you do that?"

"Give me a list of the places your husband frequents."

"Why? What would you do with it?"

"And a list of the dames he knows."

"Just look in the phone book. He sees everyone, every day."

"Then I shadow him, and catch him in the act."

"Will he stop? If you do catch him?"

"Sure, baby. Sure."

The detective took himself away with his camera and his note-book and his gun. He followed the curvature of the earth until he found the sun. Hiding behind a satellite, he brought out his camera and snapped a quick shot. He suspected he should have brought faster film. Sunglasses, too.

All that day he shadowed his client's husband. The sun plodded his stately course from horizon to horizon, favoring no one. He shone on the just and the unjust, it seemed to the detective.

Then night fell but the detective was not there to see it, so intent was he on following the sun and snapping more shots. Forty days and forty more days he followed, until finally he stopped to let the moon catch up.

She was dark. She said she always felt dark, eclipsed, without the sun's gaze. The detective pitied the emptiness of her and used the darkness to develop his photos. When they showed nothing, the moon wept bitter rocks.

"Listen, sister. The guy's clean. He never even looked sideways at another woman. I dunno why he's giving you the cold shoulder, but it's not because he's got a frail on the side."

"It is me, then, I know it is."

"Okay, doll. Okay. Dry up the rockworks. Let's go back to my office. I got a copy of *Consolation for Dummies* there."

*

"What seems to be the problem?"

"I told you, my husband avoids me."

"How does this make you feel?"

"Dark, sad, empty. Like I'm nothing, a mere reflection of him."

"And how does that make you feel?"

"Like his negation. As if were we to meet we would cancel each other out. Maybe he knows that."

"Okay, how does that make—"

"Is that all you do? Ask the same question over and over again?"

"Sorry." The detective turned a page. "Trial separation? No. Couples therapy? Mmm, no." He let the pages flip past his thumb, then set the book on its spine atop his desk. When he let go, it fell open, and he spoke after reading. "Listen. I think it's time for you to move on. You were attracted to him once, sure, but it's over. Done with. Kaput." He spread his hands out, palms down. "Leave him."

"I did not hire you to advise me. You were to help me." She reached into her purse, put her hand on something inside.

The detective felt the attraction, the tidal force pulling him into her orbit. Hair sprouted. Fangs grew. "You will help me," she said.

He felt his heart heaving at the inside of his chest.

"All right," he growled. "Back off, sister. I'll take another run at it."

A sliver, a fingernail of light, glinted at him from her face. "Thank you," she said. When she pulled her hand out, it was holding a slim volume. She placed it carefully on a shelf far from his desk, but not so far he couldn't read the word "Garou" on its spine.

"No way," he said. "That's what I should have said," he said. "Take your money back. Leave me alone. Stop stealing my heart and turning me into a wolf.

"That's what I should have said," he said.

The detective slouched over the horizon into darkness. Not as surprised as he expected to be, he hurried forward to find the great dead orb. Chalk marks already in place, and the coroner scraping bits of this and that from walls and roofs and Mercury and Venus.

"It was murder," he heard, and, "Solly never saw it coming."

"I doubt that," said the detective to himself. "She's either one thing, or the other: either victim or victor." He felt tired.

She was dark, invisible, when he returned to her. He knew where she would be: a hundred and eighty degrees removed from the scene. Eclipsed.

Weak. Needing his strength.

He caught her up in his arms and carried her into his office. Put her on the couch.

"He's dead," she said, and it was not a question.

The detective nodded. "He was keeping you at a distance. He knew he was going down. He didn't want you involved."

"You did it for me."

"I—? Did what?"

"You never remember what you do," she said, "at night."

He snapped on his desklamp, its sterile cone of light lit up no more than its parabola of desk.

She struggled up. Her hand fell on one of his books, and she pushed it into the light. "*Cosmos*," she read. "Why not *The Sun Also Rises?*"

"You're mistaking the title for the territory," he replied. "Pamplona's not hot enough for me."

"Curious, that I'd find the one item I most need. You think big, too."

"Bigger than the both of us." The detective felt a glow eat his heart, a warmth a heat a burning that intensified until he was the source. His heart was no longer alone in its pull toward hers. He could feel the mass that he was, pulling at her, could see her expression melting from bleak comprehension to sour acceptance. "Not so curious," he said. "Call it inevitable." He spared not a look for the tools of his trade. The camera. The notebook.

The gun.

As the building around them melted away he rose and she with him. Together they rode into the sky, no longer separated by the planet between them.

HEDGING WITCH

The day her family tells Holly she's a witch is a crazy day. No doubt. Its highs are higher than any other day she can remember, and its lows lower than any other. Just crazy. Even its mundane parts feel like the most mundane—

Well, no, that would be going too far.

Breakfast: "fruit and grain and fluid milk." Or so the flyers say, touting West Virginia leading the nation in providing breakfast for families that are among the poorest in the United States. Holly, sitting in her favorite spot, manages to wolf down a banana before the twins Esther and Hester seize her granola and milk. Maybe they need it more, or maybe they're just picking on her as they do every day. She'd like it to be the former. They've always looked needy.

Classes: fifth and sixth grades together because less than a thousand people live in Kellar County. It's mostly all woods, just off the Appalachian Trail. That's the only reason there are actually two cafes in Black Oak: all the hikers and ultra-marathoners.

Classes: right, classes! Math is good, Holly 100% grasps algebra, the quadratic equations folding and unfolding as if they were wire puzzles in her hands. Just like she doesn't get English: authors saying one thing and meaning another makes her confused.

Lunch: sloppy joes and potato chips. Mum, who besides being her mother is one of the two lunch ladies, tells her in a quiet moment that she's a witch just like all the women in her family going back to Scotland and probably wherever they were before Scotland.

More classes: Spanish is eh, social studies is eh, PE starts out good with Holly scoring a dozen points in basketball, then missing an easy shot that gets scored on the rebound by Ruth, who almost never gets points on the board.

And all afternoon Holly is clutching this new fact. She's a witch. She's a witch? Everybody wants to think they're special, so maybe she is one. Almost like flipping a switch she decides to believe it's true. What does it mean, what can she do, and does she get a black cat like Sabrina?

After school: homework and chores. While poring over Spanish tenses she wonders if she'll be reading spells. While herding the cow in with a switch she swings it like Harry Potter in the movies, murmuring *wingardium leviosa* to the wind. While chopping carrots and onions for stew she pesters her mother and aunts with questions.

A hedge witch, she finds out, means she'll learn from the land and its spirits. She is likely to be good with herbs, with healing, with following her instincts to help balance nature and the needs of humanity. Maybe, says Aunt Rose, she'll be adept at crossing over to the spirit world like Grammy Clematis. And maybe, says Aunt Ivy, she'll go into midwifery like her cousin Juniper over to Johnsontown. What she won't be doing is joining any coven; hedge witches aren't big joiners. That's okay with Holly; she's always had trouble figuring people out anyway. Math is easier.

Pop comes home from work, tries as best he can to scrub auto grease out of the wrinkles in his hands and face, says what's up. Mum tells him food'll be on the table in ten minutes and by the way they weren't sure before but now they are that Holly is a witch. They can all feel it, like Mom did all of a sudden at lunch time. Soon enough maybe some god will tap her on the shoulder. Pop says good luck with that, it's a lot of responsibility, and by the way did Mum tell you not to share this with folks outside the family? There's only one gas station in town, one grocery store, one Dairy Queen & Joe's All-Day Diner, but there's five churches and one or two of them are not overly fond of witches.

Supper: the stew is good. Holly doesn't remember ever getting a meal at home that's been less than tasty. She's been asking more and more to make meals, knows now it's part of her gift.

The evening passes in more homework and watching television over her parents' shoulders. Then bed, where she spends the time before sleep in imagining the delivery of babies, poulticing animal bites, casting love charms, and enticing plants to grow. None of these activities sound all that appealing.

More chores, ones of a witchly nature, settle themselves on Holly's shoulders over the next few weeks. Going out with Aunt Rose in search of potent wildflowers. Studying family histories with Aunt Ivy. Even making meals starts to involve a deliberation bordering on meditation.

And lectures about balance. Karma. Kismet. Fortune and misfortune. Holly comes to understand that her family evens out luck in their area. Not consciously, or not *always* consciously. The things they do keep any one person from being too unfortunate. Accident-prone Beth gets to make the occasional basketball goal. Hester and Esther, terrors that they are but also often going hungry at home, chance to find girls who have enough extra food to share (or to be extorted from, more accurately).

Holly grows unhappy. She doesn't want to believe in a world where all her skill with a basketball isn't enough, where what's hers can be taken just because it puts the universe a little more into balance. Chaos shouldn't lead to order, she thinks.

She dumps a lot of pepper into the soup one night, but it turns out the turnips would have been too bland and the extra spice helps even out the flavor. At the next basketball game she dribbles, she waits until Beth is nowhere near the basket, she shoots, she scores. And coming down she feels a moment of dizziness and twists her ankle, sitting out the rest of the game while Beth gets one easy layup after another. She finds a new place to eat her lunch, but a third-grader named Judith looks so hungrily at her sandwich that she sighs and shares.

There are things she could do that would be too much, but Holly isn't the sort of person who could set things afire or steal things or kill small animals except the chickens they need to eat. So she grumps around the house, doing her chores and deciding maybe she doesn't like basketball all that much anyway.

Then the idea comes, late one night. There really is only one thing she's been forbidden from doing as a witch. If she did that one thing it would put her on a different path. So on Saturday she goes to visit churches.

Black Oak Baptist Church: Pastor Ned Swanson doesn't believe in witches. He says most modern churches don't believe in them either, that children often feel a need to be special, and maybe if he just talked to her parents they could find out some way to help her. It would be useful just then to make his pipe sprout a flower or all the paper in his office fly around the room like birds, but she can't do those things. Putting more balance into his life is not exactly a noticeable phenomenon. She says she was just kidding, and to please not talk to her folks. They have enough problems, and she'll go see the school counselor, okay?

Trinity Presbyterian: Minister Wallace Lemayre believes in witches, and says they have their own way of finding God. Holly says okay then, good to know.

Perfect Unity Bible Ministry: When she says there might be a witch in town, Priscilla Lodge looks so fierce and pounces on her words so ferociously that Holly tells her the possible witch lives on the other side of town from their house and leaves as soon as she can. She hadn't thought dying could be a result of being truthful. In most movies and books honesty is rewarded (her brain takes a while to add "eventually rewarded").

She doesn't go to the other two churches.

Holly skips basketball. She drops her lunches on her usual bench and walks away. She avoids her aunts and then her parents, contributing as little as she can to chores and meal making.

Gradually, the world goes gray.

*

Four days later, Holly comes home to find her entire family waiting in the den for her. When she stands, just waiting for them to harangue her, they instead gather around and hug her one by one. At first she puts up with it, then pulls away to sit in her favorite spot.

They've all felt the imbalance, even her Pop. He says it doesn't take a witch to see when someone's miserable. They say she doesn't have to be a witch. It's a choice; Great Aunt Dahlia gave the life up and became an architect back in the day. But if Holly stops being one it doesn't mean she won't be affected by balancing forces. They'll spin her around, those forces, and make her dizzy, because she'll know what they are and be unable to affect them.

On the verge of saying yes she'll quit, Holly hesitates. Instead, she says she'll think about it. And by the way, she adds, she told a few church people about witches. Her kin look from one to another to another and say not to worry. They try and fail to look not-worried.

The word is all over school the next day. Perfect Unity is hunting witches. They say it's not to harm them, of course not, it's just to help them, to show them the error of their ways. Even Holly, who takes most things at face value, understands the threat. Beth Swanson, who's the daughter of the Baptist minister, tells Holly her pa accidentally mentioned Holly when Priscilla Lodge came to call. Mum, at lunch, tells Holly to cut out the back way of the cafeteria with her and meet the rest of the family outside town.

Mum and Holly find Pop and the aunts and the dog in two cars packed with as much of their belongings as they can fit. One of the car's theirs, the other is one Pop had bought with an eye to reselling at the station. Silently, they all look back at Black Oak before driving away forever. Pop cries, giant tears working their way down the wrinkles in his cheeks. The aunts hug one another and the dog. Mum's more stoic.

All they say to Holly is that this sort of thing happens to witches and their families a lot. Moving's kinda sorta in their blood. The young almost-a-witch still vows to herself never to let the black cat out of the bag again.

They stay with family in Lockhart, South Carolina, while Pop finds a mechanic job farther south. Some other branch of the family sells their house and the station and the cow & chickens in Black Oak and gets them the money. The town is all up in arms over witches though Aunt Ivy says it ought to settle down now they're gone. Some day soon another family of practitioners will move to Black Oak and put out the word (quietly). People need their charms and their herbal remedies at least as much as they need balance.

Holly tells her family she's ready to be a witch, but she feels like she'll be a new kind of witch. What she wants, she says, is to study how witchcraft makes balance work. What she's really good at is math, and she wants to use it to figure out their craft. Mum says maybe it's Seshat, goddess of mathematics, who's whispering in her ear. Aunt Ivy says it could be Nike while Aunt Rose holds out for the Celtic goddess Emer.

Holly thinks maybe there are gods, or maybe "balance" makes witches think there are, or maybe witches are just extremely intuitive. And, maybe, that's something she'll find out soon enough.

PARACHUTE KID

I pegged the big black woman as trouble immediately. She had that oh-so-concerned look people only get when they're about to screw you over. She came into our trig class with Principal Peters and walked directly to Mr. Brown's desk. They went into a huddle just as Lee snapped the paper football I'd folded past my ear, and held out two thumbs-up. I wasn't watching because I wanted to keep one eye on that huddle and the other on my path to the window. I figured it was the second fastest way out of the room, in case it was me they were after. The fastest I'd reserve for a *real* emergency.

"He scores!" Lee followed with that sound that's like a faraway crowd cheering.

"Lee Tsien Chen," said Brown, pointing our way. "Second row."

Lee froze. The woman lumbered over and he used both hands to pull himself out of his desk and to his feet, looking down. If there's one hard and fast rule about dealing with adults, that's it. Never look them in the eye. It makes you harder to call on, it pisses them off, and you don't have to look at their wrinkled skin. Three for the price of one.

"Hello, Lee," she said. "My name is Margaret Carter. I'm with—" She saw me watching, and lowered her voice. I still caught it. "Immigration and Customs Enforcement. Come with me, please."

Lee shot me a look.

ICE. I knew she was trouble.

*

Lee didn't show up the rest of the day. I hustled to my bike and rode to his apartment, part of a large complex that was all empty fields not long ago. He and his "aunt" live clear on the other side of Costa Mesa, not far from John Wayne International. I'd like to have a car to drive to high school, but there's too much paperwork involved; too many ways I could screw it up. On a bike I'm just another kid.

His paper auntie opened the door and said something in Chinese. I took it for an invitation and entered. As usual it took my eyes a minute to adjust. The bright sun outside would have a hard time competing with the dazzle of red and gold inside Lee's home. They're lucky colors, and his parents were more than wealthy enough to buy him the best of everything, so long as it was in shades of gold and scarlet.

I walked to his room. The apartment always smells wonderful, part open-air spice market, part fishing boat. I often eat there.

Lee was in his room, asleep on top of the Lakers bedspread. Weird thing: he'd shaved his head. I saw clumps of hair all around the bed as I was waking him.

"Sam! Aw, Jesus." There were tear tracks down his face, and he coughed a couple of times. "She's going to send me back."

"Back" would be bad. China was as familiar to him as Mars was. He'd been in Southern California for ten years.

"We'll get you hidden away," I said. "Stay with me tonight."

He didn't argue, he never does. He just threw a few things into his backpack and grabbed his keys. On the way out the door he said something short to his auntie. She shrugged.

We threw his pack and my bike into his gold BMW and peeled out.

"What's with the hair?" I asked, shoving the cap forward on his head to rub at his bare scalp. He swerved back and forth, trying to swat at my hand.

"We do that to get ready for tests," he said. "SATs are next month."

"We?"

"My people."

"Oh, suddenly you're all Asian."

"Fuck you."

I guessed what he'd been thinking. If he was going to be sent back to China as an "unaccompanied minor," at least he could look like he'd been studying. Like he hadn't been staying out all night with me at the 24-hour noodle shops in Chinatown. "Tell me about that Immigration woman."

"She's a bitch, wants to send me back, end of story." If the steering wheel hadn't been made of metal, it would've snapped in his hands. Then, softer, he said, "Something tipped them off. They found out both my parents are in China, and that the woman I'm staying with isn't a relation."

"Shit." I looked out the window as he turned onto my street.

"Another couple of months and I would've graduated."

That's when I saw the guy.

"Lee! Don't stop in front. Drive around the corner."

He was startled, but used to doing what I said. We parked in the alley behind my place. Once in the house, I ran upstairs and into the front bedroom. Getting down on all fours, I crawled to the window and raised my head until I could just see over the sill.

In our neighborhood, we keep to ourselves, nodding at each other while mowing our tiny lawns or taking out the trash, but not speaking. We all know each other, though, and I didn't recognize the guy sitting at the bus stop across the street. He obviously *didn't* know that buses stopped coming through here years ago. The graffiti would've tipped him off, if it hadn't been everywhere else too.

He was watching my house. I figured he was another ICE agent.

Lee crawled up next to me and looked out. "Why's he got a raincoat? Is it dripping?"

A wet raincoat? Now, in Orange County? It hadn't rained in weeks. "Shit!" I jumped to my feet and started waving my hands, but just then an SUV drove by, and when it was past he was gone.

"Where'd he go?" asked Lee. There was no place the guy could have run to fast enough for us to miss him.

He'd *twisted*, but I wasn't going to tell Lee that. I hadn't told him who I really was in the four years since we'd met. Now was no time to start.

The next morning, I was up before Lee and scratching together a breakfast when somebody knocked at the front door, then rang the bell. I ignored it. I'd decided to pretend nobody was home while Lee was here. I grabbed plates and silverware, setting two places.

I was finishing up a half hour later when the knock came again, then the doorbell. Same pattern, so I figured it was the same person. I ignored it, and carried my dishes to the counter a few minutes later.

There, looking in the window over the sink, was ICE Agent Carter. I dropped my glass. She smiled and gestured for me to open the kitchen door.

I figured I could always *twist* if she was here to take me into custody. Well, try to, anyway. So I opened the door.

"Hello. You're Samuel Nelson?"

"Yes," I said. "I saw you yesterday."

"My name is Margaret Carter—"

"Tell me something I don't know."

"They told me at your high school that you're Lee Tsien Chen's friend." She walked past me into the kitchen. She looked at the extra place I'd set at the table. At the eggs and the pancakes waiting there. "He's in the United States without supervision, in violation of his student visa. It happens a lot in Southern California; we call children like him 'Parachute Kids.' Where is he, Samuel?"

"Beats me," I said. "My pop just finished eating." I indicated the dishes in the sink. "He works nights, so he has to get his sleep." I hoped I wasn't going to have to prove a point by eating Lee's food, on top of my own breakfast.

Her sharp gaze darted around the room and she poked her head into the den. I was sure there wasn't anything downstairs to rouse suspicion; I'd always kept it clean and innocuous. Gramps had taught me that, just as he'd been taught in his own youth.

There was a cough from upstairs. The watchful look left her eyes, and I silently thanked Lee for his quick thinking. He'd hardly make noise if he were hiding.

"Well," she said. "If you see Lee, tell him his mother needs him in China. He should be there for his father's funeral."

Funeral. So that was what had tipped ICE off. Damn, no wonder he'd been crying.

Lee coughed twice more as she was leaving. By the front door this time.

I took the stairs two at a time. Rounding the corner to the back bedroom, I started talking before I got there. "Damn, Lee! Good idea, but don't overdo it, huh?" Then I got to the door and stopped.

Lee was on the floor next to the bed. At first I wasn't sure if he was breathing, then saw him take a shallow breath and break into racking coughs. When they subsided, he stayed on the floor.

I got him to the bathroom, where he retched weakly into the toilet.

He slumped down against the wall.

I poured him some water and squatted down across from him. "You need to go to the doctor."

He shook his head, probably afraid talking would start his cough again.

"If I call nine-one-one from here, that ICE agent might find out you were here and deport you. If I drop you off at Hoag Hospital anonymously, you should be okay."

He shook his head again, then coughed. Coughed. Hugging both arms around his chest, he knocked his head back against the wall several times, muttering "damn" between the last few coughs.

Finally he stopped coughing and hung his head between his knees. Spreading from the bridge of his nose outward a faint red rorschach grew, like a light sunburn. It had the shape of a butterfly.

I got up. It was time to call for an ambulance.

Just then there was a pounding on the door. Not the front door. The bathroom door, right next to me.

I couldn't help it, I was so startled. I *twisted*.

I wouldn't be surprised to come out of a twist one of these days with my head on backwards.

This time it wasn't so bad. I took a quick assessment of myself. There was a pain in my left side, like I'd stretched too far the other way, and my back hurt over my right shoulder blade. I pulled at my shirt and found a large hole with rough edges. There wasn't much blood. Like I said, not so bad.

I was on the ground in a small stand of trees, mostly mesquite, walnut, and loblolly pine, so I pegged it for the Southwest. The grass was well-tended. It looked like a park, so I hadn't gone too far back. The sun was low; it was early morning or late evening. I knew there was a fire nearby, or soon would be. There always is, after a blind twist.

I'd barely made my way through the trees, to find a sidewalk bordering a street, when there was a tremendous explosion from beyond the low buildings across the way. Two of the buildings were simply thrown away in the shockwave like matchstick houses. I saw a plume of thick black smoke shoot skyward. Luckily I was protected by a sturdier structure, a bank. In glancing back down, I read the bank's name, and knew with a chill where I was. *When* naturally followed.

Texas City, Texas. April 16, 1947.

*

I had to see the heart of the conflagration. I closed my eyes, took a half-breath, and let the fire pull at me. I twisted.

I landed on my feet right up against the railing that ran along the edge of the wharves. Nobody paid attention to me, all eyes were on the ship. In the harbor, the *Grand Camp* had been burning for more than an hour, sending up flames that captivated everyone. They were the most intense orange anyone had ever seen, the orange of ammonium nitrate bound for wartorn Europe.

The crowd of men and women—and many children—around me was still alive. They wouldn't be much longer. They were watching the firefighters arcing their paltry columns of water at the blaze. I peered around, looking through the crowd, watching for—

There! A flicker in the air and I was seeing a shape come into being and drop to the dock. A five-year-old boy with blood starting to well to the surface on his upper arm. He was naked and grinning. People around him backed away.

I had less than twenty seconds. That first blast, the one I had seen from the other side of the bank, was coming. I had twisted back in time almost a minute. I ran, pushing people aside, and grabbed the boy and he was squirming against me trying to turn his head to look out to sea at what we both knew was coming what we could both feel building what drew us to itself and I screamed as the explosion blossomed and hugged him to me and

twisted

—London. Horses squealing, their carriages and the houses all around blazing. Twist.

—A forest. They all look alike to me when they're on fire. Twist.

—New York. An early September morning. One tower was aflame and we could both hear the other jet. Twist.

—Texas City again. The day after my first twist, just after midnight, and the *Grand Camp*'s sister ship *The High Flyer* was about to explode, taking with her the *Wilson B. Keene* and the Monsanto plant. Twist.

—Another forest, this one not yet ablaze. I could feel it coming, though. It was in the air, so charged that I felt all my hair lifting away from my skin. The boy squirmed in my grasp, not trying to twist away but looking all around him for the spark, the fire, the explosion.

The trees were all around us. No clearings, nowhere to get away from the inferno I knew was coming except to twist. But I was so tired, so scraped up from traveling through time.

And then it came, lightning stabbing the towering tree behind me, and so close I could feel the energy blasting through its root system and into the soles of my shoes, throwing me up and away into another tree. Dazed, I lay there for a long moment under the spruce, hearing nothing except the roaring in my head.

I sat up, rubbing my forehead and looking at the fire as it crackled through the fir's branches to neighboring trees. That's when I caught the familiar shimmer in the air as another Sam Nelson dropped into existence. He looked about fifty, much older than the Sam that Lee and I had seen outside my house. Dressed in a supple yellow Nomex approach suit, boots, and hardhat, he trained the video camera he carried on the trunk of the burning tree, tracking up, across, and down to spot me in his viewfinder. He peered around the side of the camera, as if unsure if I was really there. Lowering it, he walked to where I stood and led me farther from the fire.

"Sam? What's going on?" he asked. "Aren't you a bit young to be fighting fires?"

I was glad my ears had cleared enough to hear him. "Wild twist. It was an accident."

"Aren't they all?" He hooked a thumb over his shoulder at the fire.

"Where am I? And when?"

"You can't tell? Come on, what kind of trees do you see?"

"Fir." I nodded toward the burning tree. "Spruce."

"Grand fir," he corrected. "Be specific. Sitka spruce. And over there is a yellow ceder. And there's a black hawthorn behind you. It's August 10th, 1034."

"British Columbia, then," I said, looking down toward my tennis shoes. When the hell had I gotten so superior and condescending? "When are the rest of the Sams coming?"

"Coming?"

"To fight the fire." I imagined them, Sams of all ages arriving with axes and heavy-duty extinguishers. I was surprised they weren't here already; we tried to catch fires as early as possible.

"We're not fighting this one. It's necessary for the environment. Cleans out the understory." He turned back to the spreading fire. "I'm just studying it." He started to raise the camera again, then paused. "Is that yours?"

"What?" And then I saw the small nude figure staring raptly up at the fiery rain of needles and cones all around. I ran to the kid and pulled him away. Older Sam was ignoring both of us, so I closed my eyes, concentrating on a certain place and time and

twisted

—Newport Beach, California. 1977. A two-bedroom house. Mine, but unfurnished and new, suffused with the smell of fresh paint. I could feel the boy trying to direct the twist, to send us once more into flame. I grabbed a doorframe and yelled "Stop!" Something worked; maybe he was just too tired. We were both covered in abrasions, and I felt fresh blood on my cheek. I'd been wrenched in every direction. So had he. The boy held up his right hand and screamed; the index finger was gone, down to the second knuckle.

"I'll take care of that," said a voice, and the old man stepped through from the kitchen.

"Gramps."

His face and neck were covered in masses of scar tissue, his left sleeve was pinned up, he walked with a cane. He limped over to the boy. "Sam. Hello there."

I'd heard that voice, saying that name to me, so many times. Tears pricked at my eyes. Gramps had taught me English, had shown me how to read—hell, he'd named me. First the fires, then the old man. My earliest memories.

I had to get away for a minute. I walked upstairs to the front bedroom and grabbed the first shirt I saw. Most of them were still in plastic. When I got back to the kitchen with it, Gramps had the kid seated at the table and was clumsily bandaging him. I draped the shirt around the kid's shoulders while staring at his damaged hand. Then I looked at my own—complete—hand.

Gramps—the oldest Sam I know—had a different pair of fingers missing on his remaining hand. Time is just the weirdest thing ever.

He finished with the kid and pulled down a loaf of bread. Sam tore into it like he hadn't eaten in days. I took a slice, too.

Gramps picked up the ointment again and looked at me. "Your cheek is bleeding."

I put a finger to my cheek, looked at it. "I'm okay," I said, holding up my hand to ward him off. He started for me anyway, and I backed up a couple of steps. That stopped him.

"I'm dead, aren't I?" he said.

"Yeah. Three years ago, my time."

He looked me up and down. "Looks like I've got about a decade, then."

"If—" I said.

"Yes, I wish it were that easy. No, strike that, I don't."

Neither did I. Then what we did, all we Sams, would be useless.

Gramps smiled. "At least you're not staring at my feet anymore. Nice to see your face."

I looked at him and he at me, and the kid chewed and looked at both of us. I broke the staring contest first. "Well, gotta go."

"I've got him," said Gramps, laying his hand on the kid's—on Sam's—shoulder.

"Goodbye, Sam," I said to both of them. I twisted on out of there.

*

I turned on the television and got the date and time off of the cable directory channel. It was early afternoon two days after I'd left Lee upstairs.

I checked, just to make sure. He wasn't up there.

I pulled off my bloody, torn, and abraded clothes and threw them away. Then I took a shower and treated the worst scrapes. I looked—and felt—like I'd been dragged behind a car. Getting dressed again, I noticed Lee's keys on the dresser.

The drive to the hospital was a memorable one, considering Gramps had only given me a couple of lessons before he died.

Lee was out of intensive care, the nurse at the desk told me. She was polite, but adamant that the details of his illness not be discussed with anybody but family. But yes, I could see him.

He was sitting up in the darkened room, alone with the beep of the heart monitor. "Hey, Sam." His expression was blank, like he wanted to see which way I'd jump before committing himself.

"Hi, Lee. I'm sorry to hear about your dad."

"Yeah, well. It's not like he was ever around." He was fooling with the cord that ran from his finger to the monitor.

"So how'd you get to the hospital?"

"That guy, the one who was knocking on the door? He was the same one we saw earlier. His raincoat was still dripping. Water and blood both. Weird." The monitor started beeping a little faster. "He looked just like you, only older."

"He *was* me."

I told him. About me, and about being found by me when I was five. Or apparently five, older mes have been looking in the past, especially around fires, but haven't found a me younger than the Sam I'd rescued. I told him about being raised by Gramps. And then I told him about my mission in life, and he broke up.

"Oh, that is excellent," he said. "You, a fireman! All by yourself!"

"Yeah," I said. "Except when I put a fire out, it stays out. You heard about the Kyoto Inferno? Five years ago?"

He shook his head.

"The Los Angeles firebomber? In 1980? Apollo 11?"

He was still shaking his head. "Didn't that one go to the moon?"

"Now it did. I have as much choice about what I do in the past as you do about what you're going to do tomorrow."

"Color me freaked," he said, but the heart monitor had slowed back down. He looked toward the door, and I turned my head to see that there were shadows on its pebbled glass. The handle turned, and a nurse walked in followed by a Chinese woman.

"Màmà," said Lee. He and the woman, his mother, talked together in Chinese.

The nurse turned to me. "Excuse me, dear. I think you'd better go."

Lee held up his hand. "Could he stay? Please?"

"Well—" said the nurse, but Lee and his mother had already gone back to their conversation. Tears were streaming down both their faces.

The nurse dithered, then left, and after a while Lee introduced his mother to me. We held an awkward conversation, translated through Lee, which broke off when a woman doctor came through the door accompanied by a young Chinese man.

"I'm Doctor Meade," she said. "And this is Lawrence Fong, a graduate student from the University of California. He'll be translating for me."

"I can do that," said Lee.

"Some of the medical terms are pretty complicated. I want to make sure your mother understands your condition completely."

Lee had something called Systemic Lupus Erythematosus. "Or SLE," said the doctor. "It's more common in women than in men, but it's also more prevalent in people from China. There are eleven warning signs, and Lee has four of them, including fatigue, the facial rash, and loss of hair. That's more than enough to make a fair diagnosis." She talked about an immunosuppresive regimen, and said the chances of his surviving were very good. "Eighty percent of people with Lupus live past ten more years," she said, like that was a good thing.

Lee's mother shook her head. "He must come back with me for treatment in China," Fong translated. "She doesn't trust western medicine."

"He would be better off here," said the doctor. "He's likely to die of an intercurrent infection."

Lee's mother was adamant. Finally, in obvious frustration, the doctor agreed to sign Lee out. They all left.

"If the doctor were a man," said Lee. "He might have talked her into it."

I didn't know how much time I had. "The doctor said that if you go back to China, you'll die."

Without a pause he said, "Then I'm not going."

"She'll make you."

"Not if I'm not here." He pulled the sheet away and yanked the lead off of his finger. Immediately, an alarm went off on the monitoring unit. "Crap," he said, trying to get to his feet. He coughed. Coughed again.

Allegheny General Hospital in Pittsburgh specializes in Lupus. I figured, as long as I was twisting, that we might as well do a little research and get him into the best institution. So first we went to the library, a few years up the line to see who'd had recent breakthroughs in the disorder, and then I took him to Pennsylvania.

I got him there a couple of months before we left the hospital in California. You wouldn't even know about the bar fire there unless you were local, but it helped pull us to the area. I made sure to get him a male doctor. Then I jumped to six months later and met his mother again for her first time.

When he was well, he asked me to take him back to before his father's accident. He thought he could stop it.

I said I'd consider it. Maybe I'll take him. If it works I'll get introduced to his mom for the first time again—as well as his dad.

Twisting back home, I went through the ritual of undressing, showering, bandaging, and dressing. I was on my way to check the date and time when there was a knock at the door. I ignored it, finding out I had arrived a week after Lee had gone into the local hospital.

The doorbell rang.

Tired and sore and twisted all to hell, I couldn't think of any reason not to answer the door. Twisting away from ICE and the end of high school would be a pleasure.

"Hello, Samuel," she said.

"Agent Carter," I said.

"This is Maralee Consualves of Child Protective Services. I called her as a concerned citizen. May we come in?"

How far could I string them along? "I don't know," I said. "My father is asleep upstairs. Please come back later." I bet myself that Carter had very sensible black pumps, and that the hightops Consualves wore were a riot of color. But I didn't look. I'd stopped looking down.

"I fear we really must have this conversation now," Consualves said. "We have been trying to contact you for several days."

So I let them in. They preceded me into the den, looking around at the photos of various Sams at various ages on the mantel, then at the inexpensive furniture, the television, and through the door into the kitchen. I saw Carter point out the stairs to the other woman.

They sat on the couch. I took Gramps's recliner.

"Now, Samuel," said Carter. "Your school has had no contact with your parents or a guardian in several years. Your grades have been good, so they haven't felt any need to call someone in. But now, you've been skipping school for a week." She grinned, obviously convinced she'd caught me, another parachute kid just like Lee.

Consualves took over. "You seem quite mature. But it is my job to ensure that no minor is in danger or without the help he or she needs. I will ask you right out: do you have someone to watch over you?"

I opened my mouth.

"Of course he does."

I turned to the stairs, as surprised as the two women. An older me stood on the bottom step, removing his wet raincoat. He dropped it, and advanced on Carter and Consualves. "I am his father: Samuel Nelson, Senior. His mother is sadly gone. Has Sam done something to precipitate this meeting?"

"I fear he has been missing school lately," said Consualves. "It worries us when there is no reason given."

He shot me a reproving glance, so I tried to look contrite. "We will discuss it, he and I. But—isn't that something for me to take up with the school? Not you?"

"Actually—it is." Consualves got to her feet, followed several seconds later by Carter. "There has been no official complaint. We won't keep you any longer. Come along, Margaret." The tone of that last line said plain as day that Carter had run out of favors at Child Protective Services.

Margaret went along. She paused next to me, looked in suspicious bafflement at the wet raincoat on the floor, and went on to the door. Once there, she turned. "One last thing, Samuel. Have you seen Lee Tsien Chen?"

"Not recently, no."

"The police are looking for him," she said. "And so is ICE, for deportation. You seem to have been the last person to see him. I'll make sure your address is in our system." She left.

I was right about their shoes.

*

Dinner was quiet, just the five of us. All Sams, of course; even Gramps and the kid—maybe three years older, maybe four—twisted here. They want me to go back to school. "Back" as in back a week to make up the lost time. After graduation, they'd like me to apply to the Massachusetts Firefighting Academy. I said that my application had to be in nine months ago for consideration.

We all laughed. That was the easy part.

I don't know how other writing pairs work, but Edd and I are a tag-team, sitting together and taking turns writing a page or two at a time. Most writing is like watching a movie in which you play all the parts, but collaborating is more like improvisational theater. In improv, the rule is, no matter the question, the answer is always, yes, and . . . You need to let the story unfold in ways you hadn't thought of, to find a way to get to yes.

One of the best things about writing collaboratively is challenging and supporting each other to stretch your limits. That was definitely true of writing "Silver and Scythe." We had been invited to submit a story to an anthology of stories about magical folk: fairies, elves, pixies and the like. Neither of us had ever written that kind of story before. So, naturally, we said yes.

I had been reading Celtic lore for another project, so I was familiar with the story of how the fairies of Ireland were displaced by human mortals—a great war between the Duatha de Danann (the Fair Folk) and the Sons of Mil, invaders from Spain. After reading five or six versions of the legend, we were off.

When we were done, someone asked me which parts were whose. Apart from a clever detail here or a well turned phrase there, I really couldn't tell. This is not the story either one of would have written; it is more than the sum of its parts.

—Manny Frishberg

Manny Frishberg is a science writer, book editor, struggling novelist, and the editor of two science fiction and fantasy anthologies. His solo short stories have appeared in magazines and anthologies since 2010. He is the other half of Vick & Frishberg.

SILVER AND SCYTHE

Edd Vick & Manny Frishberg

Fenod grumbled to himself and slapped cold hands to colder arms. "A Brownie am nae meant to slog through half-froze mud," he grumbled.

King Pellaidh, as grimy as his elderly servant, looked up through a patch of flowers to where a party of Elves sat mounted on pristine stags. "All the fey races are here represented," he said. "We kings had to ensure the council of war was in a spot equally as distasteful to all." A faint burst of laughter came on the wind. "But hark, the scouts return."

Sweeping into the camp, a trio of blue Fairies spun to a halt, the wind that carried them dying in a patter of clods and leaves. Their leader brandished his spear. "It is true!" he said. "The humans make iron."

"Aye, for weapons nae doubt," Fenod muttered. All present knew the metal was a mortal poison to their kind. His sentiment echoed among the assembled spirits.

"Not proven," Crom Cruaich said. The crook-backed god lifted his head as high as it would reach. "Not even alleged yet," he shouted to be heard over the throng.

Queen Medbh gathered her robes, the color of the sky just before first light, and stood up from her throne, blonde braids held in place by a chased gold band around her forehead. "Then let the fairies speak."

"They have melted the stones and seen fire pour in yellow rivulets," said Aelfric, spearing the air with his fine silver lance for emphasis.

"The Sons of Mil gathered the black branches when the light died and they cooled," Hefeydd said. His pale blue eyes grew wide with unfamiliar dread.

Kheelan straightened to his full twelve hands and waited. All around, the Sidhe and Fair Folk looked from one to another, Water Sprites gurgling softly from their brook. The Elves' steeds shuffled nervously in the stillness. "They fashion knives from metal," he said, "and they make axe-heads."

"Weapons!" several said, and "They're baneful vipers," shouted an elf. "Kill them all," yelled a nearby kelpie, transforming in her anger from horse to shaggy dark-haired maiden and back.

Pellaidh leaped onto a hummock. "Wait," he said. "Knives and axes may have peaceful purposes. Do we not eat with silver knives?"

"Some of us do," Fenod muttered.

"Do we not fell trees and shape our houses with axes?"

There was a murmur, more of dissent than approval, among those present. Many Sidhe lived wild, and most avoided any contact with the invaders. What commerce the Fair Folk did have with the mortals were with hapless boys who were led to Tirn Aill, or maidens snatched away to Tir Tairngire, the Plain of Happiness, then back in their beds before dawn. Pellaidh's people, alone among the Tuatha Dé, had regular contact with the newcomers. The Gruagach, Brownies, found the mortals entertaining and, on occasion, Fenod or his brethren would ease their toil as they quaffed the milk the humans left for them.

"What would you have us do?" said Queen Medbh. "We and the Children of Mil have coexisted for aeons—but uneasily. We Elves and Sidhe have our gifts, but we are few beside these humans. If they are forging iron weapons, we must strike soon or see our lands and lives taken from us. So again I ask: what would you?"

All regarded the Brownie king. His voice low, he said, "Consult Frige."

"Frige," said one, then it passed all around the gathering, "Frige." It was a beckoning, a plea more than a command. "Frige."

A tall, lithe woman appeared then and glided through the crowded spirits. All bowed deeply as she passed to take the center of the throng. The ancient goddess surveyed her kith with patient resolve.

"We endure," she said, her voice a flowing stream over smooth stones. "The Milesians have been among us long enough for us to see what frail wisps they are, like dust in a fairy horde's wake, they live a short while, then return to the surrounding earth."

One of those gathered, feeling emboldened, spoke up. "What challenge does the wind face from a dust mote? What are men? A gall on a leaf hanging off a branch of the Great Tree."

"And yet," said the goddess, "where a single mote of dust is beneath our notice, massed into a plain of mud they drag us down." Frige spread her arms and turned her face toward King Pellaidh, and a golden beam connected them. "Are they dust?" she asked. "Or mire? Are they stone?"

"Truly, Goddess. I do not know."

"The Sidhe are not lightly called to war." Frige lowered her hands, one now holding an arrow, the other a feather. "Sound out their nature, and answer like with like." And then she was gone.

Everyone looked at King Pellaidh again. They had no doubt who was assigned the task.

"Blood and thunder," said Fenod. "A quest."

"You have a week," Crom Cruaich said.

The business settled, several broke out their harps and silver whistles, drums and uilleann pipes, filling the glade with riotous melodies. Dancers circled in the meadow, tall fairy princes clutching the hands of gnarled leprechauns, spinning water sprites spraying a fine mist, tinkling with their laughter.

The gray light of just-before-dawn stirred Fenod from his dreams. He blinked, still groggy from too much Fairy mead. He knew better than to quaff a hornful but he also knew he would be dispatched to seek out the Sons and Daughters of Mil's true intent, so it would be days before he would have another taste.

Pellaidh sat under a tree, already dressed in his travelling clothes, a tawny green tunic with a sash of oak leaves, an oaken scabbard topped by the hilt of his silver pommel and grip, slung low on his hip, his brown acorn cap tugged down almost covering his right eye.

"Time you were up, Fen," he said, rousing the aging servant with a slap to his rump. "Prepare to end humanity, or save it."

Fenod glared at the sound of his king's far too fervent humor as the sun crested the horizon. "Oh, my old bones," he said, pulling himself erect. The rest of the Fair Folk lay in sodden stupors. "Ready, sire," he said.

Pellaidh whistled up a pair of trout in the river nearby and sat himself astride the larger one. Fenod was grateful his laird would not subject his head to a lengthy walk. He clambered aboard a feisty overweight fish. But their steeds' frequent exuberant leaps shortly robbed Fenod of his optimism.

Far inland, they left the fish in a bywater and, a league on from the stream, the pair crossed a bridge, imperceptible to the Sons and Daughters of Mil, into their realm and time.

Fenod and his laird crept through the open field of grasses. The old retainer licked his lips when he saw a pair of cows switching their tails near one of the huts. But, instead of gathering wild fruits or going off in hunting parties as they always had, the Children of Mil engaged in a new occupation.

As the brief human days unwound, some poked sticks in the ground, gouging long rows through the sod, tearing up Earth Mother's hair in clumps. As nights followed days before the Fae watchers, men and women came back along, casting handfuls of wild barley corns onto the tortured ground. Plants took root and tiny flower sprites woke and danced around the ripening seedheads while the corns grew fat on their tall, stalky limbs. Fenod and Pellaidh laughed at the antics of the little plant spirits.

"Human ways are strange," Pellaidh said. "Yet, they do no real harm that I can see." By now the human sun was racing along its arcing path faster, the moon rising and setting both in the darkness. Pellaidh, grinning, pointed to an earthenware bowl set outside a house's door. "Milk, I'd wager," he said. They skulked closer and feasted on the offering left them.

Then, the humans committed an inexplicable horror—returning to the field with curved iron blades, they swept across the plain, slicing through the narrow stems, oblivious to the panicked screams of the barley sprites.

Pellaidh turned away from the scene of slaughter, but Fenod forced himself to watch. He gaped with a rising sense of dread as the narrow stalks were felled. The fragile spirits that inhabited them were torn in twain by the black metal blades. He watched their essences drift up to the clouds and wondered if they were returning to Elfhame or dispersing like motes of dust to fall to the ground like mortal things.

Eventually, the human sun fell below the far edge of the earth and their foul occupation was done for the time. The king and his retainer watched their departure from the killing fields with a boiling rage for these intruders, their offerings of milk be cursed.

"I have nae need to watch these creatures for even one of their short evenings more," said Fenod, kneeling.

His king stood silent, bent over by grief, still refusing to face the grounds where the sprites had so recently cavorted; the creases of caring strained his face. The Fae sun fell toward the Earth, bathing the shorn ground first with shimmering gold, darkening to red, then indigo, recounting the tragedy in the theater of colors. Were they humans, they would have cried.

When the curtain of night had fallen, King Pellaidh bade his servant away and they marched back to the Fae bridge, shrouded in a cloak of silence. At the brookside the laird summoned their fishy steeds again and they rode through the fairy night to report the horror they had observed.

They arrived, by their own time, not much after the assembly had risen from another night of folly. A few Elves and darker sorts of Sidhe who favored the night time languished, but the major share of the Tuatha Dé Danaan were breaking their fasts with nectar and ambrosia, still harmonizing with airs played through the long night.

Crom Cruaich noticed the travelers first. The elder Sidhe fell quiet as he caught sight of King Pellaidh, whose face still wore its stricken look.

"What news do our scouts bring of the Milesians? Are they of a peaceful bent, despite their truck with the black metal?" He spoke with the hopefulness that had carried the day before the pair had left, though his reading of the Gruagach laird's countenance already told him all he needed to know. Queen Medbh, herself of a more bloodthirsty bent, grinned darkly.

Pellaidh squared his shoulders, composed his features, and simply said, "Humans kill our kind, I know not why, and they do it with iron." Fenod helped him to the place they had used before, and settled him on his hummock.

Some few younger Sidhe turned one to another inquiring what killing was, but all elder Tuatha Dé did not. They had fought the Firbolg, who had held these lands from time immemorial, and the Fomorian giants. Elfhame had gathered to its shores more than a few fallen Fae in those battles.

"War." The chant started low, from the Cu Sith, the Eaches, and other such fierce tribes. It was taken up by Elves, by Kelpies, and grew. "War." Medbh raised her arms, her green eyes darkening, while Cruaich lowered his head, his heavy brows beetling. "War."

Medbh turned once more to the assembled Fair Folk and silenced the mob with a gesture. "Are there any among you who cry peace?" Not a voice replied. "Then war it shall be! Gather your tribes at Magh Tuireadh."

Word went out by runners and riders on fishes and forest creatures, on the waves and the wind. Silver pikes caught the glint of the sun as they swirled up in the fairy wind, and stone battle axes swung from their hips as they rode and walked, swam and flew. The warrior throng assembled, readying itself to march on the human settlements.

On the other side of the veil of time, human seasons passed in the course of a Fae day. The Children of Mil multiplied in their brief moments in the sun, grew tall, aged and died but their numbers always increased, like their auroch and goats, cattle and sheep spreading over the hills. They tore up longer and wider fields to seed with grains, and the Tuatha Dé heard the plaintive cries of the plant spirits each time they were felled. The lament made their blood turn cold in their veins but it sharpened their resolve as they hurried forth to battle.

Crom Cruaich beckoned Pellaidh and his vassal. "My kin, the Brownies," he said, "think you that, mounted on rabbits or foxes, you could be our scouts? None of us know the human lands as well as you."

Pellaidh nodded. "You may count on us."

Pellaidh and his small force of Brownies sat their mounts ahead of the horde, watching the settlement sleep. They rode, splitting up as they traveled. Dawn's earliest light found them in the foothills, where they encountered their first surprise. Pellaidh's fox and Fenod's badger both shied away from the smell of humans far sooner than the Brownies had expected. They stared in amazement at a wide road made of beaten dirt, its center paved with worked stone. Looking uphill, they saw a great wound in the side of the mountain.

"They are quarrying," said Pellaidh. "But who could need so much stone?"

"I'd need that much if I were commemorating every step I took," said his companion, nodding to the road.

Pellaidh shook his head, then turned his fox's head away from the quarry. "Our answers lie downhill."

They rode, not on the paved way and not even on the dirt bordering it, but in the forest to one side, riding quickly, dodging trees, heeding birdcalls and fairycalls, smelling the freshness of spring.

Barely half a human morning was gone when they saw a large agglomeration of stone buildings, a henge of tree trunks at its center. A bell tolled.

"Firbolg's Teeth," said Fenod. "These Sons and Daughters of Mil certainly can multiply."

"And build." Pellaidh's jaw was set. "This will not be so easy a nut to crack. Come, we report."

Fenod's badger, unused to long journeys, sighed as they turned about.

Queen Mebdh declared the need for a war council and runners went through the camp, calling out those Fae who had battled at Mag Tuireadh uncounted millennia past, to aid in strategizing. She led them across the bridge of time to where the humans dwelled in their brief allotment.

"For too many centuries our battles have been festive events, tournaments to display our bravery and practice skills long past the needing," she told the most elder of the assembled elves, fairies, and assorted tribes. "Now we must recall the days when we made war for the right to this land, for things have come to that turn again."

"Our jousts may be but jest these days," said Crom Cruaich, "but these silver lances we carry can still win the day." He brandished a finely chased silver spear, as delicate as lace and sharp as obsidian, that glistened in the moonlight. Another hoisted his battle axe high to catch the reflected light from Crom Cruaich's spearhead, and send it dancing on to an elfin sword swinging wildly, slicing through the cool night air.

"Enough," shouted Pellaidh. "We don't lack mettle; it is a plan we need." At that the crowd settled down and the Brownie Laird drew the human villages as he had seen them last. In the truncated

Milesian night, they drew out lines of attack, rubbed them into the dirt and retraced new lines until, in the last fading starlight, they had a stratagem all could agree on.

The Fae horde crossed into the human realm when the moon was new and the night so dark that even a fox could not see its own feet. In the western mountains they formed their ranks, the Fairy archers to the rear, Bucca in front, wielding their picks and stone hammers the size of a giant's fist, a legion of Elves and other Fae in the center hoisting their pikes and battle axes, dirks and broadswords above their heads.

Fenod felt a chill pass down his back when he thought of the upcoming battle. His king was young enough to have seen only the last of the battle against the Giants of Fomor, when Fae forces were in the ascendant. The elder Brownie remembered darker, more uncertain days. Then he thought of how few humans there were, how weak they were without magic, and was cheered. How could the Tuatha Dé not carry the day? He looked to King Pellaidh, barely visible with the glamour on him.

Pellaidh's voice came. "Look there, 'tis the signal." And when Fenod turned, he saw a shining arrow head appear far overhead, produced with Elvish magic. "Let us go," said the King, and though he spoke calmly his words carried easily to all Brownie ears.

They attacked at night, and chose the first town Pellaidh and Fenod had found, a middling-sized place, as their target. A river passed through it, the better for water-dwellers to use in their assault. Pellaidh and his kin led the Queen's forces to vantage points and to roads that could be blocked, while other more ferocious Fae silenced humans at farms, inns, and other outlying dwellings. The merest sliver of a moon looked down as a fir darrig and a brace of kelpies slew the guards at the town's main gate from behind, then the main force of Fairyland swept down to dash through streets soon brimming in blood. Not a human was left alive; magic and fine senses aided the Fae in seeking them out to the last man, woman, and child.

Fenod and his liege stood on a hillside overlooking the town at daybreak. They had not seen most of the slaughter, being assigned as couriers and scouts, but now they could both see and smell it. Pellaidh shivered, almost as if he had awoken from a nightmare. "I like this not," he said. "I thought I had a stomach for battle, but this is butchery."

"Is it not necessary? You saw with your own eyes what the Children of Mil do to our kin."

"They killed Sprites, 'tis true. Yet they've never harmed a Brownie, nor an Elf, nor any other. Truth be told, I simply do not understand them."

"So far, so true." Fenod plucked a blade of grass as long as his forearm, first making sure it hosted no fairy. "Excepting for Sprites with the misfortune to be born only to be reaped."

"As we have gleaned here, this night past. And like these mortal interlopers, they are cursed to see but a scant few days before their time expires, while we watch the ebb and flow of time's tides."

"Aye." Now Fenod, too, felt a shudder pass through him. "But what alternative do we have? Stand with the humans? I think nae."

"I am no traitor," said Pellaidh. "Yet I feel there must be a third way between total peace and utter war. But hist: the horn. We are called."

Queen Medbh assembled the other sovereigns in the dale just past the bridge tween lands. "Fine sport, this," she said. Her auburn hair matched the gore she'd squelched underfoot. "And only three Tuatha Dé killed, all by their accursed iron weapons." She turned her face westward, watching a human day pass, then another. "Let us away, and kill again."

The Sidhe assembled their ranks on her order and crossed the barrier between their realm and the humans' to march on the next settlement and drive the Children of Mil back across the sea. The night was barely half spent in the human lands when Fairy archers lined the hill overlooking a small village, barely more than a rough circle of stone huts, thin trails of wood smoke rising from their thatched roofs.

Squat Elves raised their shields of copper and their silver-bladed war axes, while swarms of other Fair Folk gathered clan by clan in squared off rows, ready to charge into the gap at the call of trumpets. On a signal from the queen, horns blasted and the hordes of immortals streamed down the hill into the undefended village.

Except the village was not undefended. At first the Tuatha Dé met no resistance as they ran toward the central square—barely more than a patch of tamped-down earth filling the space between huts. But as they found themselves confounded by the absence of enemies to slaughter, humans came streaming out their doors, screaming cries so shrill and wild they rivaled even the Ban Sidhe's wailing. In answer to the clamorous call more humans, as many as a field has flowers, ran at the archers from behind. They had smeared their skins with sap and mud to baffle the attackers' senses.

Into the fray the Sons and Daughters of Mil carried whatever they had at hand—some struck the immortals with wooden pitch-forks and cudgels, causing the elves to roar with laughter. But others wielded metal implements: butchering knives and hatchets for chopping kindling, scythes and shears that cut through Fae bodies, leaving a trail of carnage in their wakes. In much less than a human hour the queen called a retreat and the Fair Folk withdrew to behind the veil between worlds.

Amid the keening for lost kin, the queen sought out King Pellaidh. "Speak to me of these humans. Our second attack was on a smaller village than the first, yet it ended in disaster. How can this be?"

Pellaidh tugged at his beard, then pointed at the barrier between worlds, a shimmering wall through which the world of the Sons of Mil could be dimly seen. "Look you," he said. "See how their sun races across the sky? For the folk we just battled, a year and more has passed since our battle. They prepared for our second assault during the year that passed after the first. A single human has so little time, and so treats it as precious, more precious than the Five Talismans are to us. We while away our long days in games and sport and banquets—all quite worthy, of course—but they fight the earth itself and their own fleet lives just to survive, to reproduce, and to multiply."

"Our magic makes our lives easier. I see." She nodded. "So, how are they to be exterminated?"

"Your pardon, fair lady," said Fenod, who had kept his eye on the veil. "Another, more pressing concern comes to mind."

For there, in the cup between mountains, were gathering a horde of humanity. As each moment passed for the queen and her fellows, an hour and more passed beyond the barrier. And for each of those hours, another throng swelled the ranks of the enemy.

"They trailed us," said Pellaidh, "or I expect there are those who remembered where they were taken for our sport."

"So many," she whispered. Then, aloud, "To arms, all!" She whirled her spear on high. "The enemies are at our door!"

Fenod tugged at Pellaidh's sleeve. "Look," he said. "See how much iron their army carries."

"This will be a mutual slaughter," he said.

"Yes," said Fenod, gazing speculatively at the barrier between worlds. Then he spoke low and urgently to his king. Pellaidh at first shook his head, then stilled and listened, and finally at the end gave a short nod. He patted Fenod on the shoulder and scurried after the queen.

"Milady!" King Pellaidh said without his usual decorousness. "We stand no chance against this horde of humanity. And their numbers only swell, while ours are diminished and threatened with extinction. They are ready to drive us into the Western Sea."

Several Buccas and Leprechauns muttered their agreement with the Brownie King, while others vilified Pellaidh. Aelfric was the first to raise his voice above the chatter.

"We have fought to defend our place here for eons past, but never before a foe that would not accept honorable defeat. These Children of Mil breed like the mayflies they resemble in the brief-ness of their lives. Without the time to learn honor, they bring no glory in their defeat, yet know no limit in their aggressions."

"True enough," shouted Kheelan from beside him.

"Do we cry done after one lost battle?" asked the queen. "This is unlike the proud Tuatha Dé by whose side I fought 'gainst gods and giants."

"Look at them," said Pellaidh, gesturing at the gathering multitude of humans. "They howl for our blood, as we thirsted for theirs. Even were each of us to slay a dozen of theirs, they'd still carry the day. They've learned the potency of iron. If we meet them, we will all surely die. Mark me, I do not fear death; but if all die then it is for nothing."

As they watched, scouts from the human side approached the divide between lands, carefully feeling before them with staves. When one felt the different quality of the bridge, he called to his fellows. A moment later an Elvish arrow took the man's life, but it was too late. Horns sounded, and a column of the enemy formed, ready to advance on the bridge with shields held high. All this had taken but seconds from the Fae's perspective.

"Soon 'twill be too late," said Pellaidh.

"We should leave them to their accursed fields of slaughter and have no more truck with them," Hefeydd added. "We have lands aplenty. Let us retire to Tir Tairngir and curse these humans to never enter the Plain of Happiness."

"Enough," said Mebhd. Her quiet voice cut through the clamor. "Let us consult Frige." That silenced the throng and they waited for the goddess to have her final say.

When she appeared, Frige's dour countenance captured the attention of everyone present. "I hear the lamentations of the dead," she said. "And I feel the grief of the living." She turned a slow circle, catching every eye. Then she nodded.

In her right hand appeared an arrow, now in her left, a bow. The goddess raised her bow, set arrow to string, and loosed. The arrow became a shaft of light, then lightning. When it struck the bridge, a blast of sound swept across the lands, both human and Fae, and when it passed the midspan of the way between worlds was no more. Frige led her subjects on their march away from the portal and the human lands.

Long and long in vain did the humans seek to cross the bridge, to carry their enmity to the Tuatha Dé. Years passed, and decades and centuries, and the Fae faded into myth and memory.

A Fairy moon rose and set, waned to a sliver and waxed rotund again and the immortal Children of Danu celebrated in their various ways. Pellaidh approached his old retainer where he sat on the edge of Tir Nan Og, staring across to the far shore of the Western Sea, at the world left behind.

"Do you yearn for another place, old friend?" the Brownie king asked.

"Nae. This is the land we are best suited for. Nor have I any hankering after times that went before. But I indulge myself by recalling the strange, short-lived folk we abandoned, and wondering how they have fared all these days."

Pellaidh saw right through the elderly elf. He chuckled. "You wonder if they still set out their saucers of milk." Fenod made a show of being shocked at his laird's suggestion. After the hardship they had caused, no Sidhe had countenanced having any dealings with the Children of Mil.

"I have thought the same myself," the king confessed. "Let us walk their lands."

The mystic bridge was in ruins, but little enough trouble for agile small folk who after all didn't mind getting wet. Soon they were wandering fields and roads worked by mortal hands. Avoiding contact with humans and marveling at the quiet of a night without spritesong, they came to a small group of cottages and watched as the candles in the windows were blown out one by one.

"I will miss these lands," the King Pellaidh admitted, more to himself than his companion.

"Aye," said Fenod, "'Tis as honorable an end as could be wished. These Children of Mil won fair, but yet they are a sad lot. Unfortunate breed, they toil through their fleeting day while we frolic and sport through ours."

A door opened at the nearby steading, drawing Fenod's attention, then a few moments later closed. "An offering," he said.

Pellaidh smiled. "Go ahead."

Arriving at the hut, Fenod took off his cap to dip up a small amount. He sipped. Thinking to cheer his majesty, Fenod carried a capful back. Together, share and share, they finished it off.

"I wonder sometimes why they do this," said Fenod.

"Who can divine the ways of humans?" Pellaidh pulled at his beard.

Fenod shrugged, licked his lips, and crossed the yard for another hatful. As he noticed a hated iron blade dug deep into a section of tree trunk, he cursed the humans and their dreaded metal. Scattered pieces of trees were more evidence of their perfidy.

He noticed a thin trail of smoke rising over the roof and crept to the window, still thinking of revenge. In the middle of the room a tiny flame sputtered in a smoky pile of tree segments. Sympathy for the humans' miserable existence washed over him when he saw the puny fire.

As he crossed the yard again, Fenod waved his hand and the wood split into smaller chunks. Then he stopped to draw himself a last cap of milk.

"Our lot is nae so bad," he told his laird.

"It could be far worse." King Pellaidh took another draught. "We could be humans."

CHOICE CUTS

I believe I've chosen. Bring me the tenderloin, a caesar salad, a glass of your house chablis, and make me female. The Mediterranean pearl-diver, I think."

"Yes, ser, and how would you like that cooked? Oh, and what skin shade, if I may ask? We have a special on olive tonight."

Robin finished ordering and set aside his menu. As always, it would take a little time for the machinery to engineer his Change. It wasn't like he'd imagined, so many times, as a depressed teen. Down would come the magic, and touch him, and up would sweep the Change, from toes to scalp, narrowing his feet, denuding his legs—he'd somehow thought women weren't subject to leg hair—widening his hips, inhaling his penis, budding his breasts, and so on up to hair that would be long, lush, and full.

On the contrary, the Change was surprisingly mechanical. Make the order, wait for the vat-grown body to be altered according to taste, and squirt his mind into it. It was almost like putting on a form-fitting leotard, if you didn't mind stripping down to your psyche.

A sudden hush came over the restaurant, and Robin looked up. Two people, a man and a woman, stood in the doorway. Something was obviously wrong with them, besides their archaic clothing, but Robin couldn't put his finger on it. The headwaiter stepped forward and spoke to them briefly, then recoiled in shock. There was a word, something one of them had said, and it spread around the room like wildfire.

"Pregnant."

The headwaiter motioned them to one side, into the hallway leading to the toilet. Conversations resumed in the restaurant, but to Robin's trained ear they sounded artificial, strained. A man at the next table said, "What do you get when you cross an unChanged man with anything?"

"That one's a hundred years old," said his companion. "Babies." They both laughed.

Robin saw his server approaching, and stood to meet her. She was nervous, he could see that, and before she could say anything he held up a hand and nodded. She looked relieved, then turned to lead him back toward the hallway. Once there, she tapped at a side door marked "Private" and opened it for him.

The couple was there in the office with the restaurant's owner, a heavyset person of indeterminate gender, who scowled at Robin with evident distaste.

"Robin Coope? You're a Trainer?"

"Teacher," said Robin. "'Trainer' is a Belter word. Did they ask for one?" Then, before the ser could answer, he turned to the male—he couldn't quite force himself to face the pregnant female—and asked, "Were you looking for a teacher?"

The man nodded. "We just want to find somebody who can help us. I'm sorry, this is the first place that would even let us through the door. We, Molly and me, we grew up on the Ceres colony. They—the Colony Pregbureau—weren't going to let us keep the baby. They said the chance of it having a learning disorder were more than ten percent, and so they wouldn't let us try again, and we'd heard how Earth was but we thought maybe we'd have a chance here, that maybe you'd let us birth him, so we stole a shuttle and—" Suddenly the words ran out and he sat, trembling, clutching the arm of the female, reminding Robin of a flat photograph he'd seen long ago of an aboriginal couple on their first airplane ride.

The restaurant owner hauled serself out of ser's chair and loomed over Robin. "I want them out of here."

There came a rapping at the door, and Robin's server poked her head into the room. "Your order is ready, ser."

Robin sighed, then turned back to the owner. "I haven't Changed in . . . well, in quite a while. You know how it is." The man—Robin suddenly realized the restaurant owner was male—nodded reluctantly.

"All right. We'll expedite your Change, but you can forget the food. It'd be wasted on that body, anyway. Just be quick about it." He beckoned the server. "Hook him up at my terminal."

Robin looked back to the couple, forcing himself to see them both. "Look, Molly and—I'm sorry, I don't know your name."

"Johnny. I'm John, John Farmer."

"Johnny and Molly. Well, Johnny and Molly, I'm about to undergo a Change. You know what that is?" He waited for their cautious nods. "It's really nothing, like putting on a new set of clothes, but you know I'll look different when you talk to me next. Just sit on that couch, don't interfere, and I'll be back to help you as soon as I can." That done, he followed his server to the owner's desk and watched her as she skillfully passed her hands over a series of lightbuttons.

"Just sit back," she said. "And this'll all be over in a few moments."

Robin felt his usual anticipation preceding a Change. He stared at the mandala pulsing in the air before him. Its projectors subtly sensed his mood and matched its beats to his alpha rhythm. Then it came, the snapping, tearing sensation, and he cried out briefly.

When Robin came back to herself, she was an elfin, olive-skinned naked girl.

She dressed, then hurried to meet her new clients. Something had changed then, slightly, in her perception of the couple, and she found herself suddenly smiling. She ran a hand over her flat belly. It might be nice to use the skills she'd been trained to use, and it could turn out to be remunerative, too.

She waved gaily to the other Changed guests she met, turned

once more into the hallway, rapped briefly at the door, and entered the office to find two servers wrestling Robin Coope's body out of the owner's chair. "Be done here in a sec," one of them said. The Farmers were watching, both aghast. Robin walked over to them, and suddenly she found herself smiling again: at them, smiling at Molly, and at John, and at the obvious bulge that was their off-spring.

"Molly? Johnny? I'm Robin Coope. Again."

It took the better part of the afternoon to get the Farmers registered with the Web as immigrants. Robin arranged for living quarters, paid for by one of the few remaining anthropological teams extant on the Web. She got their ident cards printed at a public terminal, listed them with emergency assistance, sold their shuttle to the Smithsonian, and bought a muumuu for Molly. She felt livelier than she had in years.

She even wangled a stipend from the anthro team to hold her over while introducing the Farmers to 22nd Century Earth.

The next morning, Robin entered her brand new office. The room was spacious, almost four meters square. The cameras were innocuous, the couch low and inviting. The only intrusion was the tiny machine riding in Robin's inner ear that passing on comments, questions, and judgments from her likewise invisible patrons. "The Farmers are at the door," announced the room a few minutes later.

Robin ushered the couple into the room. "I hope you slept well."

"Oh, we did," answered Molly. "Thank you, Miss Robin." She blushed.

"Just Robin will do." She offered them seats and showed them the table's automenu on which they could order breakfast. "Just press any picture, and the kitchen will deliver it to you. Are you comfortable? I mean, with talking about your situation?" She waited for a nod, then went on. "Ceres cut all ties with Earth right after Changing became popular, so I'm not sure exactly where to start."

"We know about NullPop," offered John. "You don't birth anybody until somebody dies. I mean, *really* dies."

"That's right, we stabilized the population at twelve billion, and we don't allow pregnancies any more. We use the same technology that we use in Changing, except we allow a personality to grow in the vatbody."

"Why didn't anybody meet us when we landed?" Molly asked. "If one of you had flown all the way out to Cereville we'd have turned out the whole place to welcome you."

Robin cocked her head, listening to a dozen voices, then stilled them all by saying, "We don't like surprises. Suppose—suppose you are somebody who's lived a hundred and fifty years, and you know that, by jumping from body to body—by Changing—you can live as long as you want. You do one of two things: either you go out and do everything, experience as much life as you can; or you shut down the part of you that wants to do new things, because there's too much of a chance that you'll either run out of new things to do, or one of those things might kill you. And, sure enough, over a century and a half, most of the people who want to try new things run out of luck, leaving the rest of us."

As she sometimes did, Robin tried to pin down her vague memories of sports, pre-Change. Skiing? Maybe. Surfing? Her thoughts shied away from the image of roaring surf. She had tried camping, a sudden flash came of sleeping under canvas, of wrestling a trout from a stream. She hadn't enjoyed it; someone had talked her into it. She hadn't been that outdoorsy, that daring. Maybe that was why she was still alive. The memory slid away, as if it belonged to someone else. Which, when she thought about it, it had.

Molly shifted uneasily on her cushion, and studied the menu. "I'm getting a chocolate milk." She offered the device to John, but he shook his head.

"Over the years," Robin continued, "We get into ruts. None of us look around at our neighbors, much less up at the sky. About the only change that's acceptable is *the* Change, because that's what keeps us alive."

"What happened to your body?" Molly interjected. "Your other body, I mean."

"Oh that?" Robin waved her hand. "It was just meat." A strangled noise came through her link, and she winced. "That was insensitive of me," she added quickly, leaning forward and making eye contact with Molly. "We don't have much respect for flesh, I suppose, considering we put it on and take it off so readily. I was in that male body for two years, and was a female before that. But we really don't have the resources to bury or waste good flesh like that, even when it is a little on the old and stringy side."

Molly's drink had arrived, and she made a production of sniffing it and setting it aside, before turning a half-frightened, half-determined glare on Robin. "You all are very different here on Earth, but it all comes down to this." She patted her belly. "Do you have respect for this baby of ours? Can we bring it into the world, and love it like we ought to?"

Robin chose her words carefully, aware she was trying to span the vast void between their worlds. "We understand your attraction to your . . . offspring. While we have no intention or desire to interfere with familial attraction—"

"What?"

Robin sighed. "We know you love your baby, but you have to understand. Population Control, NullPop, is not a flexible agency. We—they—have rules for immigration; they'll just delay two personality implants for you. But there is no option open for natural babies; it's not just illegal, it's unheard of. Everyone on Earth is made allergic to embryos. You'll have to give it up."

John was standing, folding his fingers into the palms of his hands in a way that made Robin vaguely uneasy. From behind him, Molly said, "Give up our baby? I don't want to give him up for adoption."

"Adoption?" Then the meaning of the word came to Robin, courtesy of her ear-machine, and she laughed in shocked delight. "Oh, no, it'll have to go in the hopper, of course. It's a rare delica—"

The movement was sudden, caught only in Robin's peripheral vision, then the man's folded hand caught her on the side of her head and neck, knocking the much smaller woman into the menu console, off which she bounced to crumple to the floor.

That's something else we've gotten rid of in the last century, said a voice in her ear she barely heard before chasing darkness down to nothing.

"They call it a 'fist.'" The doctor was hesitant, obviously as rusty at his skill as she was at teaching. "He appears to have used it to break a vertebra in your neck. I don't believe you will be able to move anything from there down."

Robin stared at the ceiling. "Where are they?"

"The Farmers? Oh, they were Changed. Some kind of law having to do with violent offenders, whatever those are." The doctor shone a light in one of Robin's eyes, then flicked it away. "Of course, they're much happier now. Are you ready to Change?" The question was a formality; already the mandala was forming in the air above Robin's eyes.

"I suppose," she said. "I suppose I'm ready now. Would you make me a male, please? A large male? With big hands." As the doctor refocused the mandala, Robin's last thoughts moved back to her teenage years, when she had been suicidal, sure that her wish to be the opposite sex had been perverse. She remembered, keenly, imagining the magic coming down and changing her: sprouting hair on her face, flattening her chest, narrowing her hips, sprouting her clitoris into a penis, and so on. The thoughts, newly minted, were yet ones she remembered from all the female bodies she'd had. It was comforting.

"What happened to the Farmer's baby?"

The man wheeled a portable terminal to the bedside and ran a sure hand over its diagnostic lightbuttons. "I'm not sure. I suppose I could check."

"No," said Robin. "Don't bother." She knew what had happened to it. Then the snapping, the tearing, and soon Robin came to himself.

REBEL THE FIRST
AND ONLY

This here's a story about more than a few things, but mostly it's about Duane Fuller, who we all call Reb so you might as well forget I told you his real name anyway. Now as with most stories about Reb it's got a few things in it what don't make no sense nohow. You're gonna have to bear with me over some of the rough spots; I expect you'll know 'em when you see 'em.

But lemme tell you it from the beginning, which is where I come in.

There we are at Slow Jack's Place lifting a few, Reb and me. The Place is a converted railroad passenger car. Jack painted all the windows black except the one at the end in the door, so it's dazzling to look that way when you're in there in the daytime. It gets dimmer the farther you get toward the back under the box air conditioner he bondoed into the metal wall.

We're at the bar, about halfway down where Jack left out some of the seats. Nobody's in there but us and Jack. Reb's on my left so the low sun throws the brown shadow of his bottle all the way down past mine. I get to thinking and turn to him and say, "You know, I don't recall seeing you around the last month."

Reb says, "I was in Italy. Didn't you hear?"

"No," I say, because I hadn't. "Maybe did you and Maybelle go away that week I was up to Tulsa visiting my niece?" Maybelle, that's his wife.

"Most likely," he says. "It *was* kind of sudden."

It all started—says Reb—with that box of Cracker Jack.

*

Now normally (Reb says) I don't eat the stuff, what with getting popcorn bits between my teeth and just generally being able to take peanuts or leave them. But when a guy's drinking the fancy imported beer that his son brought all the way from Arizona because he wants his pa to like the slip of a girl he's bringing along—why then a guy's just got to have something to wash that beer down with. So I opened the Cracker Jack and passed it around. Let me tell you, it washed that beer down mighty fine.

Soon enough we got down to the bottom of that box, and all that was left was the prize, a teeny puffy paper pillow with something heavy inside. I tried to give it to my boy Dallas and he gave it back, and I tried to give it to that girl Patricia of his, and she gave it back. Finally Maybelle up and said so open it already.

About then my boy Dallas asked if we've started keeping cattle that are maybe given to stampeding and I said no.

And after that Patricia asked if we're prone to earthquakes here in Anthem, Texas and I said no.

And then I tore the end of that prize off and tilted it so what was inside rolled out onto my palm. Turned out it was a ring, gold-plated and looking mightily expensive. I resolved then and there to buy Cracker Jack more often. There was a folded piece of paper in the envelope, too, so I asked Maybelle to fetch me my reading glasses.

She was on her way to get them when she happened to look out the window and she said law would you look at that? Dallas and Patricia, they ran to look so I went to fetch my glasses my own self.

Maybelle yelled something about her pea patch. I ambled over to the window, unfolding that paper as I went. When I got there, the window was rattling fit to burst. I looked out and what do you think was landing out there? A helicopter, that's what, a big old jobber like they use to fly whole tanks around.

Well, we all gawked for a long second or two, afore I remembered the paper in my hand. I looked down at it.

Congratulations, it read, *you're the new Pope.*

"The Pope," I say to Reb, peering up at him and setting my beer down. "Imagine that. I thought they'd have a fancier system for picking 'em." I pull out my spiral notebook what the *Daily Sun* gave me and start writing.

"Seems they do," says Reb. "It's got to do with them taking votes of people they call 'Cardinals.' Not like the Arizona variety, I reckon they're more like Senators. And they vote and they vote. If they don't decide in eight votes, though, they're deadlocked. And blamed if that ain't what happened this time. First time since Jesus appointed Saint Peter the first Pope, they said."

But I learned all that later. Just then we were all in a tizzy about having unexpected visitors. The pilot set that helicopter down pretty as you please between the pecan trees, the Well of Youth, and the pea patch, although he did blow over a few trellises. Old Blue the Fifteenth lost his doghouse, but the Good Lord knows you do make sacrifices. Maybelle said law she was going to have to break out the good china now and Dallas went to get his camera. Patricia asked me did we get things landing on the lawn often, and I said not since that roc-bird back in sixty-nine. You remember, Buddy, that's when we lost the first Blue. Or was it the second?

Anyway.

You never saw the like of the troop that come out of that helicopter. There were guys in black suits who held one hand up to their ears, the spitting image of the folks who guard the President. And there were these guys in armor carrying spears, setting up one of those whatchacallits, an honor guard. And then they unrolled a red carpet. I kid you not, a red carpet just like it was the Academy

Awards on television or something. A guy came out waving a ball that had smoke coming out of it. I figured they didn't want skeeters bothering them.

The last one out was a man in red robes with a hat like a gimme cap but it didn't have a brim. Wouldn'ta kept the sun off his neck none, hope to tell you. He took one look around and I could tell he didn't particularly cotton to what he saw, and then he marched to the house surrounded by the black suits. I figured, let them knock, and after a little bit that's just what they did.

Dallas let them in and we served ice tea all around in the cups we brought back from the Alexandria Library. Red Hat introduced himself as Cardinal Matthew Carlino. He said did I get the invitation and I said I got the ring if that's what you mean. He said that means their gee-pee-ess dingus was working just fine.

So Carlino asked me did I want to be Pope and I said I thought they'd already decided themselves. And he said sure *they've* decided but I have to say okay too. Now as it happened I was between jobs at the time, so I said yes.

"Neighborly of them to ask," I say.

"Right neighborly, except I do keep forgetting to ask what a job pays before accepting it. But anyway, then they asked me if I was Catholic."

"You aren't, are you?"

"As it happens, I was." Reb looked down at the bar for one whole entire minute. "The janitor at the high school, Mr. Herrera, remember him, he's the one got sainted last year? He was a Catholic, and he and his wife used to have me over for pie or cake after school. They were the ones who converted me to Catholicism with a—whatcha call, a confirmation and all. There was a time I'd do anything to piss off the folks." His pop, the pastor of First Anthem Baptist, that's who he really meant. "Cardinal Carlino seemed really relieved, and I wondered how many people he'd been to see in that fancy helicopter of his before he got to me. I kinda figured he'd bring up my being married next, since I never heard of a married Pope. But no, he slid right past that subject. So then he said what name did I want to have as Pope."

"How's that?" I say, fixing to get indignant. "They wanted to give you a different name?"

"I didn't get that either, so I just told 'em that the name my buddies gave me in high school was good enough." Reb slaps the bar, raising a cloud of dust that swirls around in the air like dirt behind a big rig. Slow Jack looks over and waves a finger at him all slowlike; he likes it quiet in his bar. "Anyway," Reb says, "from then on they all called me Pope Rebel the First."

"The First," I say. "The One and Only is more like it."

"That's what I like about you, Buddy, you're none too subtle." He lifts the bottle to take his last swig.

Well now that sounds like a compliment to me so I up and buy him another Coors.

We all trooped out and got on that helicopter, which took us to DFW airport, where we got on a jet, just the five of us and the Cardinal. Boy, howdy, how we all howled—especially old Blue—when that plane took off straight up! I looked out the window and its jets were pointing straight downward, just like a rocket's. That jet took us to a Vatican aircraft carrier in the Gulf, the Saint Agricola of Avignon they called it, which took us all the way to Italy. I remember the name of the ship because I kept one of the cocktail napkins for a snotrag.

And then there we were docking in Port Civvy-something. It's near Rome on the west coast of Italy. They got this hummer with tinted windows, which it took us to a subway station. We didn't have to buy tickets, though, that place was there just for us and whatever other muckitymuck wanted to go to the Vatican. Blamed if that subway car didn't look just like the monorail at Disneyland, excepting there weren't no Mickey painted on the side. Instead there was a painted cross with Jesus on it, all bloody and looking mightily pained.

We took that subway forty miles to Vatican City, on the west side o'Rome. Carlino, he told me the subway's been there a couple hundred years now. It used to be a secret, a back way into the catacombs, he said, but now they let big celebrities like Judge Judy use it. Her and the president and Dwight Yoakum and all.

Pretty soon I knew what them catacombs Carlino had mentioned was. The subway started up and we're driving between twin walls of bodies, all turned to bones and stacked up like cordwood. I figured the stink in there would be worse'n anything, if the windows was open. But instead it was dark and cool in the car. Restful, like. I reckon I wouldn't mind being planted there myself, once I'm dead that is. For a second I wondered what the smell reminded me of—kind of piney actually—and then I saw they had one of them tree-shaped freshener things hanging up front.

It was a pretty quick trip. Soon we pulled up at a subway station with velvet walls and tile floors, and an escalator that took us up to the pope-house. It was like being at the mall excepting there wasn't hardly any people.

Things happened pretty fast after that. We were all tuckered out from the trip, but Carlino, he up and dragged us out to this balcony overlooking the front yard. And boy was it full of people, let me tell you. They put up a yell when they saw us, just like as if we were football heroes, and I looked to see if they were going to do the wave. But then a chimney nearby let out this plume of white smoke, and they gave a yell that puts the first one to shame. Just as they're letting up, Carlino he sneaked up behind me and put a mile-high pope-hat on my head, and that made 'em bust out all over again.

"White smoke," I say. "Smoke *signal*, more like. Sounds like that's their sign that you're the new Pope."

"Got that right." Reb is in profile to my left, the setting sun outlines him in light so's I can't hardly look at him. He turns toward the light, tapping a nervous few times on the bar, then looks back down. Then Slow Jack turns on the fluorescents which come on in ones and twos, buzzing like spring somewhere where there's flowers. "Got that right," Reb mutters again into his beer. "At first—"

At first it was a cake walk. Maybelle she found out about the shopping in Italy, and faster'n you can say Jack Robinson she was off to the stores with some Swiss guards. I had thought they were there as real soldiers, but Carlino said they were trained but really mostly for show. If a Catholic hurt me he'd be excommunicated—thrown right out of the church. They keep better watch over the Pope when he's away from the Vatican. At any rate, soon enough Maybelle was bringing back leather coats and shoes and purses and I-don't-know-what-all, enough to outfit an army of wives.

Dallas and his girl, all they needed was a room, if you know what I mean. My dog Blue, well, he got the biggest thigh bone around. Wouldn't surprise me to hear it was from some kind of dinosaur.

That just left me. The first couple of days I was sitting in a red throne of a chair while people come up to kiss my ring. I hope to tell you, I never seen so much hand-kissing in all my born days. The first few times I fixed to slug whoever it was planting their lips on my hand, but after a while I got sorta used to it.

And I was signing stuff I couldn't read. Sure, Carlino would tell me what they were. Investitures, renewals of treaties, encyclicals—he said those are just letters that go to a bunch of people, like pizza place flyers, I guess—things like that. Who woulda thought I shoulda taken Italian back in high school, instead of Shop?

That put me in a stew. I like to know what it is I'm signing. For all I knew they were trying to put one over on me, like that time the Devil came to Anthem. If I'm going to do a job I like to do it

right, so I asked Carlino if all them documents could be put into
English. He squealed about it a little, saying it'd take time to do and
that's not how things were done, and how if anybody was to write
anything anti-Catholic I'd never see it anyway because they'd be
excommunicated so fast it'd make your head spin. Seems their answer for everything was to throw a guy out of the Church. Finally
he came around when I told him right then and there to translate
one of them suckers out loud. I expect he knew I'd just ask him to
read every single one of them for me.

From then on they were in English, but of course it was all still
lawyerese to me. I pondered my way around each of 'em as best
I could, signing maybe five things a day, and not doing much of
nothing else. The in-box turned into an in-crate mighty fast, but I
just don't like doing things halfway. It didn't take much of that for
me to remember I hadn't asked Carlino what the job paid. Boy did
I slap my head over that one.

"Don't tell me," I say. "Let me guess: they expected you to work
for nothing." Reb and I had done community service that time
when we were teenagers and got caught stealing unicorn horns
from the Goodwill. I figured that's how this job worked too.

"Naw, it was worse than that," he says. "You're right that there
wasn't a paycheck, but we had room and board, and could have just
about anything we asked for. Remember what I told you about
Maybelle's shopping for clothes? Whenever she'd pick out a new
pair of shoes the store owner would just give them to her. When
I had a hankering for one of Shorty's barbecue sandwiches, they
flew him on over to Italy. If Dallas wanted a chocolate-covered
Labrador Retriever, he just had to ask and it'd be there inside of
an hour."

I look at him.

"Not that he ever asked for such a thing," Reb adds, studying
the new beer closely. "That's just a for instance."

"I don't see what's so bad about getting whatever you want," I say. "Sounds pretty cushy."

"It didn't bother me so much at first, either. It took Maybelle to point out the problem." He turns to face me. "Let me put it this way. How do you know if your stories for the *Sun* are any good?"

"Well, the paper pays me."

"Exactly. If they just gave you a paycheck because of who you are instead of how good you can write, would you feel so good about what you'd written?"

I go hmm.

Exactly. I got to thinking that made this job a lot like welfare, where they give you money just for being poor. Now Maybelle brings in enough at the Save-a-Lot to keep the wolf away from the door. How do you think she'd feel if we had to go on welfare? Pretty bad, I reckon. We worked hard to get where we are. I could have lived with that, but it did kind of eat at me.

And then there was, well, the sermon. For my first one Carlino suggested I preach from a text they'd worked up for me, and I said okay. He delivered it so fast I figured it was a standard speech. I practiced it up in front of a mirror a dozen times, then delivered it to the family who said I did okay by it. A couple of weeks after we got there my usual clerk Tomas rousted me out of bed on Sunday and dressed me up in my pope-robes. When I got up in front of those thousands of people, though, I just lost it. My mind went blank and the notes in my hand looked like they were written in Martian. That's when I winged it.

"Winged it?" I ask all innocent-like, and if there's a grin on my face it's all on the inside, where Reb can't see it.

"Yeah, I stared out at all those people, and it got to looking like when I was little and my dad made me stand up near the pulpit and announce the next hymn. All I could think of was his hellfire and damnation sermons, so that's what I gave them.

Unfortunately I didn't really remember everything just the way he put it, so I might have added a few things from *The X-Files* and *Terminator* and *The Weekly World News*. I can't say for sure, it's all a bit hazy."

"How'd they take it?"

"I wasn't sure at first that most of them understood me. The translator gave up a minute or two in. Everybody—but everybody looked pretty dazed when I was done, though; they just kinda sat there." Reb looks toward the window. The sun's gone down outside, and I figure he's going to want to go home to Maybelle before long. She sets a great table when she gets home early enough. Then he sighs.

Monday rolled around. We'd made pretty good friends with the guards and the folks who served up the grub, so usually we'd be joking and making faces at each other because most of them didn't speak English. That's not how it was on Monday, no sirree.

You'd think I'd turned into Johnny Cash the way they looked at me. Everybody tiptoed around like I was gonna burst into song or punch somebody out at any moment. Now it doesn't take much of that to rile me, so I up and ordered everybody out of the room. There was a television there that we got American TV on. They'd piped it through a couple of Vatican satellites. Patricia switched on CNN, and we found out right away what was up.

The announcer was talking about "the astounding pronouncements of Pope Rebel the First." All about how I'd said that aliens from the future were after our embryos, or something like that. They had a picture of me and Blue; the one where I'd put the pope hat on the dog. Dallas he laughed at that until Patricia kicked him.

Tomas came in to tell me it was time to get to signing paperwork. At first he was quiet like the rest of them had been. He's usually chatty, though, and I guess that's a pretty hard thing to recover from, so we were only a few steps down the hall when he up and asked me what to do about the aliens.

"What aliens?" I said, then I said, "Oh, those aliens. Well, I reckon you'll just have to build some anti-time machine rockets."

"Oh," he said. "I suppose we'll need to talk to the Americans about that," and I agreed, just to play along.

When we got to the office, everybody else was still pussyfooting around, except for Carlino. Him? Well, he was just looking thoroughly pissed. "Let me show you something," he said, and led me to the office next door.

This it turns out was where I answer my mail. And by "me" I mean a bunch of clerks were sitting there typing letters into computers. Carlino told me the Vatican gets a couple thousand letters and emails a day addressed to the pope. Only the most important ones are passed on to the man himself, the rest are up to these guys to answer. "Care to guess how many email messages we received today?" he asked.

That's not the kind of question somebody asks when they're looking for a wild guess, so I kept quiet. "Four hundred thousand," he said. "And counting. I can only imagine how much we'll be seeing from the mail and Federal Express this week."

I allowed as how that was a pretty big number.

"Half of them will be cranks of one stripe or another," he said, "and the other half will want to know what to do about the aliens from the future."

I didn't get it for all of ten seconds. Then I did, although he helped by spelling it out for me.

Turns out I couldn't make a mistake. Or wasn't allowed to, same thing. It's called "papal infallibility," in case you want to write that down. It means most Catholics take everything the pope says like it comes from God's own mouth, and those that don't keep mum about it. I asked him if we couldn't send out a newsletter cyclical-thing that said I was only joking, and he said it's hard for a pope to unsay something. The last time a pope gave out with a joke it started a war.

Still, it did seem pretty unfair to let everybody think what I'd said was gospel. I wanted to make it right. I would've taken to that job a lot more if I hadn't taken it so damn seriously.

I decided it was a good time for a family meeting. When we were all together I started out by asking how everybody felt about this whole Pope hooha. Maybelle, she looked like she wanted to say something, but Dallas spoke up first and allowed as how he was just fine with it. He'd fattened up a bit on that Italian food, and wasn't in no hurry to give up the good life.

Maybelle spoke up then. She was of two minds. She loved the free clothes, and how she could make them Swiss guards jump just by saying boo. But she was missing her pea patch and her hell-hounds and the other checkers at the Save-a-Lot.

I told them about my morning with Carlino, and that sobered them up some.

Patricia was the one that surprised me. I'd expected her to go along with Dallas, but she up and said she was planning on college and wanted to make something of herself and she was going back to Arizona, fiancé or no fiancé. Dallas he looked stricken at that, and changed his tune pretty damn quick. He said he was just kidding before and he thought living in Tucson sounded like a fine deal.

Once we'd all agreed that I needed to give up the Pope gig, it was time to talk to Cardinal Carlino. I didn't expect him to be too broken up about it. I'd only been signing a few things a day, and my sermon had not been what you call a rousing success. Plus there was that whole papal infallibility thing.

Sure enough, he was ready to be rid of me. He said he expected there wouldn't be a problem getting the rest of the cardinals to agree to my successor, now they'd experienced the alternative. We talked over ways for me to get shed of my Popedom. I figured it was just a case of me saying I was quitting, no harm no foul. But he said that wasn't something a pope had done before, and it might not work, infallibility or no infallibility. When I asked him what he meant he said that whole other churches had sprung up like weeds when there was more than one person claiming to be pope, and there might be a lot of people who wouldn't accept my quitting just like that. It would have to be something more drastic than that, he said.

"Drastic" didn't sound so good. I asked him if he was talking about my committing suicide. I thought that'd bring him up short, but he just laughed and said if I were to wait a few days I wouldn't have to kill myself. Somebody else would do it for me.

Now I didn't like that line any better than I had suicide, so I asked him if he was planning something. I kinda *loomed* over him when I said that. If he was bothered he didn't show it—he just said that he knew for a fact there were a couple dozen would-be assassins on their way to Rome already.

That did kinda bring me up short. From his expression, Carlino might be okay with opening all the doors between them and me.

He said it would've been better if I'd never gotten to be Pope. Then he said it would've been better if I'd never been born. I was about to let him know that was mighty unmannerly of him when what he said rang a bell. I knew then what to do.

It was the easiest thing in the world, once I though of it. There was a surefire way I could get the church to say I didn't exist. All I had to do was excommunicate myself.

"Didn't that cause more problems than it solved?" I ask.

"How's that?"

"Well, if you were unfoolable, then you were right when you decided to kick yourself out of the church for telling a whopper about aliens from the future. But if you were pope, nobody ought to be able to kick you out, 'cause you're unfoolable." I pull a few shelled peanuts out of the bowl Slow Jack keeps on the bar, and pop one into my mouth. I suck the salt off of it and then crunch up the stale nut.

"Infallible," he says, "not 'unfoolable.' Oh, I didn't excommunicate myself for telling a lie or even for making a mistake."

"No? Well then what did you do?"

"Remember the guards? How they were just for show because nobody would dare hurt the Pope for fear of getting thrown out of the Church? Except for assassins, evidently. All I did was bang my fist really hard against the wall. It hurt like hell, so after I got it looked at I excommunicated myself for hurting the Pope, and we all came on home."

I give him that look I save for city councilmen who think they're putting one over on their constituents by lowering one tax and raising three others. "How come I never heard about any of this?"

"Well, *hell*, Buddy," he says. "You were in Oklahoma." He takes a last pull off his bottle of Coors. "They let me keep the ring. See?" And he pulls his hand off of his bottle to show me. Boy howdy, what a sparkler. His finger's welled up around both sides of it like a cheap radiator hose around a clamp.

"I thought sure they'd of kept that," I say, scribbling furiously in the notebook.

"Nah," says Reb. "Usually they break the old one up and melt it down to make a new one for the next pope. But this one wouldn't come off my finger, on account of my fingers being so thick and swelling up so much when I punched that wall. They lemme keep it." He raps the ring against the counter. "Better'n what you usually get in a box of Cracker Jack, any old day."

Slow Jack, he takes the sound for Rebel calling for another round, so he brings 'em over. That reminds me that Reb's usually home eating by now, so I ask him why he's still at the Place so late.

"I had dinner already," he says. "Maybelle brought home Chinese food from the deli at the Save-a-Lot." It's long after dark, but I see a halo around his head like the one when the sun is coming through the Place's lone window, and I lean back to look past him.

Several reporters are jockeying with a rabbi and a monk, all trying to get through the door at once. Camera lights are blazing and people are yelling Reb's name.

"Dadgum," says Reb. He shakes his head. "I should never have opened that fortune cookie."

As I write this introduction to "Great Depth," two whales have just washed ashore in San Francisco Bay, making a total of five gray whales found dead in the Bay Area this month. No one knows what killed them along the path of their spring migration from Mexico to Alaska.

Scientists, journalists and fiction writers are speculating about the strange deaths of creatures at every level of the marine ecosystem and what these die-offs mean for the future of our oceans. In the imaginative story "Great Depth," Edd Vick adds a non-human voice to this discussion.

Edd says that a dream he had at the Rainforest Writers Retreat on the Olympic Peninsula inspired this story, told entirely from the viewpoint of a whale. After his nameless protagonist narrowly escapes from an evil being that threatens whales and other sea creatures, she embarks on a complex and compelling quest to defeat it. Humans ("landers" in the whales' parlance) are left on the sidelines as a group of cetaceans attempt to lure the monster into a final confrontation to save themselves and their descendants.

—K. G. Anderson

K.G. is a speculative fiction writer who has sold stories to *Galaxy's Edge*, *Weirdbook*, and many anthologies. In 2012 she and Tom Whitmore accompanied Edd on a memorable book-hunting trip to Archer, Texas.

THE GREAT DEPTH

I swim in two oceans, one made of water, the other of words.

Mothers rumble the Message, a constant background pulse to whatever other news or opinion or tale is the pressure of the day. Lately most of the opinion is how brain-cracked we are, how so many of us are beaching ourselves.

This is why I dive. I'm escaping from the Message, swimming so deep all is darkness. There is a thrill to this; Mothers tell tales to calves of fiends inhabiting the deeps. I've never seen anything but fish. Some strange, to be true, but more prey than predators to one my size.

Most of the clicks I send out disappear into a profound emptiness all around me. It is fitting that this void should be where we go when we die. Finally I get an echo and snap up a pair of squid. The exquisite pressure mutes the constant background Message, drives its tone downward. That's when I hear it, a response from deep below. I take it at first for a reflection of surfaceward talk; this happens sometimes when waters of different temperatures lie one over the other.

But no. This talk is deep and slow. It speaks more to my bones than my brain. More, it is *solitary*. My world is one of millions of voices repeating and amplifying news, opinion, and tales. This is a lone voice from the deep saying things I do not understand. Worse, my body does understand. It drives downward, toward this new voice, as my blood screams in me for air. I see pale light below, and realize I am seeing something that glows in the dark. But this is no mere fish, luring smaller prey. This is large, more immense than an entire pod of whales. Beneath its skin I sense colossal columns of muscle and unfamiliar organs. Its maw gapes, a gash wider than the biggest lander shell, and even at a distance I feel a current draw me toward this beast.

While my body plunges toward the monster, my brain drifts up and away. In a dream I see myself as a tiny creature clinging to a rock. I feed on whatever the ocean sees fit to drop on me. Then, as time passes, I feel myself grow and hunger. I learn to broadcast my invitation. I am the beast, consuming all that answer my call. I see a tiny animal.

My perspective changes again. The animal is me. The creature is the one drawing me toward it with sounds that are poison to my mind. Slowly, deliberately, I shift my consciousness back to the creature. Using the malleability of dreams I convince myself/it that the small animal is toxic.

When I wake, it is to find myself swimming strongly, more energetically than I ever have, tired to the marrow yet using every jot of energy to drive myself forward and up. Forward to—

Forward to land. I see it ahead and not so far away. I shove myself through the water, sudden furious pain slices at me from stem to stern, and I know that I've scoured myself bloody over a coral reef. I want to stop; I try to stop, but my body disobeys. Now the land is closing, and now small human shells are rocking in my feverish wake, and now the land is here, and now—

I drive myself up onto a beach in the early morning moonlight, crushing a small shell meant to hold less than a dozen landers. Sand flies into one eye, and with the other I see shore birds burst into the sky in disarray, screaming their various alarms.

My body presses heavily on the shore. I've never felt this strange pressure, pulling so strongly in one direction so my organs all sag and my lungs labor. The urge to kill myself subsides. I thrash, trying to save myself, to return to the ocean. It does nothing but grind me into the sand. With no way to save myself I prepare to greet the Great Depth. Birds return and perch on me to peck and pry. My slowly drying, filming eye tracks the sun as it broaches the horizon, and then they arrive.

Landers. Improbably balancing themselves like porpoises on their tails, they move around me, making thin, shrill sounds. None of their noise penetrates deeper than my skin.

Their motives are opaque. If they were fellow whales, they would be crooning in sympathy, supporting my body until my spirit had floated away, then accompanying it as deeply as they could. But these landers, I have no idea what they think, why they act as they do. Fear grips me, but I soon reduce it to a minnow and release it. I intentionally turn my attention away from the landers. Nothing matters but making my death the best one it can be.

I look into the sky once more, seeing a cloud that looks like a manta. My brain slows in time with my faltering heartbeat, my only regret that I can fall no farther than this beach. Another cloud, this one a crab.

A tug, a pull, and I focus once more on the landers. Something is binding my tail, heaving at me. For a moment I panic, contorting and bucking. Then I realize that the pull is seaward. I welcome it. Improbably, the eye facing downward sees the sand slide past. I see a smear of my blood.

I enter the water. It is too shallow yet to swim, but I can twist enough to see a lander shell, puffing clouds, pulling me with nets that surround much of my body. The humor of the situation strikes me, and I snort through my blowhole. These landers: when my kind are in the ocean they want to take us out, but once I am ashore they work to return me to my home. I doubt they will accompany me down, though.

We reach deeper water, and mats of something like damp kelp float off of me. I realize that while my mind was drifting the landers had put these on me, moistened to keep me from dehydrating too much. So they are not merely returning me to the ocean to die, to fall into the Great Depth. Strange as it seems, they mean to help.

The nets are unwound by landers who keep a prudent distance. Their shell repeats the same nonsense syllables over and over, though the sounds seem fainter than usual, even from so close. I thank the landers, sure they don't understand me, and dive down and away, flinching from the pain of salt water in my wounds.

The minnow of fear I thought banished returns. My blood pounds in my ears, and I have to surface again because I want to, I need to, breathe. I am here when I notice—

All the sea's sounds are muffled. I have injured my hearing, perhaps by diving too deep, perhaps on the beach. I send out clicks, trying to see the ocean bottom, needing to orient myself, and they come back vague and muted. So even this sense is damaged. I dive, I breach, I breathe, I dive again in what I hope is the direction of open water.

Days pass, and life returns to nearly normal. Seasons pass, and I listen, with difficulty, to news, to opinion, to tales. Years pass, and I tell of the deep-sea monstrosity, of my beaching and rescue. I breed, and give birth to a girl calf. I chase fish.

One day I am in cold waters when the Mothers approach. Even impaired as I am, I have heard them coming from half the ocean away, and I wait. After greetings, they speak to me in high-pitched tones that do not carry. At first I am shocked; this way of speaking is private, more befitting a mother speaking to a calf. Then I understand; they have news only for me. But who speaks privately?

More sisters and brothers are vanishing or dying every year, they say. Some starve, some are disoriented and damaged by collisions with lander shells, but many more are beaching themselves.

The Mothers blame two offenders. Landers still venture out in their shells, making their appalling racket. They drive us to desperation. Something, say the Mothers, must be done. Eventually.

But the more immediate problem is the beast from the depths. They have heeded my news of it. Explorers sent to listen for the beast have not returned, and a greater and greater area of ocean has become devoid of life. Fish disappear, porpoises disappear, and the whales that do not likewise disappear heave themselves onto beaches to die. Pods everywhere mourn their dead or vanished members.

The Mothers have heard my story; they know of my impairment. More, they know me as a fellow mother now. I have a new standing and my story a greater value. They are convinced that the beast is to blame.

Part of my story was of the beast's enticing call. Now I share what I before reserved: the dream of being the monster, of inducing it to believe I was poisonous. After my encounter I thought this more hallucination than experience, but if I have had a permanent effect on the monster then this could explain the increase in beachings.

I feel guilt that fellow whales may have died because of me. The Mothers look at me in a way that makes me feel insignificant, like krill, and say I have probably deprived the monster of many meals. Then I feel guilt that I may be the reason the monster is surfacing. One mother looks at another and says that some people will feel remorse because the moon is too far away, and some because it is too close. Their laughter is short and contains undertones of urgency to return to solemnity.

We reach a consensus. I leave them, and spend several days thinking about the plan we have decided on, and how to bring it to pass. I lurk at the edges of the lifeless area, which reaches almost to the surface of the ocean. Then I call.

From near and far young whales arrive, prepared by news and opinion. I instruct them privately, as a mother does her young, for fear our own speech may draw the beast to us. I learn their gifts: which are fastest, which strongest, which have the sharpest hearing, the best sense of smell. We disperse, diving deeply in areas yet alive to find the wreckage of lander shells. We bring the largest parts we can carry back to the dead expanse, some of us even working in concert, and drop them above the dead area. We do this over and over, as quickly as we can, hoping to kill the beast or weigh it down or block its call or chase it back to its deeps.

For three days and nights we go about our task. Our tails grow bruised from bashing shells to pieces, our mouths become sore and lacerated from the loads we carry, our muscles ache from constant use. We tire.

I know we have failed when one young male disappears, then another. They are the ones with the keenest hearing of my impromptu pod. They have doubtless succumbed to the beast's call. I instruct the rest of my workers to draw away from the lifeless zone and send out news of the disappearances. If I am lucky the males will be discovered mindlessly fleeing the beast as I did, and may be gently brought back to themselves.

We are not lucky. The dead area expands and reaches the surface. The hapless young ones are gone forever, food for a monster of the deeps now hungry for more or maddened by our barrage of wreckage. I am happy that I have sent my own calf far away to another ocean.

We send news, a warning to all that the beast is imminent. I instruct the fastest swimmers to spread the message to other oceans, up rivers and into bays, wherever civilized life exists.

The beast breaches in the dusk. Though we are a half-day's hard swim away, those of us left feel the swell of the water it displaces, we see the dark smudge on the horizon so like a faraway continent. Its voice rumbles through the water, enticing all who hear it into its maw. It is terrible, frighteningly alluring. I nip at those around me who listen, who turn toward the beast. I drive them away, telling them all to amplify the news.

Then I turn to face the beast. When one of my kind is friendly, when we are paying attention, we turn to the side so our eye may see the one we're addressing. Facing another is only for fighting. I take a breath, submerge, and thrash my tail to drive me toward the behemoth. Its voice beats at me, bids my body obey and submit. Likely it thinks that is my intention.

I send out clicks, but they aren't echoed. There is no sea life left anywhere near; it has all fled or fed the beast. I swim on, toward the enemy, finding it all too easy to do. Then I turn.

It is difficult. The beast's hold on me is bone and sinew deep. This is like fighting a current, but fight it I must. Slowly I curve through the water, taking many times my own length to do it. I can feel that I have the beast's attention. Its voice pounds at me.

I swim, slowly, parallel to the beast, then pull away. I can barely move; all the fatigue of three days exertion without respite weighs me down. I surface. Resting, I turn slightly, to look at the beast. It bulks in the distance like an enormous iceberg, and I know that like an iceberg the vast majority of it is still beneath the water. I could take a breath; I could sink; I could look at the thing, but if I do so I might see that hideous maw.

Then its voice batters into me again. I can actually feel the water throb in time with its bass notes. I yearn to throw myself into its mouth. My damaged hearing barely mutes its overpowering summons.

I hang there on the surface, at a distance, just breathing. Deliberately, I cast my perceptions adrift, as I did before on my long dive. I am sucked into the beast's mind as quickly as previously, as if the thing wants to devour me entire, thoughts and all. Then I feel its revulsion. I am poison! Indistinctly I feel my pulse race, my body tremble, preparing to flee.

I will be happy to bolt. I must retain this feeling, but more, I must change the beast's image of me. I remember happier days, days of chasing schools of fish, of feasting on a thousand swimmers small and large. Picturing myself as one of those prey is all too easy, as is imagining the beast as the predator. Heart racing, I make myself the beast and focus all my hunger on that small, small thing that floats in the distance. It is not poison, I say, it is the most delicious of creatures.

Slight ocean waves jostle me, and I know it is now moving. Toward me.

Flexing, I turn to swim away. My goal is the beach where I ran aground after my first encounter with the beast. It is so focused on chasing me that I think I can get it to follow into water too shallow for it to survive. If I am extremely lucky there may be a way I can slip past it. I will likely not be lucky, and will join my fellows in the Great Depth.

I send out a notification, warning everyone ahead of me to flee. The seas are so empty; my workers have done their job well. What there is of the Message is swamped by the creature's beckoning call. I move on. Most of a night later I pass a lander shell, one that is several times my size, but I know no way to notify them of the impending danger.

Soon after, sounds of rending metal reach me through the water. I look back. The beast has turned aside to assault the landers. I watch, perturbed, as it seems almost lazily to butt the shell, which breaks in two. Fire and thick clouds of dark smoke rise from the wreck against the early morning sun and a pressure wave gives me a sense of the enormity of the explosion. I realize that I do not have even a vague notion of what the beast looks like, beyond its gargantuan size, its exotic internal structure, and that huge mouth. Briefly I am reminded of the tale of the six whales who had only the use of their eyes while trying to describe a kraken.

Now is not the time to satisfy my curiosity. It turns, questing, my way. Again the water's swell notifies me it is pursuing. I turn. I swim.

My advantage is that the beast is out of its depth. I am familiar with the surface, while its origin is the deeps. I know where I am going: the shore where I almost died years ago.

We are passing land, a group of islands home to many landers. When I was young I would play in the currents flowing between them, memorizing which channels were passable even in low tides, which were dangerous even during the highest ones. An enchanting new plan occurs to me. I slow, allowing the monster to close.

I may not have to die after all.

I curve so sharply that my wake breaks like a whitecap. Taking a quick breath, I submerge and use all my remaining energy to force myself through the water with the speed of a barracuda. The echoes of the clicks I emit tell me that the beast is turning with me, closing now as my course is not taking me straight away from it. There is a triumphant tone to its voice, or perhaps I'm just imagining it.

I struggle to remember the layout of the islands. I calculate the level of the tide. I strain to recall what news there has been from younger whales who have frolicked in the vicinity more recently. Furiously, I issue a stream of clicks at the rising seabed ahead of me. I do all these things at once.

Then I pick my passage.

I swim just below the surface to minimize chop that could slow me down. Passing a spit of land from the island on my right, I curve to pass between it and another island. I have picked these two because there is a steep drop-off on both sides of the channel that gets shallower farther along. I remember barely making it through here when I was young.

Diving near the bottom, I push my throbbing muscles as much as possible to get me through this last strait. Black spots occlude my vision. Blood pounds in my veins. My head throbs. The channel narrows. It grows more shallow.

The beast follows.

My back breaks the surface, and I realize I won't survive. The passage is not deep enough. Either my memory or my calculations of the tide has failed.

I run aground. Scraping across a bed of pebbles and plant life, I come to rest and feel once more the terrible weight of my own flesh. Even my desperate clicks dissipate in the open air, returning nothing. At least, I think, if I cannot survive then the beast shall not.

The water rises around me, and at first I think it is merely a wave. But as its level passes my eyes, then breaks over me, I understand. The water, compressed by the oncoming monster, pushes me through the narrowest part of the passage. Walls of rock race by on either side. Soon I am floating in open water, past the islands.

I drift here, insensible for most of a day. Again I dream. Once more I am the feeder, luring all I can sense to my maw. Then the food diminishes. I am hungry. I am hungry for a millennia before I discover I can move, and chase, and catch, and kill. Repulsing the poisonous prey, I rise into a strange ocean where my body, while it bloats and cramps, is strong. Though I eat, the hunger remains, until I finally realize it is a need beyond hunger. Somewhere there is another like me. Just let me catch this one elusive animal, and I will have the strength to reach another ocean, to find that other, to mate.

The dream fades, then releases me.

It is again dusk when I stir, and turn to survey the passage behind me. I send clicks. It is blocked, and I know what blocks it. Slowly I swim around one of the islands and verify that the other end is likewise obstructed. When I get closer I see that there is a swarm of lander shells passing in and out of the channel's entry. Already there is a smell of putrefaction, as if the creature's body could hardly wait to rupture and rot on the surface.

Satisfied that the beast is dead, I head for open seas. The Message comes softly to me, speaking news and opinions and tales. I have news of my own to tell, of another monster, and a daughter to protect. I swim into an ocean full of water, of meaning, embracing both.

LYDIA'S LAST WISH

L ydia was the only teenager in the world with a wish left. When the genies were all unleashed they assigned each of their number to a newborn. As the children grew, they used their wishes, always in juvenile ways.

When she was four, Lydia said, "I wish I had a ice cream," and she had one. It gladdened her for ten minutes, then she said, "I wish I had another ice cream only bigger than the last one." When she was partway through that one her mother found her, and knew just what she'd done. She slapped the girl's hand, knocking the treat to the floor.

"Don't you want to wish we lived in a big house," scolded Mama. "We could have all the room in the world."

"Or maybe you could wish we owned all the money there is," said Papa. Her older brother Philo said that never worked because a little while later some other kid would make a similar wish. All the conflicting advice just confused her, and she kept from using her third wish.

By the time Lydia was six, only barter worked, and even then not always; some kid would wish for all the sweets, or all the toy cars, or that all the asparagus in the world would disappear. Serves them right, thought Lydia, considering they usually got buried under the resulting avalanche of sweets or toys. She sort of missed asparagus, though.

Her genie reminded Lydia every morning as soon as she was awake that she hadn't used her last wish. He perched on her laundry hamper; just a wisp of smoke with deep lavender eyes. When she was eight she tried to talk to the genie, asking it what would happen if she made this wish or that wish. What if she wished the sun was less bright? What if she wished all the ants in the world would disappear? What if she wished all the genies away?

Each time the reply was that silky voice in her mind saying, "Is that your wish?" And each time she said no. No, why would I want a cooler sun? No, why would I wish the ants away and let aphids run wild? No, why would I want to make the world less chaotic, less full of wishes, less interesting?

One day all the fireworks in the world went off a few miles south, killing a lot of people but filling Lydia with awe. She wished, but not out loud, that she'd thought of something so splendorous. She told Philo if she'd had two wishes she would have asked for the biggest meteor shower ever. But she only had one.

"Pity," said the inner voice. "That would have been spectacular, and would finally have finished all of you off."

This was her first overt intimation of the genies' darker design. Lydia thought about that remark. Days weeks months later she was still thinking about it. A hundred times she almost wished the genies would just disappear. Then one night she had a dream about one slowly turning invisible. It wouldn't be sufficient for her to use the word "disappear," she realized. Her genie could just twist her wish to its own end. She'd have to be careful not only about what she said, but about how she said it.

A week later everybody over the age of twenty-one keeled over, lifeless. "Some wish," said her genie in a rare moment of spontaneity. Mama was dead, Papa was dead, and a week later when Philo turned twenty-one he too dropped dead.

The world looked a lot less interesting to Lydia. Now it looked downright lethal.

"Lydia," said the genie the next morning. "You haven't used your last wish."

"What do you want?" She balled up her sheet in fists that shook. "Why are you doing this to us?"

"We're malign spirits." The wisp of smoke swirled, its eyes doing loop-the-loops. "I expect we'd be a metaphor for getting what you want, only not how you want it. If we didn't actually exist, that is. I'm still waiting for that last wish."

"You want us all dead. Then you'll be free. I could wish you were all dead instead."

"You got your ice cream." The smoke swelled, thinned, until there was only that voice in her head. "Twice. Is that your last wish?"

She didn't reply. She guessed that, for a child's first two wishes, the genies were less inclined toward lethal results. Sadly, she'd already broached asking for more wishes and been lectured on the Law of Conservation of Magic.

In the kitchen, later, she was scrounging through the cupboard for something to eat when there was a commotion outside. She went to look. Several streets over it was hailing dogs. They would appear in midair, and fall howling and yelping to their deaths. Lydia presumed there was a child in the center of the growing pyramid of canines who had wished for all the dogs in the world. Stupid kid. Stupid wish. Why would anyone want to bring more children into the world, if they were only going to do something idiotic like that? At least there were lots fewer kids being born now, with all the adults dead.

Once she was back inside, Lydia's throat almost closed. She hyperventilated, sobbing for all the dead dogs in the world. Poor things. She felt so sorry for them.

She caught her breath. Maybe she had an answer. With every adult gone, with supply so skewed and demand so instantly and fatally gratified, there were all too few people left in the world. Perhaps humanity wouldn't be able to recover.

Still, it was worth a try. "Genie," she said. "I wish for every genie in the world . . . no, I wish for every genie *everywhere* to love . . . no, to like humans." Two seconds passed. "Not to eat," she added in a yell.

"Is that your wish?"

"It is."

"Hmm."

A few years later Lydia was one day away from her twenty-first birthday. Her *Hamzad*, her personal genie of the lavender eyes, wept purple tears from his faceless eyes. "I'm so sorry," he said for perhaps the millionth time.

"Don't be," she said. "I've seen wonders." Lydia turned to the crib where her twins slept. The teenager watching the babies smiled, backing discreetly away. Each child had a tiny swirling Hamzad perched near it. She kissed each baby. "Use them wisely," she said, though she knew they probably wouldn't. But even the unwisest of wishes could have a benign interpretation, and now genies had only the best intentions for mankind.

Edd and I share an addiction to Bernard Cornwell's Sharpe's Rifles *series. He discovered the books through the PBS TV series, working late publishing comics for MU Press. For me, the* Sharpe's Rifles *series was more the methadone for my craving for Patrick O'Brian's Aubrey/Maturin series, though Sean Bean playing Richard Sharpe certainly helped things along. For months the "Over the Hills and Far Away" theme song was the household earworm. As new books appeared we stole them from each other to try to finish them first. We read at least one of the* Sharpe's Rifles *books out loud to each other. That shared addiction was the source for this lovely steampunk story.*

—*Amy Thomson*

Amy is the author of *Virtual Girl, The Color of Distance, Through Alien Eyes*, and *Storyteller*, plus several pieces of short fiction including the *Analog* magazine AnLab award-winning "Buddha Nature." A Campbell Award recipient, she is also married to Edd.

OVER THE HILLS
AND FAR AWAY

5 April 1812

Lieutenant Eustace Fitz-Randolph set the wooden camp
stool atop the stony cliff and sat heavily on it, feeling all
of his fifty-eight years. He and his artist were a mile south and
east of French-held Badajoz, across the Calamon River from Fort
Picurina, which had been stormed and taken by the British two
weeks before. Ever since, English eighteen and twenty-four pound
cannons had been pounding Badajoz's southern walls, breaching it
in two places. Some time after nightfall a Forlorn Hope of picked
men would attempt those breaches. Attempt, and likely die, while
making it easier for those who followed to take the city.

Eustace was relieved the storms that had lashed their encampment the first ten days of the siege finally appeared to have abat-
ed. The creak in his bones was lessened, their forthcoming attack
had more chance of success, and best of all he could see the whole
damned, doomed city from where he sat.

His artist, Daniel Bridges, shrugged out of a small pack and
opened it to rummage inside. Pulling several sheets of foolscap and
a piece of charcoal out, he slumped down next to the lieutenant's
stool. He roughed in a sketch of the city and the British encampment. When finished, it would make a fine accompaniment for the
article Eustace would write of the attack for the *London Illustrated
Gazette*.

"I should be down there," Daniel groused. "I could ha' been one
of the first into Badajoz."

"Nonsense," said Eustace. "You'd still be in the stockade for brawling had I not bought you out. If I hadn't lost my previous artist to dysentery you'd *still* be there. You should thank the Lord you are a passable limner."

"I'm a damned good artist, or you'd not ha' done so," the man said equably. "Still, 'tis a fine lookout point we've got here. Ye've picked the tallest point in all Portugal, I'm thinking."

"That's as I like it," said Eustace, leaning forward over the escarpment. He savored the faint flutter in his stomach before settling back. "Now you to your work and I to mine."

The first intimation Eustace had that anything was wrong was when Daniel paused in his drawing and cocked his head. "Hear that?" he said in an undertone.

"Not—" was all he had a chance to reply before a press of bodies bore the two of them to the ground. Eustace, his breath knocked out of him, could only think that these were the French relief forces that Wellington had been expecting almost daily. He spat dust and forced his head around to peer over his shoulder.

His attackers were horned and glaring fiends clad in fearsome, outlandish wooden armor! Both he and Daniel were held prostrate in the dirt while one of them stood over the artist, raising a curved sword over his head with obviously deadly intent.

"*Chotto!*" The guttural command came from beyond the warriors, from someone dressed in costly robes over armor. Eustace saw him to be a man, but one of sallow hue and with curiously-narrow eyes. He stared in wild surmise.

"Daniel!" he said in an undertone, "These are warriors from the Orient. Don't anger them." The pressure on his head increased, grinding his cheek and nose into the soil. Then, at a word from the leader, they were jerked to their feet and held. The man examined their faces, muttered to himself in obvious surprise, and then looked beyond them to the city and encampment.

Then he faced Eustace and Daniel, stared into each of their faces again, and spoke a short sentence, pointing toward the city.

Daniel looked at Eustace, who looked back.

"Hell and Damnation," said Daniel to the man, "Ye're not half lost."

The British batteries shot gouts of fire, wreathed in clouds of smoke barely visible in the darkening sky. Several of the soldiers started and muttered at the sight.

Their leader turned to lead the way down the side of the hill away from Badajoz. Eustace and Daniel were hustled along in his wake. Behind them rolled the concussive blasts of the cannon.

After a walk of some few miles in the gathering gloom they crested another hill to find a strange and fantastic sight. Eustace might have taken it for a landlocked ship, were it not for the string of metal spheres floating above it like a tin centipede.

The structure was six stories tall, and horribly wounded. In shape not unlike a hundred gun man-of-war, it would have never floated, for a great wedge of its bow was obliterated, burned out in some horrific conflagration that exposed several levels of the contrivance. Eustace saw living quarters, corridors, storage rooms, and a kitchen exposed to the air, all charred.

He saw, too, as torches were lit in and around the thing, that it was indeed a conveyance, though not meant for water. It floated a few feet off the ground, held in place by ropes leading to spikes driven into the ground. Ladders were set against its side in several places, while workmen in loincloths pounded with hammers and carried rough-hewn boards.

Chivvied up a ramp into the ship's interior, they were escorted up stairs and ladders to the deck. Finally the journalist and artist stood on a vast expanse of wood, broken here and there by covered chimneys, forests of copperwork and hoses, scores of boxes, and openings down to stairwells. A low railing surrounded the space, which Eustace estimated to be as large as several dozen cricket pitches. In the center, far enough away that he had some difficulty making it out, appeared to be a tent with rolled-up walls.

Above them was a line of more than twenty enormous metalclad balloons, each fed by its attendant score or more of hoses and pipes leading up from holes in the deck.

They and their escort marched to the lantern-lit tent, which proved to be a pavilion, a canopy supported by four poles set on a raised platform. A man sat cross-legged on the blond wood, a sheathed sword to one side and a kneeling woman by his other. He was dressed in silk robes and studied a map. Their captor prostrated himself before the dais and waited to be recognized. When the man looked up and nodded, he made a brief report in a language Eustace did not recognize, displaying the contents of Daniel's pack, including his rough sketch of Badajoz.

Daniel peered around, then whispered to Eustace, "I can't see the lights of Baddyjoe from here. I expect they're hiding from us, just a'waiting for their chance to break the siege."

Eustace shook his head. "These people were surprised at our appearance. I'd wager they're no friend to us or of the froggies." He entertained a vision of this skyship being blown thousands of leagues off course by the storms that had stalked the land for days. Then his journalistic instincts came to the fore. "Imagine, though, if we could rise into the air, and watch the battle from above!"

"Not just watch the battle," Daniel snorted. "Say rather 'bombard.'"

A decade and a half before, the French had used captive balloons at Mauberge to observe and direct fire at Austrian positions, but after his disastrous Egyptian campaign Napoleon had disbanded the *Aerostiers*. This skyship, could it maneuver, promised whole new vistas of warfare.

"Hist," said Daniel, "It's his nibs."

Eustace looked around to find the robed man regarding him. The man spoke, and the woman translated his words into Portuguese, then Dutch.

"Terribly sorry," said Eustace. "Parlez-vous Francais? Sprechen sie Deutsch?"

"I speak your tongue," the woman said.

"Englishers," said the man, darting a scowl at their chief captor. He spoke on, and the woman continued to translate. "Greetings aboard the *Kumo Hiryuu*, the—" She paused and stared over their shoulders for a moment. "—the *Cloud Dragon*."

"It is an impressive device," said the journalist, gazing around again in unalloyed amazement. "Tell me, what do you use to maintain its buoyancy? Hydrogen? Coal gas? Or some other substance we have not yet recognized?"

When Eustace returned his attention to his interlocutor, the woman translated, "I leave such details to my magicians. My name is Lord Isaka Mitsui. We come from Dai Nippon."

They gave their names and Mitsui continued, "It would be well if I could have your parole and that of your man."

Eustace readily agreed and nodded to Daniel to do likewise. The enlisted man clumsily followed his example; in war only officers expected to be taken alive for ransom or to sit out the war. Men from the ranks anticipated only a quickly slit throat. Neither of them carried any weapon more lethal than a knife, which at a nod from the man were returned to them.

Mitsui waved a hand at the armored men surrounding them, and they dispersed to their various stations. Servants brought low stools for them. He placed his hands on his thighs, arms akimbo. "What can you tell me of this place? Are we indeed in your England?"

"No, you are in Portugal," said Eustace. As the man seemed utterly ignorant of both the war and the finer points of European geography, Eustace found himself starting from first principles, pausing often to let the woman translate. Mitsui quickly grasped the situation.

"I believe I have heard of this emperor, Napoleon. He is the one so recently trounced in Russia, is he not?" The woman paused. "Trounced? Is that the word? So he has placed a man of his choosing in position as daimyo, as a local lord, over this Spain, and wants Portugal as well. Your George the Third believes the French will not stop here, as you have opposed him on other fronts."

"King George commands and we obey," Daniel sang the popular song quietly. "Over the hills and far away."

"Quite," said Eustace. "You have the gist of it."

"And your position?"

"Position? Oh, I see. I'm a newspaperman." At the woman's quizzical look, he added, "A journalist. I report about what I observe."

Mitsui brightened when she repeated his words. "A writer! I thought you a mere field commander."

"No," said Eustace. "I am no longer a soldier. Writing is my sole profession now."

"Now?" The Nipponese picked up a brush and dipped it into a bowl of ink. He poised the laden head of the brush above a large sheet of paper, holding his oversize sleeve back with his other hand. He looked up at Eustace.

"I gave up my commission after the death of my son."

Mitsui murmured some words. After a pause, the woman said, "We have something in common, then."

A whiff of acrid smoke was borne to them on the errant freshening breeze. Eustace strained his ears, realizing the hammering below had stopped, no doubt due to the late hour. Try as he might, he could hear nothing from the besieged city. It was yet too early for the attack, he judged, which had been scheduled for several hours after dusk. The dais and the three of them sat in a pool of light surrounded by profound darkness. Even the stars in the bowl of sky were half-obscured overhead.

Mitsui leaned forward to apply brush to paper. In swift strokes he drew a recognizable caricature of Daniel's sketch of Badajoz, though Eustace noted that the roofs of houses curved upward at the eaves. Mitsui regarded it for a moment, then put it aside. "You are my guests for the night. Tomorrow we view the outcome of this battle of yours."

*

Hours later, Eustace awoke from a dream of falling. He thrashed about in the silken sheets of his thin mattress, then sat bolt upright. Opening his eyes, he sighed. He knew he was due another long sleepless night, the kind that in the past he had only eased by long application to the bottle. That comfort was denied him on this skyship, at least so far.

Rising, he dressed, taking care not to wake Daniel. He slid open the wooden and paper door and peered into the hallway. A guard was stationed there, but he merely inclined his head when Eustace made to leave the room. It seemed these Nipponese took parole as seriously as civilized countries did.

There was a gentle breeze making its way down the corridor from the gaping rent in the ship's side. He walked to the opening. All was quiet below, although he did see a flash of light that was likely from the door of a dark-lantern being briefly opened by a guard. He longed to escape, but he had given his word he wouldn't try. Unsure why he was doing it, he clambered up the exposed and crumbling beam-ends to find himself in a compact kitchen. Then it came to him, and he searched pantries until he chanced upon a bulbous bottle wrapped in some fibrous root. He peeled up the stopper to be greeted with an odor not at all like wine, beer, or any spirit he'd ever encountered, but potent all the same.

He sat, dangling his legs over the side, and took a cautious sip of the liquid. It burned going down, similar to whiskey, albeit smoother, and with the taste of some unusual plant. He was about to chase it with a larger gulp when a sound came from behind. Twisting about, he saw a slim, long-haired figure silhouetted in an open door. After a moment's hesitation, the woman darted a look behind her into the corridor, then firmly closed the door and crossed to Eustace.

He climbed to his feet and made her a bow, which she returned, putting both hands on the front of her knees. She rummaged in a cupboard, coming up with a pair of small cups. When they were sitting side by side once more, Eustace saw by the light of the moon that this was the same woman he had seen earlier with Mitsui. Was this the man's wife? His concubine? She poured and offered a cup, which he took and drank, and he recollected her lack of years. Perhaps she was the man's daughter. It occurred to him that no matter her relationship to Mitsui, she was doubtless not supposed to be alone with a captive, most particularly not a male one. It would do her reputation no good to be found here, and could easily doom him to death.

"What is your name?" he asked.

He received no answer, save that she poured again for him, and then for herself. "Please," she murmured finally, and "Saké," indicating his cup.

"What is your name?" he repeated, and waited.

"Reiko," she said after a time.

"Should you be here? Is it not dangerous?"

"My movements are not of concern. We shall not be bothered here. All the guards are below, or above."

"I admire your command of English."

She sipped. "My thanks. I had frequent contact with the Dutch and Chinese merchants that were allowed quarters on Desima Island, near Nagasaki. They were welcome in our home. Since I showed some slight affinity for languages, I was encouraged to learn all I could."

"I understood that Nippon—that Japan is inhospitable to foreigners."

"Yes, ever since missionaries were expelled two hundred years ago. However, some believe there should be more than commerce." She glanced aside as she said it.

"Like religion? Christianity, perhaps?"

The gaze she turned on his face was direct in the scant moonlight. "I had forgotten that your duty is to delve for facts and report them. Please do not speak of this to anyone else."

"I will not," he said.

"It was from the Chinese that we learned of secret plans to build skyships."

"Chinese ships? An aerial navy, perhaps?"

"Yes. A son of the Ch'ien Lung Emperor deposed his father some twenty years ago. He was not the chosen successor, one Japan would have welcomed, one who was dissolute and unlikely to turn his eye toward conquest. This one, though—" She shook her head. "He said he desired to expand trade with other countries, to break the Dutch stranglehold on commerce, but an expanded Empire is his true goal."

"Truly there are would-be emperors every way you turn. Was this ship not built in Japan?"

"It was captured by Lord Mitsui as it floated at anchor. We were trying to return home from deep within China; it was our, how is it you say, 'shakendown' cruise?"

"Shakedown, yes."

"We were blown off course. Worse, we flew directly into a storm that utterly disoriented us and caused a fire that sorely damaged the ship. When we fought clear of it we found ourselves in unfamiliar skies. Several people died, including Lord Mitsui's son."

"He did mention we had something in common."

"You said that your son also died. May one ask—?"

"I was a colonel in India," he said, his mind unwillingly hauled into the past. "My father had bought me my lieutenantcy as a wedding present. We Fitz-Randolphs have always fought as officers for His Majesty. I did the same for my son Victor when he announced his marriage."

He sipped at the saké once more, but held his hand over the cup when she moved to refill it.

"Victor was very pleased, especially when he found that he would be assigned to my command. Perhaps he thought I would be easy on him. Maybe he was just happy to be near me; I'd like to think that was the reason." Eustace turned the porcelain cup gently between his palms. "I was anything *but* easy on him. I expected . . . more than he could give, and I was not reticent in telling him so. Finally, it drove him to abhor the army, and me, and his heritage." Eustace set the cup aside, sure by now that he had had quite enough to drink, to be so free with his history. "Victor deserted to join the English adventurer George Thomas, who sought to unite the Mughal Empire of India under his own rule, using trained officers and native soldiers. Victor was killed at Georgegarh, when Thomas sallied out to attack the Frenchman Bourquien."

He sighed. "I resigned my commission, determined forever after to remain only an observer." Eustace yawned and stretched. "Pardon me. I suspect it is time I went to sleep."

"Yes, of course. Only you should not try to climb back down in that condition. It would invite death."

Reiko rose and crossed to the door. She opened it a crack and peered out, then disappeared down the corridor. He gave her a count of twenty, then followed. It was the matter of a few moments to find a stairway down that debouched near the room he shared with Daniel. Nodding again to the guard, he entered. It was only when he sat on his bed that he noticed he still carried the half-full bottle. He set it down and stripped once more for sleep. It was, for once, quick in coming.

When he awoke the next morning, the bottle was empty and Daniel was singing a bawdy marching song. Eustace made his ablutions, then hauled the man to his feet when a servant appeared to guide them to breakfast. The artist blanched at the food, but Eustace ate a double-portion of rice, pickled vegetables, and some kind of dried fish.

The same servant escorted them up to the deck, where they found preparations well under way for departure. The stakes had been pulled up so that the skyship floated above the ground. In the ground-hugging fog Eustace could almost believe them to be on an oceangoing ship. He and Daniel were seated on low stools near the pavilion, which was already occupied by their captor. Reiko sat by Mitsui. Eustace tried to catch her eye, but she did not look at him.

Mitsui spoke several phrases in his native language. Guards and courtiers jumped to run hither and yon, repeating orders into speaking tubes, pulling at ropes, breaking open boxes.

The hiss from the hoses increased, the deck canted slightly, and Eustace felt the wind of their progress. As some manner of lifting gas was pumped into the front-most balloon, it rose and its side-mounted fins bit into the air, pulling the ship along. When the first rose, the second dipped, the third rose, and so on back to provide an undulating motion, much like an eel through water. The ship on which they stood was attached by what seemed excessively thin metal rods to the joints between the armored balloons, so that it rode serenely, oblivious to the rocking motion above.

The craft turned ponderously and made for Badajoz.

Eustace rose from his seat and walked with Mitsui and Reiko to the ship's bow, trailed by a wavering Daniel. The others stopped a pace or two from the low ornamental railing that ran around the deck's edge, but Eustace stepped up to the dropoff and gazed down. The terrain below was rough and hilly, more rock than shrub, and still sere from the rough winter just past. He felt himself sway with the barely perceptible movement of the skyship, and leaned farther against the breeze their movement generated. Far below, a wild goat paused in his cropping as the ship's shadow passed over him.

"We're making a good clip," Eustace said, near mesmerized. "Fast as a horse over level ground."

A faint rhythmic tintinnabulation was their first herald from Badajoz. Daniel cupped a hand behind his ear and was about to speak when Eustace cocked his head and stared blearily into the haze.

"'S cannon, ain't it," said the artist.

"So it is." Eustace turned to their host. "It seems the assault last night was not successful. We should advance with care. There will be cannon fire from both sides." Reiko translated.

Mitsui was silent. Then he smiled.

"Your, er, Excellency?" said Eustace. "Perhaps you do not know, but cannon are quite powerful. The French even have howitzers, which throw bombs high into the air." He mimed the action of a high arcing projectile with one hand. The *Cloud Dragon* rose, clearing the hill where Eustace and Daniel had been captured, and they all saw the city in the distance, surrounded on two sides by river and on the other two by British camps and batteries.

Mitsui still said nothing, only giving a slight movement of one hand. It was evidently a signal, for servants brought them tables, and served tea. Eustace found the drink bitter and strong, but Daniel drained his cup and held it out for more.

"We shall discuss matters with one side and then the other," said the Japanese man through his interpreter. "I shall repair and provision my ship. More, I should like to discuss a uniting of forces."

"With the English, of course," said Eustace.

Reiko translated, Mitsui answered, and Reiko was silent. She bit her lower lip, then finally said, "The *Cloud Dragon* will decide your battle one way or the other."

"Not bloody likely," Daniel said under his breath. Then, louder, "You don' treat wi' Boney's crapauds. They take what they want." He rose and stalked to look down on the city.

Eustace saw that the ship was bearing down on the French-defended city. Shading his eyes, he made out Fort Picurina, hard-won by the British and made into their prime battery due to its proximity to the walls. As he watched, a bloom of smoke and peal of rolling thunder presaged another strike at the city's walls. Moments later he saw the cannonballs strike, and an impressive section of stone collapsed.

None of the British cannon were yet aimed at the skyship, but Eustace thought it only a matter of time. He wondered why Mitsui didn't wait until the battle was over, and ally with the winner. The skyship, even damaged, was likely well-enough armed to tilt the balance in favor of either side, but at considerable risk to its airworthiness. Too, Mitsui obviously felt no allegiance to either side. He'd barely heard of Buonaparte.

What, then, was his rush? Shaking his head, Eustace looked around for Daniel. The artist was leaning against a stack of boxes and looking decidedly green.

The ship arrived in position over the castle at the north end of Badajoz, well away from the battle, and turned into the wind. The pumps slowed their beat, and the segmented balloons above Eustace slowed their movement, holding the ship's position.

Reiko stepped next to Eustace at the bow's railing. "Some of these French people will no doubt speak English, Portuguese, or Dutch. If they do not, will you translate?"

"That, I believe, goes far beyond my duties as a captured combatant. No, I will not."

Reiko nodded. "I shall rely on their resourcefulness, then."

"Why is Mitsui determined to speak to the French first? My countrymen would be pleased to ally with yours."

The woman looked down into the city, where army officers were gathering. "He must decide which side is more powerful," she said quietly. "This is not our battle, nor is it a question of right or wrong. Nine-tenths of the world has no care for what happens here. We have our own concerns."

"Your own wars, don't you mean?" Eustace said. "I thought about your story from last night. It's too far from China to here for you to have been blown that far. You are running from some battle, I think; that's how the ship got damaged. And perhaps the victors of that battle are pursuing you, driving you ever farther to the east. Is that not why Mitsui is in such a hurry to gain allies?"

She laughed, barely more than an exhalation. "We are here. Never mind why. Is that not the important thing?"

"Then why did you go to so much trouble to find me last night and feed me that cock and bull story? Were you watching me your-self, or did the guard in the corridor signal you?"

"I do not know 'cock and bull,' but I understand your meaning. You did bear watching."

Mitsui signaled for a rope ladder to be lowered to the waiting Frenchmen. His soldiers assembled nearby, and Reiko turned away to attend him. "Be careful you do not sacrifice your 'impartial ob-server' status," she said over her shoulder.

Someone put a hand on Eustace's shoulder. It was Daniel. "Gotta go," he said. "I've got to piss so bad my fingernails hurt." He lurched in a shuffling walk toward the side of the ship.

Eustace took a half-step after him, wondering if the man was going to pitch right over the side and down into the city. "Daniel," he said, "Wait!"

The artist unlaced his breeches and pulled out his cock. He looped an elbow around one of the struts and leaned out over the city below. Letting fly, he loosed an impressive stream of piss down on the city and the gathered green-clad officers.

Outraged cries rose, and the flat crack of musket balls being fired up at them. Most of the shot thudded home into the hull be-neath them. Several whistled past to reach the top of their arc and rattle uselessly on the deck. Men near them laughed.

Then one of the struts parted with a musical note.

Response was immediate. Mitsui shouted in Japanese, and Eustace heard hatches slam open below them, then a rattle as of anchor chains through hawser holes. He felt the deck rise sharply under him.

Daniel had not given up his vantage point. "You should see this," he yelled over the racket. "There's thousands of little metal balls falling onto the city. They're smashing hell out of everything!"

Men hurried toward them.

"Daniel, come away from there," said Eustace. "And put away your willie. You've gotten us in trouble."

The artist turned, stepping away from the railing and rebuttoning his breeches. Two soldiers motioned them away from the rail while the rest ignored them, reaching instead into the boxes nearby. They pulled out what appeared to be lances tipped with canisters and trailing colorful kite tails.

"Rockets," said Daniel, and Eustace saw that it was so. These were not the crude devices he'd seen being experimented with by army engineers and artillerymen. They were uniform in appearance, milled, and it appeared there were great stores of them aboard. "At least they had the boxes already open," noted Daniel. "They was expecting trouble."

"Oddly so," said Eustace. "As if they welcome the chance to attack."

The soldiers carried the missiles to the side of the ship. In a serried line, several score of them stood at the railing. Eustace saw a similar rank on the other side of the deck. A servant passed down the line lighting fuses, and at a shouted count man after man hurled his rocket at the city below. They ignited mere yards below the deck, screaming down to explode on the city and its inhabitants.

A cheer rose from the British ranks audible even from their great distance.

"Our men will be pleased they don't have to fight so hard to take Badajoz," said Eustace.

"They'll be rapturous we're up here while they get to ransack the place." A newly-sober Daniel shucked out of his pack and retrieved his drawing supplies from it.

The *Cloud Dragon* came about, heading toward the now silent British lines, where all were doubtless wondering if this instrument of war were about to bombard their army as it had the French.

One, then another, howitzer shell arced up from the city's walls as soon as the skyship had cleared them. The first shell, its fuse sparking, fell short and exploded mere yards above the glacis that protected the walls. The second whistled up through the space between the ship and its balloons, exploding just past its arc, raining the deck and several of the balloons with shrapnel. Hose ends flopped to the deck, spewing their gasses. The entire structure shuddered as another shell bounced off the hull and exploded below them.

Skysailors ran to cap the hoses and throw sand on two fires that had sprung up. Several clambered up pipes to inspect the damaged balloons, while soldiers aimed another volley of rockets at the defensive positions so vulnerable from above. Eustace saw one, two, then three ammunition dumps catch fire and explode as the rocketeers targeted the burlap bags of powder.

Then they were beyond the range of the howitzers, sailing in suddenly placid aether above no-man's-land. They forged on, watching as the infantry, loosed on the city, ran up the glacis, across the ditch, and into the breaches. There they handily overwhelmed the meagre forces of the disorganized defenders.

Daniel put aside his first drawing and began his second. "Shouldn't ye be taking notes?" he said mildly.

Reiko strode up next to Eustace, sparing a brief glance for the work in progress. "Your leaders, are they the ones on that hill?" She pointed.

Eustace nodded. "Lieutenant-General Wellington," he said. "He's the one you will need to parley with."

Tense moments reigned when it appeared neither Mitsui would descend to speak with the British commanders, nor were they willing to clamber up to treat with the Japanese. Finally, Wellington's curiosity about this new weapon of war appeared to prevail, and he led the way up the rope ladder followed by several protesting officers.

Mitsui greeted them, sitting on his dais, with Eustace and Daniel to one side. The artist held his pad of paper in the crook of one arm and drew quick sketches of faces.

Eustace was perturbed. Something was missing. He realized that Reiko was not present. How were Mitsui and Wellington to speak, if there were no translator?

Wellington's gaze passed over the journalist with barely a pause as he advanced on the platform. Standing with the toes of his boots almost touching it, he bowed formally.

Mitsui inclined his head coldly, then made a small gesture with one hand. Soldiers rushed forward to surround the delegation. Eustace started up, then held still as a soldier rounded on him. The pumps increased their beat. He felt the deck rise under him, and saw the hill's crest drop out of sight. Eustace looked at Mitsui. The man sat, rigidly straight in posture, eyes hooded. He ignored the questions and remonstrations from Wellington and his generals. At last he looked up. That simple movement made him the cynosure of attention.

He stood, lifting his sword in its scabbard.

Eustace felt a movement at his side, and looked to see Daniel scrambling to his feet. Mitsui saw, too, and barked a command in Japanese. Two soldiers leaped after Daniel, who was already running for the side of the ship. Eustace, on the verge of jumping after Daniel, finally saw Reiko.

She stood behind the pavilion. She had her hands clasped before her bowed face, and even at this distance Eustace could see the tracks of tears down her cheeks. His vitals clenched at the sight as the plot became all too clear.

"Soldiers, to me!" He shouted the timeworn command, and drew his knife. Stabbing the nearest soldier, he yelled, "They mean to kill you all!"

Wellington and his men jumped to obey, drawing their sabers and menacing Mitsui and his guards. They started edging toward Eustace, who stared wildly about for Daniel. The artist was grappling with his pursuers, who had caught him pulling at the top of one of the boxes of rockets. At a shouted command from Mitsui they threw him to the deck and one drew his long curved sword. In a smooth, almost balletic swipe of the blade he had Daniel's head off and the sword resheathed in seconds. A wash of blood swept across the pale wood of the deck. Eustace's gorge rose.

The Viscount spun the journalist around as his generals fought a desperate rearguard action against the Japanese soldiers. "Do you have a plan of attack, man?"

"I—yes!" Eustace dragged the man around the side of the pavilion, his coterie backing in time with them. Reiko turned away, but Eustace leaped and caught her.

"Release me," she screamed.

"Tell Mitsui to back off," Eustace yelled. "I've sussed out his plan. Tell him it's a sin; that he'll go to Hell!"

"Don't you think he knows that? It's too late."

Eustace spun to face Mitsui, Reiko held before him. He menaced her throat with his knife. "Then tell him not to take another step or I'll kill his daughter."

"Too late," she repeated. "Too late." Mitsui stepped to the front of his men, eyes on Eustace, unsheathing his sword.

"Damn." Eustace began backing away, toward the side of the ship. "Tell him . . . tell him I know what you had planned! You're all Christians. You could only worship in secret—if you were found out you'd be martyred. Mitsui's plan is to make Japan so hated and feared that all Europe will turn their attention on her. He never planned to ally with either side when killing both the English and the French commanders would do. Japan would be attacked, be made to join one empire or the other, be made a Christian colony!"

"You can't know that," she cried, "I'll never translate that."

"I'll not spread his lies."

"No," she said, "You won't have to. The destruction of that city and the death of your Wellington will be enough."

Mitsui and his soldiers followed step for step as they retreated. The two who had killed Daniel moved with them to one side; he supposed it would suffice if he and the British delegation were all forced off the side of the ship, to fall to their deaths. Better, perhaps, more graphic; it appealed to the sensationalist in him.

His foot hit something, and he looked down to see Daniel's

head roll its grisly way across the deck. That meant he was near the box Daniel had breached.

"Hold her," he said to Wellington, and reached into the box. "Find a lamp," he yelled, pulling out a pair of rockets.

Seeing the weapons, Mitsui yelled in Japanese and his men surged forward, killing General Nairn and wounding a corporal. The rest of Wellington's men desperately whirled their heavy sabers, meant to be wielded from horseback.

"We've got better than that," the Viscount growled. "Dyneley! Thomas, give the man your slow match."

The artilleryman leaped to comply. Applying the slowly burning cord he always carried in a box at his waist to the rockets' fuses, he said, "Do you plan to menace these blighters with explosives?"

"Worse, I'm afraid." Eustace held the rockets' lances at their extreme ends and aimed them roughly up at the balloons overhead.

"No!" wailed Reiko, struggling all the harder in Wellington's grasp.

The rockets ignited, screaming up in tight spirals while trailing their tails. One exploded prematurely, too far below the balloons to do any harm.

The other curved sharply upward to strike and explode against a balloon halfway back. Mitsui backed away, and Eustace found himself holding his breath. It seemed they all were. The tableau held for one long second.

The balloon exploded, its armor pierced by the rocket.

Mitsui signaled to his men, who ran amidships to deal with the damage.

Wellington fixed Eustace with a look. "Allow me to advert you to the fact that we are all on a burning ship. Is there anything akin to a life boat?"

"I doubt it. Perhaps we can release one of the balloons from the others?"

The Viscount nodded. "Jones, Wrottesley, see what you can do.

Everyone else, attend to their needs." The engineers nodded and surveyed the growing conflagration.

Fire leaped from sphere to sphere above them, running with terrific rapidity through the structure. The flames ate their way down the hoses as they fell away from the balloons. Skysailors ran to unhook the fittings, but they were tragic seconds late amidships. Fire flowed past their hands into and through the deck to the vast reservoirs of lifting gas below.

"Too late," someone said.

Eustace felt it as a shudder first. The deck lifted and the ship lurched. Then fire rolled from every hatch, chimney, and porthole as a massive explosion blasted the wood into flinders. The deck under them rose, then dipped, knocking all of them off their feet and rolling them toward the side. Eustace caught at one of the stanchions and hung with it under his arm as the deck canted still farther. The crate of rockets wedged up against a stanchion and several men clung to it. Two generals slid under the railing and fell screaming into the air. He saw the aft end of the ship, burning merrily and rising into the sky, shed itself of cargo and flailing sailors alike.

Losing some handhold farther up the deck, Reiko rolled over and over down the incline toward him. He grabbed at her as she caromed off the railing, grasping hands as she fell. She arced down, pulling cruelly at his joints.

Another tremendous explosion destroyed several of the metalclad balloons above him, and deflated others. The stanchions parted with musical twangs around him one by one, and he felt the deck begin its long fall to the ground. It turned in the air, held an instant by a last few pipes. When they parted, he, Reiko, and the crippled ship fell together.

Eustace lay partly in a stream, facing east. The sun was halfway to its zenith. It seemed strange that less than a day ago he and

Daniel had stood on a hilltop and watched British preparations for taking Badajoz.

He was unable to move either leg, and his hands scrabbled ineffectually at the dirt by the streamside. Then a shape moved into view.

Reiko. She rose, dripping, from the water, and stumbled to loom over him. For a long moment their gazes held one another's, then she dragged him out of the stream. She dropped to her knees and folded her hands in the familiar posture of prayer.

Eustace breathed the hot, smoke-laden air. Somewhere behind him a blaze was devouring the thorn trees and what was left of the skyship. His torso, arms, and head were warm, but his legs were without sensation. Something in the distance caught his attention.

A horde of tiny dots moved out of the low-lying fog in the distance. From the east came a hundred skyships, and a hundred more behind them.

And doubtless a thousand more besides. The invasion was on, albeit not the one Mitsui had planned.

GUY, SKY HIGH

Guy Frost dies on a Friday in Spring. One walk to the end of the block, one tiny blood vessel ripping open in his brain, and he doesn't come back. Not alive, anyway.

His wife, Lois, notices right away that he is missing. "No, Leaper," she tells the cat, "no chance whatsoever he'd be out after dark. His show's on." After fifty years of marriage she's got Guy's routines down pat. She has the television all warmed up for Guy, his cigar handy, and the remote control clicker placed just so on the arm of his recliner.

Leaper sits atop the set. He swishes his tail back and forth across the screen, where Agent 99 is holding a gun in her lazy grip, too close to her body. Max raises his hands along with the KAOS agents until 99 wearily says, "Not you, Max."

"Not you, Guy," Lois parrots, then startles herself by glancing wildly around the room to be really sure he's not there. It would be so like him to jump out of nowhere at her just as she's mocking him.

For Guy, death is an instant headache at first, the worst he's ever had. Then dizziness, then his vision goes double. The sun is setting over the new vacant houses that replaced the hayfields on the east side—no, wait, he thinks, the *west* side of his two story ranch house. East? East is his own house and the entrance to their newly paved cul-de-sac, and he is turning to see the house, trying to put one foot behind the other so he can spin. A military about-face. It is a little like being drunk and a little like being feverish and a whole lot like being in the wrong body. Plus, it hurts.

Warm and cozy inside, Lois laughs at the reflection of Max and the Chief under the Cone of Silence. The reflection is in the den window, where she's gone to look out into the darkening yard for any sign of Guy. Her eyes keep refocusing on the televised antics and finally she sits down to finish out the episode so she can tell him what happens.

Leaper leaps. He makes it to the top of the armoire, then down to the mantel, where he threads his way between the photos showing Guy: Guy with Lois at their wedding, Guy with a baseball bat, Guy leaning on the hood of his Corvette. Leaper pauses to sniff at the stuffed trout mounted above the fireplace, then threads Guy's bowling and shooting trophies. He vultures down at Lois from his perch.

Guy sits down. Guy flops over. His body spasms and ejects a trickle of vomit. Then his body dies there on the recently seeded lawn three doors down. At first it strikes him as a surprising thing to happen.

And then it surprises him to be surprised. He had supposed that after death came nothing or something. If nothing, there wouldn't be a him to be surprised. If something, he'd always rather vaguely thought he'd know whatever he needed to know. As a boy he'd imagined a drive-in screen showing him clips of his past, most likely focusing on the sins.

Inside the house, the end credits come up and Lois's vague anxiety grows into genuine concern. When she opens the door to call his name, Leaper dashes past her, then freezes on the doorstep, staring up into the sky and thrashing his tail.

Her first thought is, "what are you up to now?" Then "how the hell did you pull *this* one off?" fleets into her brain, followed by what she says aloud. "Guy," she says softly, "now you've done it. You've died."

The western sky is Guy. He rises translucently thin above the woods and new construction like a Ray Harryhausen giant, all head, torso, arms, and hands. He raises those hands and looks from them to her.

"Lois," he says, and his voice is intimately close to her. "This is just a dream. Honest, it has to be." That voice has always been what she's loved most about him; it is low and musical and always seems half directed toward her no matter who he is talking to.

Lois can see a cloud passing in front of Guy's throat. Jupiter gleams through his right ear. His waist intersects the treeline. So far as she can see he might just end there.

"We'll just see about that." Arms akimbo, she glares up at him. "Where have you left your body?" For once, she feels in charge. He's the one stupid enough to go off and die somewhere.

"Where?" Guy leans closer to her, head as large as a football stadium, bleachers and all. "Oh, there it is, near that elderberry."

She shakes her head, then uses one foot to shove the crouching cat back into the house. She pats her pocket to make sure she has her key, then closes the door. Then she walks. Halfway there she remembers her slippers, next to her chair, but the tickle of the lawn makes her glad she doesn't have them.

"That's you, all right," Lois says when she gets to Guy's body. She nudges his cheek with the bare toes of her right foot. "All dead. And you missed *Get Smart*."

"Really? Did Agent 99 have her baby yet?" It amazes them that the actress Barbara Feldon would be allowed to be pregnant in the show, just as she is in real life.

"Twins!" says Lois, knowing he'll be thrilled at the revelation. "I wish you could have seen it." The comment encompasses a multitude of wishes. I wish you could have grown old—older along with me. I wish we could have died together in a romantic jump off a cliff somewhere. I wish you'd leave; it's embarrassing talking to a dead man. She feels that his essence trembles on the edge of dissolution, a soap bubble of a husband.

Guy laughs, low and almost inside her ear. It tickles and she swats at him. "I see more now," he says.

Lois thinks of what he might see. It's a list in her mind: angels, my soul, heaven and hell, God.

"I can see all the way to downtown," he says. She hears the humor in his voice. Then it's gone. "I can see beyond the end of the earth."

"Can you see your way back to me? Back down here to my size?"

"No." His answer is given just a little too quickly.

They are both silent.

"Why, then?" Lois pulls her sweater tighter around her shoulders. "Why are you still here?" Is it just to exasperate me?

Guy tries to find a reason. He stands upright, head lost in the stratosphere. From here he sees the moon, and the lunar lander base left only a few months before. He sees Vietnam and the White House.

"Beats me," he says, finally.

"I suppose I'd better call the police."

"You won't need to," he replies, looking toward town. "They're on their way. Them, and a lot more people besides."

The sun is truly gone now, even the hint of red in the west has faded away. Sodium vapor lights flicker to life, distributing their orange glow over Lois and over Guy's corpse at her feet.

Are *his* feet somewhere a mile down, she wonders, toasting in a vein of lava? If she walked into him, would she see arteries and bones? Would she feel anything? Would he? Then she blinks, and again he looks miles away, like a rainbow receding as she advances.

Reporter Karen Paul arrives first. She'd been on her way home when half the sky had turned into Guy Frost. When she screeches to the curb in front of Lois and hops out, pad and pencil at the ready, she doesn't know which of them to look at first. Then she sees the body, and whistles. "Didja kill him?" are the first words out of her mouth.

"Certainly not," Lois says.

"T'was beauty killed the beast," Guy says, low and inside, making Karen jump.

Then the police arrive, then the town's one ambulance, then

some teenagers, and then it's a tossup between the mayor and a news crew in its van, who collide at the end of the street, get out, and begin yelling at each other.

"Okay, then," says Karen, with a speculative glance at the wrecked newsvan. "Just tell me in your own words what happened."

While Guy talks, Lois steps out of the way of the ambulance crew, who inspect Guy's body all too briefly, then bundle it into their vehicle. When they turn around and head away, she takes two automatic steps toward her Plymouth 88, then remembers that her husband isn't in his body any more, and stops. Lower lip caught between her teeth, she turns back around.

"Just tell me where to be," she says to herself. "Do I mourn you or laugh at your jokes?" That's the story of my life, right there, she thinks.

"It was a little like being drunk," says Guy to Karen, who scrunches up one shoulder like he's blowing in her ear. He looks at Lois, and she is sure he heard her whisper. "And a little like being feverish."

Two policemen stand and tilt their heads way back. One teen-age boy is running toward Guy. Lois blinks and it's like she's refocused her eyes. He's suddenly on the other side of Guy's spectre, still running flat out and yelling like crazy.

Guy's loving this attention. He winks at his wife as he puts down a 16-wheeler of a hand near the tangle of cars and vans at the end of the block, the other hand at his hip in a pose she's seen so many times in the flesh. In the car, leaning over to kiss her. On the bed, critiquing her wardrobe choices. At a picnic. Camping. They slideshow through Lois's mind.

And he's happy. He smiles down at her and tells his story to Karen and races the teenager and rests in the ambulance and blocks traffic and lords it over all creation.

TRUER LOVE

My lover Dieter came to Duvall last month. I never expected him to drag his chain this far north; but such is love.

Dieter only speaks German. His lover Minette had learned the language to please him, and translated.

"He says his idol has died, Carl. He says he never stopped loving you."

We were sitting on rickety chairs in what had once been a Safeway. It was the largest space in the town, so we'd set it up for daycare and as an indoor playground. I was watching the toddlers that day. I handed Dieter a little girl that had been pulling at his shirt.

"You know I gave up loving," I said.

"He says it's not that easy. He's fixated on you again and wants you to join the circle." She looked me over. "We're a lot longer than when you were with us. After Anne died and you left, we linked with a chain in Colorado."

Anne.

"I don't care how long you are. You're not a circle—if you were, you wouldn't need me. I don't do that any more." I waved my hand around at the kids, from the napping babies in the defunct dairy case through the six-year-olds playing tag, to the five teens near the registers who were pretending to study but were instead sneaking peeks at the chain of people that had come to recruit me. "This is what I do. You know how important it is."

Dieter set the girl on his lap down and spoke for a minute in German, while Minette focused laser-sharp on him. "Dieter says he can't live without you. You are the one he loves, Carl. You've been in the chain. You know what it's like." The jealousy was barely visible below her placid exterior, but it could hardly be gone entirely. It was in her narrowed eyes when she had to turn to speak to me. Dieter was her world, like Anne had been mine.

They were in the chain, thus nearly impervious to logic. I ran my fingers through a little boy's hair over and over until he protested and pulled away. Yes, I knew what it was like.

One of the teens, Manny, rescued me. He was fourteen, and we adult celibates had been expecting him to fixate any day. He got up, put his book on his seat, and walked over. "Hey," he said, looking at Dieter and Minette and the other people behind them stretching away like beads out the broken doors and down the unused highway. Most of them carried food or packs, and some of the other celibates had gathered to barter with them.

"Yes?" said Minette. She knew what he was going to ask. He could barely stay focused on her, so ready was he to be off and seeking his idol. I hoped he wouldn't have to trek too far.

"Do you have any advice about loving?" he said. "Can you tell how far a person usually is from his idol? What if my idol is on the other side of the Atlantic?"

"There are still some small circles and chains maintaining and flying airplanes," she replied. "They can take you across the ocean, if you have to go. Nobody can tell you how far away your idol is. You're going to feel that pull until you find him or her, and then you're never going to want to leave." She reached out a hand to trail across Dieter's shoulder, but he shrugged it off. He only had eyes for me. "Take heart. It's unlikely you'll have to go far. Back when there were scientists they said everyone had hundreds of people in the world they could fixate on. You just have to find one that's not already someone else's idol. When someone fixates on an idol, nobody else can."

"Go away, Dieter," I said wearily. He knew what that meant; he'd heard it from me often enough. "I'm not going to be your idol." I stood and turned him around firmly. He shivered under my touch, and looked over his shoulder at me. I stepped away. "Minette, take him away. Find him another idol. I have work to do."

I told Manny to watch the toddlers, and walked briskly to the back of the store and through the swinging doors. My wife Laura was there; she'd seen what was happening and she embraced me briefly before stepping out to enforce my order to leave. As mayor she had the authority.

Deep down, I knew that wouldn't discourage Dieter or his chain. I just hoped he'd find someone easier to fixate on.

Two days later I was feeding some of the babies while Katherine taught the teens. Her words echoed around the empty space, vying with the racket made by the twins who were follow-the-leadering over the top of the empty frozen food cases.

"Nobody came forward to claim responsibility for the virus," she said. "But before the news media broke down they reported that its origin had been traced back to a research laboratory in Toronto, Ontario. That's up north, in Canada.

"Some people speculated that a geneticist had been trying to make people tamer. Less violent." She held up some old issues of *Newsweek* with photos of terrorists and soldiers. "Not like these people. But some think he, or she, had replicated the genetic basis for stalking."

I could tell that none of her students understood that word.

She must have, too. "Stalking is following someone. Trying to learn everything about them, because you can't live without them."

"Like loving?" asked Manny.

"Yes," said Katherine. "Just like loving."

I'd finished spooning mashed potatoes into the last baby, so I went to the door and picked up a water jug. One of the reasons the celibates picked Duvall was its location next to the Snoqualmie River. We never lack for water. When everybody walked off the job to find their idol, utilities died just as fast as national economies and every other industry.

I walked across the decaying road, after ten years still looking both ways, and picked my way down the slope to the river. Young cedars and Douglas firs shaded it on both sides, and cottonwoods grew right up out of it, spread from a pulpwood project started a couple of decades back. It was early summer, and sunny days were still rare enough that I lifted my face to the sun with closed eyes.

Listening to Katherine's speech so soon after seeing Dieter just made the longing stronger to find an idol and love her—or him—with all my might. An article I'd read back when we still had the internet had said the virus was incredibly sophisticated. It targeted most lobes of the brain in very specific ways: the emotional response governed by the frontal lobe; the sense receptors distributed in several areas of the brain, and especially the sense of religious ecstasy experimenters had found in the parietal lobe. Scientists had focused magnetic fields and made volunteers feel the presence of a greater power. The virus did that for all but a few naturally immune people, but the 'greater power' for us was the idol, the person we loved. The only problem was the idol didn't love the lover back; circles were just giant cluster fucks without the sex.

I wanted to find my new idol, another Anne. I wanted to swim across the snowmelt-cold Snoqualmie and start walking across the fields. Instead, I pushed the jug under the surface of the river and filled it before walking back. Laura met me at the door. One look at my face and she grabbed my hand to pull me along the street. I set the jug down outside the Safeway near the empty newspaper racks and followed her.

Laura led me to the nearest house. We left all the doors in town unlocked. She dragged me upstairs and helped me pull off my clothes. She maneuvered me to the bed—I looking out the window all the while—and pushed me onto it. She rubbed my prick to hardness and mounted me. I didn't want her but my body did.

Afterward, she held me. "We need children," she said, but the corner of my brain still concerned with her knew she needed more. Her gaze was pulled to the window, too.

*

Manny left the next day. We loaded him down with supplies; our strawberry crop had reaped generous barter from the nearby circles, so we had plenty of food to spare.

With each person that left, Laura got a little more desperate. "You know why we're here, we celibates?" she asked him as the rest of us stood between him and the highway. "Sex. Pure and simple. We're here to make sure that enough babies get born so the human race will continue. We raise and educate kids like you. The lovers don't want babies, it gets in the way of their pure, simple loving circles. They don't want to love and care for children, just like they don't want to have a job or watch television or do anything else. All they want to do is lavish affection on their idol.

"If your idol dies and you can get away, if you can in any way leave a circle, please find the nearest celibates. Join them, please. Help us stay alive."

Manny nodded uncomfortably, his face pulled inexorably away from us. He turned south down the old road, state highway map in hand, headed for the I-90 pass over the Cascades.

I watched him patter away, barely able to keep from breaking into a trot myself. Manny had more hormones, less control, than I did. But not by much. I turned away with an effort, and saw Laura. Unshed tears glistened in her eyes.

"He'll make it," I said. "The pass in summer is going to be a breeze."

She nodded, looking at me, then away.

A small part of Dieter's chain surrounded Duvall the next morning. I suppose they were concerned that someone would hide me far away if they'd been seen coming. I'm glad now we didn't think of it, or if someone did, that they didn't carry the plan through.

Celibates had tried to defy chains and circles before by kidnapping an idol, and had been wiped out. Lovers formed chains with tens of thousands of members; our little towns rarely had more than a few dozen citizens.

"I just want Carl," said Dieter through Minette.

Laura looked at the solid mass of lovers surrounding her town. Then she crossed her arms under her breasts and glared at Dieter. "Your chain is no longer welcome here. No one will trade with you. We will tell the other celibates you have stolen one of our own."

Dieter heard her tone of voice, so he looked to Minette, who nodded and translated. He smiled, then laughed with childlike joy. Reaching into his pack, he found a pair of handcuffs. One cuff went around my right wrist, the other on his left. Laura's threats meant nothing next to his love.

"Let me say goodbye," I said. Laura brought me the baby and the twins. I kissed them all. Our hugs were awkward, constrained by the chain.

"You won't be cuffed for long. Just until we get you an idol," said Minette. "We have a few possible ones in Seattle. Then you'll be free."

"Carl. This is Natalya, she's from Minsk."

I stared at her. Natalya was short and stout and middle-aged and gray, by far the most beautiful woman I had ever seen. I would never want to look anywhere but at her, ever again. I reached out to touch her, but she backed up a step. "I love you," I whispered hopelessly.

"She was in a small circle," continued Minette. "Forty people. They operated a fishing trawler, but it sank off the San Juans. She made it to shore and the LaConner Circle helped her out before sending her our way."

That was how it went. Any chain got passed all the single people that weren't celibates, in case one of them was the one that could extend the chain. Maybe be the special one to turn it into a circle. Chains met tail to head all the time for the same reason.

She was something like the fortieth person they'd hauled in front of me. Dieter was staring at her with the same expression of distaste that Minette had for me. Everybody disliked their idol's idol. It would be funny if it weren't so goddamned sad.

"Do you speak English?" I asked.

"A little," said Natalya. The sound of her voice sent a shiver through me. My penis was heavy and hard.

"I just want to touch you."

"No. You will not." She waved a finger. "No touch. Just give me all."

"All," I said. "Of course. Everything."

The walk from Duvall and across the floating bridge had taken two days. Our chain was doubling on itself; we'd passed hundreds, thousands of people. They greeted us in passing as they sat on streets, yards, and highways. When night fell they each set up their tiny shelter and slept next to the ones they loved and the ones who loved them.

Dieter unlocked the handcuffs, sure that I wouldn't leave him now.

We started south the next morning. The tail of our chain was in Santa Barbara, far to the south. When we got there Natalya would be introduced to whoever was at the tail. If we were supernally lucky, that person would be Natalya's idol, and our chain would become a circle, every lover an idol, every idol a lover. Until someone died and the whole process began again.

Circles were much more stable than chains, but lovers died, breaking them. When a chain came apart, it unraveled from the front since the first idol didn't have an idol of their own. What the head of a chain did get was a sense of near-completion in the knowledge their entire chain was focused on finding them an idol, and all the best stuff. I say "stuff" because they got everything. Lovers passed the newest clothes, the tastiest food, the best toys to the head of a chain, idol to idol to idol. Most chains didn't unravel very far. Such is greed.

Evening found us just south of Boeing Field. An earthquake several years back had damaged the runway, but near the north end. None of Seattle's skyscrapers had yet fallen but it likely wouldn't be much longer. Everybody was still waiting for the Big Quake.

We built a fire on the median and forty or so of us sat around it while a heavily bearded man in a wheelchair stirred a stew. His lover cut carrots and potatoes with arms that looked like Popeye's from pushing him everywhere. Similar fires stretched down the dark highway.

"Natalya is a doctor," said Jo, Minette's lover.

"That's lucky," I said. Chains and circles were happy to have anyone with medical experience, or woodsmanship, or just about any craft.

Jo was a talker. "Yeah, she worked in a hospital in Minsk before the virus."

"Maybe she could have saved Anne," Minette said. When I glared at her, she smiled sweetly.

"Anne? Your original idol?" asked Natalya. "How did she die?"

"He killed her."

Natalya sucked in her breath and put both hands to her mouth.

Everyone looked at me. All of them knew the story. Everyone but my love.

"Anne was a lesbian," I said. "She was also into S&M. You know what that is, Natalya? She liked—loved—women, but in a certain way. She wanted her lover to hurt her; it made her feel loved and protected to be hurt in ways she controlled. I don't pretend to understand. It's not easy to put this simply for you. She would have her lover tie her to the bed. She loved the blindfold." I saw Natalya didn't know the word. "A strip of cloth across her eyes, so she couldn't see. She wanted to feel pain or pleasure at the will of her partner. Her lover might tickle her with a feather, she might cut her or strike her or caress her clit or pinch her nipple. She might—" My voice broke.

"Anne was forced by the virus to leave her partner," said Jo. She laid a hand briefly on my knee. "The first idol of her affection was a man, which scared her even despite the attraction. She did not like men, but was forced to love one. Then Carl fixated on her."

Ten years ago, when the virus struck and the implications had been aired on CNN, all anybody wanted to do was to find their idol. Word was: the President had walked out of the Oval Office and fixated on a visiting school teacher from Kenya. The world organized itself around vast dating circles. All transportation was co-opted for use in shuttling hordes of singles around until they could find their idol, no matter where that person was. I'd been handling cargo at O'Hare, my first job. Then it was rush rush around the country by bus and plane and train. Finally, in San Francisco's Golden Gate Park I'd been found by Dieter, then I found Anne and her idol, all in one week. So lucky, I'd thought.

Tears spilled out of my eyes. "Anne was in love, but unhappy. She couldn't stand being near me, but she saw how to get away. She taught me how to love her, her way. She made me cut her, tie her, blindfold her. She m-made me choke her."

Jo saw I was all out of words. I leaned far forward, hands covering my head as if to ward off a blow, as she continued the story. "We took over a hotel in Sacramento. We'd completed our circle, just under three hundred people, and were so proud of ourselves. We drank wine from Napa Valley and ate the best steaks we could find. Everybody got drunk, but of course no idols let their lovers have sex with them, because it would interrupt their fixation on their own idol. No idol except one. Anne. She let Carl make love to her."

"He choked her to death," said Minette.

"At her command," finished Jo.

*

"Before we leave Seattle," I said, "could we visit the mall?" We trudged south on Interstate 5. Around the next hill we'd be in sight of Southcenter Mall and the huge shopping complex that had grown up around it.

Minette shook her head. "Natalya is the leader," she said. "It's for her to say. But any mall will have long ago been looted."

"A house then. Can we look in some houses? I just want to get Natalya something nice." I heard the whine in my voice.

Minette did too, and smirked.

Natalya looked around from her place ahead of me. "He may find things for me. A dress, perhaps. More."

That was that. The leader had spoken. Different chains had different ways of making decisions, but most deferred to the head idol. It kept them happy and everyone knew they were the one with the biggest drive, the drive to find an idol of their own. Soon enough we would continue south.

Tukwila was the suburb nearest us. It hadn't burned like most of West Seattle and some of the towns on the other side of Lake Washington. We walked down the offramp at Interurban Avenue, and wandered west into a neighborhood heavy with apartment houses and smaller residences. The houses on the major roads around here were picked over, so we wandered up a side street, leading our chain of lovers. The blackberries had taken over the neighborhood, even cracking the pavement in many places. We squeezed past them when we could, hacked at them when we had to. Avoiding homes that looked too difficult to break into, we eventually found a street with older, larger houses. I picked one that had a jungle gym in the yard, figuring I was more likely to find women's clothes there, something nice for Natalya. We broke through a picture window and several of us scouted through the house. Jo waited anxiously at the window.

I ran up the stairs after Natalya, Dieter after me, and found the master bedroom. "Up here," I called.

The light was fading, so we grabbed armloads of clothes from the closet and dresser. Dieter stepped into the bathroom and came up with a razor, some soap, and other sundries.

Back in the yard, we built a fire and looked through our spoils. Natalya picked three dresses, several pairs of nylons, and a cashmere sweater. No doubt she'd make me carry them. I looked forward to doing that for her.

I woke up well before dawn, chilled. We had dragged a mattress out of the musty house and Natalya slept on it. I lay nearby, fully clothed; I hadn't yet started carrying enough covers to be comfortable on cooler nights. I crawled to our pile of castoff clothes, pulling along my ground-cloth, and looked through it. We hadn't thought to bring any men's clothes down, but I figured I could pull most of the pile over myself and get warm that way.

The fire had burned down but the moon was near full. I pulled at the clothes, and then I saw them. Scarves. I picked one up, then another, drawing their smooth silk through my hands. They were beautiful, some patterned with bold flowers and birds, some pastel solids. I shivered in the cold.

I walked to Dieter. He slept nude. He always had, but he had silvery sheets to protect him from the weather. I shook him, and he came awake under my hand. He looked up at me, abject love in his eyes. He made a motion to offer me his sheets, but I shook my head. I put a finger to my lips and beckoned him to follow.

He came after me to the jungle gym. I turned my back to it and he was so close to me that our breath intermingled. I reached out and touched his stubbled chin, his cheek. He trembled; I had never touched him before except to push him away. I put a finger on his lips, then on mine.

I held out the scarves to Dieter. "Hurt me."

He shook his head. Those were words he knew. I used more.

"You love me." I touched his hand, enjoying the quiver that ran through it. "I know you do."

And he did. He tied one hand high up on the steel structure, then the other. He knelt to secure my feet, and I said, "Don't." I was ready.

"My neck, now."

He couldn't pretend not to know what I was talking about. Shaking his head, tears streaming down his cheek, he whispered 'nein' and backed away from me. But not far.

"Come here . . . My neck. You saw what I did to Anne. You love me."

And he did. I could see his cock up and straining toward me. The depth and power of his love was horrific. I didn't want it to be the last thing I saw. I didn't.

"My neck. Now."

He passed a light-colored scarf around my neck and put the ends together.

"Tighten it."

He did. He took the two ends of the scarf that had been passed around each other and pulled. He twisted them. Did it again.

"Tighter."

His hands moved. He sobbed aloud. The scarf grew tighter and I could hear a humming rush in my ears.

I forced air past the block, whispering, "More." The band around my neck constricted. I realized I couldn't see the moon any more, then I realized the world was going away.

I woke to birdsong. I opened my eyes. Natalya leaned over me, clinical concern evident on her face.

I choked, bile rising into my throat, and rolled over on my side to vomit into the grass. One wrist was still circled by a scarf, but the one around my neck was gone.

Sitting up, I accepted the cup of water Natalya offered. Surrounding us was a circle of lovers, watching in the early dawn light. I looked around, finally rising to peer over the first rank of people. People stepped apart, and I saw him under the jungle gym, the blade from his razor in his hand. His neck was open from one side to the other.

"Dieter destroyed himself," said Natalya. "He thought he had killed you."

As soon as she began speaking, I whirled to focus on her. My love for her was as complete as ever.

"Sit down," she said, so of course I did. Hands nearby handed us bread, cheese, and jam; I didn't look away from her. We fixed our breakfast together. I gave my half to her; it would have hurt too much to swallow, anyway. After the first bite, Natalya looked around.

"We are a chain of two now, not connected to you."

A sigh went up around us. They knew it, but didn't want to know they knew.

With Dieter gone we were no longer a part of their chain. Minette was now their head. "You took him away from me," she said. Her eyes were dull and she held the almost physical pain in with both hands across her belly. It wouldn't last, I knew; soon she would feel the kind of anger I'd feel if anyone tried to take Natalya away from me. And then would come the compulsion to find another idol.

"I free you, Carl," said Natalya.

I knew what she meant. But I couldn't accept it. She just couldn't have said what I thought she'd said.

"You are celibate now, Carl. I will find another chain, one that can give me more than you can. I will go south with Minette's chain for now. You will go north, back to your little town." She stood and so I did. She motioned for me to turn away, then gathered up her few possessions and walked off.

If I looked around, I was lost. I'd follow her anywhere. I stared straight ahead, then took one step. One became two, and soon I was walking back to Laura.

I hear that there are three circles of two people in the entire world. I think it's an urban legend, but if it's true then those are the luckiest people. Imagine perfect feedback. Imagine loving your lover.

I'll take Laura. I ache to turn around, but I'll take her.

CALL TO ORDER

The assassin, sweating and shaking in fear, stalked the halls of power. He knew where his target was, knew his habits and his haunts. Micah Kent, one of the nine Justices of the Supreme Court of the United States, would be with the others in their shared chambers this morning as they discussed the latest cases, debating which to hear, which would be denied certiorari.

He pushed a cart loaded with cleaning supplies. It was the best disguise, it made him invisible. But behind one of the cart's doors was a pistol, loaded with nine bullets, though he would need only two. He would kill Kent, the most conservative Justice, and then himself. The Democratic president, after a due period of mourning, would choose another, a more liberal judge. The balance of power would tip just enough.

A passing guard, a member of the Supreme Court Police Force, eyed him. The assassin could feel his sweating palms slipping on the cart's push-handle. He took a better grip, straightened his back, gave what he hoped was an unconcerned smile to the man.

The guard nodded. "Hiya, Phil," he said.

The assassin dipped his own head in reply. He cleared his throat. "Morning, John," he said. "How's your son doing?"

"Oh, fine, fine. Looking forward to turkey day next week, of course." He glanced at his watch. "Little early for this wing, isn't it?"

The assassin shrugged. "Some kind of cleanup in one of the offices." One of his eyelids twitched.

"Got it." The guard waved him past.

Phil swallowed past a lump in his throat. His own son would soon enough be told his father was some kind of monster. But he had to do this! Justice Kent had been in office for thirty years, dispensing bile in the guise of opinions, nudging the country to the right decision by decision. It was insanity that Supreme Court judgeships were granted for life. And Kent never went out in public, never came into contact with the horrible outcomes of his decisions. But then, he would probably laud those ends.

Giving a little wave of acknowledgement, the assassin resumed pushing his cart whose wobbly wheel quivered in time with his racing heart. Turning a corner, he stopped in front of the justice's office door. He fumbled the keys out of his pocket, almost dropping them, and opened the door. Once inside, he stashed the cart in a far corner of the room, stooping to retrieve the pistol. With trembling hands, he checked the magazine, made sure a round was jacked into position.

He'd bought the gun two months ago, passing the background check easily. The vetting for his job three months before had been far more stringent. Phil had found time to make it to a gun range in Delaware several times before breaking the pistol down to sneak it in piece by piece. He hadn't fired a weapon since the army thirty years before, and his aim was awful. But then, he wouldn't be called on to shoot the justice from a distance.

After killing the man, Phil would shoot himself. He didn't want to endanger hard-working men like John, and he certainly didn't want to be subjected to the media circus that would await an assassin. He'd left an incoherent screed on his computer that would make him appear a deranged libertarian. The way would be clear for the president to appoint someone who would protect civil rights, immigrants, and the poor. No more deportations for people like Phil's adoptive sister. The world would be better for what he was about to do.

Phil roamed the plush office. Should he sit in Kent's high-backed seat? Wait behind the door? Finally, feeling a little foolish, he settled down to wait in one of the swiveling visitors' chairs. He wondered what he'd do if Kent came to his office accompanied by someone. That was a bridge he'd cross when he came to it. The die was cast.

He almost fell asleep. Maybe he did. He had a vivid vision of the Supreme Court's Call to Order. "Oyez! Oyez! Oyez!" He'd watched it so many times. "All persons having business before the honorable, the Supreme Court of the United States, are admonished to draw near and give their attention, for the court is now sitting. God save the United States and this honorable court."

Well, he had business, and he'd drawn near. Nothing, not even God, would save the man he had come to kill.

A key grated in the lock, startling him to full wakefulness. He hadn't locked the door again after entering! Would the man notice? Would it put him on his guard?

The door swung open. Justice Kent's thin body slipped into the room. He was alone.

When Phil raised the pistol, when he stood, when he said, "Close the door, please," the man did not appear shocked. He complied.

Justice Kent was tall, with close-cropped hair, narrow lips, and a strong jaw. He didn't look nearly as old as the eighty-one years his judicial biography claimed. He still wore his judicial robes. His piercing blue eyes darted to the cleaning cart, to Phil's uniform, to the gun, and back to his face.

"Did I leave a mess in the toilet?" he asked, arching an eyebrow.

Phil narrowed his eyes. "Don't be funny. You're not getting out of here alive."

Kent smiled. "Well, then, have your say."

"You're a monster. You've been in office more than thirty years, always siding with corporations, with religious fundamentalists, with—with authoritarian fear-mongers." The pistol trembled in his grip.

The Justice took a step toward Phil. Their eyes locked. "I understand," he said in a voice so soft Phil strained to hear. "You're afraid. You've been hurt somehow, maybe you've lost someone close to you."

"You don't know me." Phil edged forward a step, the better to target the man. "Don't pretend to."

The smile had never left Kent's face. "I'm just trying to see things your way." He cocked his head. "Can you do that for me? Have you ever tried to comprehend my world-view?"

"I don't want to. I don't need to."

"I see. Your mind is closed. You're just bracing yourself to fire." Kent moved another pace closer to Phil. A bare three feet separated them. "Well, while you're doing that, let me at least try to get through to you. I used to be like you. I won't say 'bleeding heart,' that's insensitive, but I used to think every little person mattered, that everybody ought to have their say. But my opinion changed, almost overnight." He leaned a little toward Phil, fixing him with a penetrating gaze, one full of conviction. "Now I understand so much more. People don't see the big picture. They don't want what's best for our society as a whole."

"As a whole? But your verdicts have supported polluters! War-mongers!"

Kent gave the tiniest of sighs. "You don't get it. We're territorial. We must defend our land and our herds." He glanced down at Phil's hand. "Isn't that handgun getting heavy?"

The assassin had almost forgotten the pistol. "Never mind," he said, without heat. "What does defense have to do with pollution?"

"It's simple." Flecks of red appeared in the justice's eyes. "Follow the research. High levels of CO_2 affect the intellect; it makes you humans dumber. I won't say docile, but we don't really care if you fight among yourselves. We just don't want you organizing to oppose us if the word gets out about our real nature. It's the same with religion: gives you something to look forward to in the next life so you don't kick up a fuss in this one. And a strong national defense keeps others of my kind in their own countries unlikely to invade mine."

"Your," said Phil, "kind?" When Kent held out his hand, Phil dropped the pistol into it.

"Ranch owners," said the justice, smiling just enough to show a canine that was a little longer than the teeth on either side of it. "Of a kind." He put a hand on Phil's shoulder. "Do keep this little talk private, hmm? Think about it all you want, but no discussion, no emails or texts, and certainly no diary entries. Let's keep this between us." His gaze burned into Phil's soul for one year-long second, then he blinked. "After all, appointment as a Justice is for life, and I expect to have a lot more years ahead of me."

Phil moved to the cart. He vaguely wished that Kent had let him keep the gun. He felt like he would have had a use for it.

FIRST PRINCIPLES

Werner Heisenberg lies abed in his rented flat, fully clothed, and watches the second hand of his pocket watch make its three hundred and fourth revolution. He is aware, as I am, of his advancing age. An odor of cabbage being cooked drifts up from the room below. There is a hole in the fabric of spacetime or possibly in one wall of his room, a small hole. He does not know that it is there. Through it I watch him, and through it I hear his telephone ring.

It is a new kind of device, with mouthpiece and receiver all in one unit, and a button on the base for summoning the operator. He picks it up, and his end of the conversation goes something like this, translated from the original German:

"Heisenberg." He sits up.

"Yes." He stands.

"That was tomorrow, I thought."

He sighs. "I have said this before. DeBroglie was wrong. Uhlenbeck and Goudsmit were wrong. Schrödinger, though better, was wrong. Indeed, I may be wrong. Physics is not—you will pardon my witticism—an exact science. That is entirely my point."

He listens for a long time, then cuts in. "Yes, yes, I can understand your impatience. We all age. Time is short for me as well."

"Very well. I will be there."

Heisenberg, sparing one last glance at his watch, adjusts the set of his clothes, picks up cane and hat, and leaves. I follow him at a discreet distance. The streets of Heidelberg are narrow, thronged with youths newly escaped from the University this evening. When this war Germany has started gains intensity, there will be no time for them to stroll; they will march. But I have nothing to do with them; my eyes are only for the professor. Looking about the street, he ducks into a beerhouse.

I enter behind him. Waiting for him to settle into a booth, I lurk behind reality or find a suitable table from which to watch him. When a woman enters and sits down across from him, I take little note of her, but adjust myself so that I may read his lips. What he says is approximately this:

"Lily! A pleasure to see you again."

"There was someone else I was waiting for."

"No. No, don't go, it is good to see you."

He peers around the room. "I suppose not. The war has interfered with it. The highlight, I would say, was in the twenties. *Then*, there was freedom. *Then*, I could concentrate on my studies. I developed matrix mechanics in 1925, and two years later my principle of . . . but you do not want to hear about this. The point is—" Finding a beer in front of him, he sips. "The point is, well, it is just that it *is* good to see you. Tell me, what have you been doing the last thirty years?"

He listens, but his eyes are on the move again. They flit past me, then move on. He does not find the person to whom he spoke on the telephone.

When he speaks again, it is with the beer again to his mouth. When he pulls it away, I see, "—why we never stayed together. I always felt there was someone, some force, keeping us apart. I could have married you, I could have taught at the University and enjoyed a tenured round of children and parties and hofbraus. But instead I lost you, then I lost myself in my studies."

There is a question. He laughs, then says, "Of course not. We've each gone our own way, and there's no gaining the time back. I enjoy what I do—" Yet he avoids her eyes. "—very much."

A man comes in, not the one Heisenberg is looking for. Lily waves to him, and they leave for the theatre laughing.

Grabbing up his cane, Heisenberg shoves his way to the door.

The crowd parts reluctantly, and swallows him up leaving me behind in my pocket dimension or inside helplessly hemmed by humanity. I pick him up outside, though, and follow him as he stumbles down the street toward the Reichsgarten. Newfound strength careens him from statue to riverside to bench, tapping petulantly at concrete and grass alike. Finally, he finds a seat free of late-night lovers saying their wartime goodbyes, and collapses on it.

He sits for some time facing the statue. Pulling out his watch once more, he sets it beside him on the bench, but doesn't look at it. An hour passes and the darkness deepens, yet he is sitting in a pool of light under a lamp. Just as I decide he has fallen asleep, or into a deep malaise, he straightens and speaks in a conversational tone. What he says is something like this:

"I know you're there. I've felt you all around me, guiding my work and watching over me. Why?! Why pick me?"

He picks up the watch, looks at it. "Am I someone special? Or does everyone feel there are beings out there? Are you angels?"

Jamming the watch back into his pocket, he sits forward, cane between his legs, to blurt, "I don't believe in you. Go away. Leave an old man alone. You know I am to work on this new thing, this bomb. This wondrous bomb designed from my notes. I could have been—but no," he says it with no belief in his voice. "—you do not exist. There are only the fundamental forces. No devils, no angels, no gods."

The statue glowers down at him in the darkness.

"Only atoms."

I say nothing. I am nothing if not discreet.

The night lengthens. Heisenberg finally stands, hand to his back, and taps his way back to his lonely room, then to the factories at Rjukan. Choice has left him far behind.

TÉNÉRÉ

Edd Vick & Manny Frishberg

I

Yahira Salak gazed at his dead camel for a few moments, then turned to regard the dry oasis. Muscles worked in his throat, desperate for a single drop of water to dampen the dust and sand. Not four months before the wadi had been a palm-sheltered haven. Today it was a crazy quilt of desiccated mud surrounded by bare scorched boles.

Even late in the day, the sun was merciless. Everyone in the caravan was dehydrated, and their expected salvation was no more. The next oasis was fifty kilometers farther and, for all he knew, just as inexplicably dry.

Salak released his breath slowly. The world of 2030 was drier and hotter than ever, but the *Imazighen,* the desert tribes, had lived on the edge of destruction for centuries. This caravan had been their final act of defiance, and he would lead it until they reached their goal or perished.

Beckoning a pair of men, he directed them in butchering the dead camel. As the sun set, they feasted on its meat and strained its urine to drink. Being Muslim, they wouldn't consume its blood, and even the meat was not as blood-free as it should have been. They went into their tents to sleep, all but Salak, who remained outside with the camels and his thoughts.

His decision for this caravan to be as traditional as possible was apt to spell their doom. Riding camels instead of trucks, they had no satellite phones or GPS, preferring to orient themselves by the stars. He climbed a dune to consult the heavens. The problems of a burning earth meant little to a limitless frozen universe.

He read the familiar constellations, then saw something unexpected. A glow came from beyond the dunes to the east; it was the kind of light pollution a town produced. But they were farther from Timbuktu than any city besides Taoudenni, where they'd come from with their load of salt.

Salak's heart leaped. They were saved! He remembered a scientific compound being built somewhere in the area, yet another no doubt futile attempt to combat climate change. Allah was indeed merciful. Even Westerners would honor the old traditions of hospitality in these conditions. There would be water and phones, even transportation for those who were ready to give up the caravan. Salvation was a mere few kilometers away.

Turning, Salak saw the silhouette of the dead wadi. His hand moved to the ceremonial dagger at his waist. It didn't take a scientist to see a connection between the new complex and the destruction of the oasis. They would go east tomorrow so they might live. But what happened after they got to the compound remained to be seen.

II

Azeez paused to wipe sweat from his forehead and neck. He looked again at the report one of the technicians had written. The incidence of rusting equipment on the west side of the collector farm was much higher than on the east side. The water table here, he knew, was far too low to account for the damage. He stooped to sift through Saharan sand with his gnarled left hand, flash roasted in a few seconds in one of the solar collectors. At least he could still use it to grasp when he pounded and shaped the intricate bracelets and pendants that were his family's heritage. Engineering had been a natural path for an *inadan*, a traditional tinkerer.

He inspected a couple of the collectors, and indeed found more rust than the newness of the equipment should warrant. Shaking his head, he looked off into the middle distance trying to account for the discrepancy. Glancing up, he saw that the sky was much paler than usual. There was hardly a hint of blue. He wondered whether climate change could account for the rust, but dismissed the thought almost as soon as it surfaced. The world was drier, not wetter.

The sun, so efficient at powering the Licht Process, pounded down on his back and neck. If he were wearing the traditional *tagelmust*, the tribal combination turban & veil, it would not be so effective. But he'd given that up when he went to university in Paris. He didn't want to appear provincial.

His phone beeped, and he tapped it. "Monsieur Azeez, we have an issue," said the plant manager, Miriam Dufour. "Meet me in the Control Room."

"I am on my way."

Madame Directeur Dufour was the only real authority, and so the most influential person in the six hundred kilometers between Taoudenni and Timbuktu. He had no problem taking orders from a woman—in the tribes women were often in charge. But it grated when she treated him as hired hand rather than team member, as she did more and more often these days.

The massive BASF carbon fiber plant was expected to be a godsend to a once proud nomadic people who had plied the desert like the ancient mariners had crossed uncharted waters. Yet, even now, only *inadan* like himself and the *éklan*, the manual laborers, worked at the BASF facility. The upper classes of the tribes shunned the place, preferring their traditional towns, trading stations, and farms. Pastoral existence had not served his people well and their futile revolt against Mali's government at the turn of the century had just made things worse. Yet, so many clung to old values.

The chemical company saw the desert, which most pictured as empty, and had seen everything they needed to make carbon nanofibers, virtually spinning air into gold. There were wide open spaces, unclaimed by anyone since the last of the salt caravans in the 2010s, virtually unlimited solar energy to power their facilities, and air—like the air everywhere on the planet—saturated with carbon dioxide.

He walked to the wide-tired cart he used to crisscross the vast conversion plant. The drive from the atmospheric concentrators where he started, into air conditioned warehouses, past clean rooms and 3-D fabbing areas to the plant's command center took twenty minutes. The chilled air had a faint tinge of ozone, incongruously set against the sunburned skin of the desert outside the wall-length windows. During the drive he only saw five people, plus plenty of utility robots. He wondered, not for the first time, if the promise of jobs for his people were illusory, beyond the dozen or so he knew by name.

"Finally," Mme. Dufour snapped when he entered the Control Room. Two techs sat nervously drinking their coffee. Monitors displayed several dozen views of the plant, both interior and exterior. A camera facing north showed a group of about fifteen or twenty men in blue turbans, and several camels with large stone slabs roped to their sides. The men all carried automatic weapons, not uncommon among the scant desert people. *No one travels that way anymore,* thought Azeez. *No one in their right mind.*

"I called you the moment Jacques reported them approaching," she said. "Now they're just sitting there." She pointed at a close-up. "They look like an old Tuareg caravan," she said. "What is this? Halloween? Purim?"

"I expect they're part of the New Azawad Liberation Movement," he said, reaching past one of the techs to zoom in on one of the "stones." "They are reenacting a salt caravan to Timbuktu. They're a throwback—romantics out to make a statement."

Azeez decided not to say anything about "Tuareg" being Arabic for "abandoned by God," again. "They want to resurrect the past. But they're no real threat. I expect they're curious about what we're doing."

Outside, two of the men were hobbling the camels while the others stood in loose formation. Their leader was still sitting far above them, though Azeez noted the camel he rode was carrying salt, not a fine racing camel as he'd expected.

"Let us inform them," said Miriam, leading him to the building's entry hall. "The more locals we can connect with, the better." Still, she used her phone to page a pair of security guards to meet them.

"This may take a while," Azeez said. He touched a button at the unmanned security desk, and the inner door swung open into a wide, short hall with a second door on the far end. They went through the airlock.

The heat struck them, and the sun's dazzle, which was even stronger for the paleness of the sky. Azeez hoped they could get right down to business, but knowing the tribesmen, he expected conventional greetings, with the usual formalities and cautious lack of inquiry into motives. The chain-link fence stretched before them delineating the perimeter of the installation against the broad open horizon. Miriam tapped an app on her phone, and the gates swung open. They walked halfway to the rebels, letting the others close the rest of the distance to meet them.

In a sign Azeez took as positive, the leader of the force had his camel kneel. Like most high-caste *Imohag*, he fairly dripped with silver. They made their *salaams* and grasped hands to show they hid no weapons, although guns and other arms were abundantly visible. Both sides politely ignored this.

"You and I are strangers," said the leader, short-circuiting the usual dance of greeting. He glanced at Azeez's injured hand, then let his gaze travel up his plain robes to his bare face in an act just short of rudeness. "I travel carrying salt to Timbuktu. Our water is gone and the *wadi* is dry. Several of our camels have died." He spoke in Northern accented *Tamasheq*.

Azeez glanced at Dufour, who nodded for him to take the lead. "The *ténéré*, the eternal emptiness that is the desert, is not kind.

You are welcome to our hospitality." As the others dismounted and started to lead their beasts to the building's covered car park, he added, "We will bring you water, and contact anyone you wish." He didn't want those guns inside the building, but it would be a considerable breach of etiquette to ask their visitors to part with them. Just as it would be improper to ask the leader his name.

What Azeez knew so far was: the man was carrying salt, likely NALM, he came from Taoudenni, and he was using camels instead of trucks. His party was sizable, which, along with his abundance of jewelry and the traditional cut of his robes, meant he was a man of some stature. No, he could not ask the man's name, but there were fewer than a million tribesmen left in the desert. Anyone of note was known to all. He could guess.

"Are you a cousin of Elhadji Salak?" It was a safe bet the man had some relationship to the local chieftain.

"I am, my name is Yahira Salak. And are you related to Aghaly al Boula?"

"Sadly, no." Azeez did not even know the name, and wondered if Salak had merely made it up. He'd been associating with westerners so much he actually chafed at the roundabout discussion. He offered a hint. "My tribe travels most commonly in Niger."

Dufour had been trailing in their wake, obviously catching little of what they were saying. "Azeez?" she said in French. "Should I call ahead to have water brought out?"

"Yes, please," he said.

"Azeez," murmured his companion. "Azeez Kemil?" When Azeez nodded, he said, "You went away, to university in the north." They reached the car park. Camels picked their plodding way between jeeps and trucks, happy to have shade.

The moment Dufour ended her call, Salak made a small gesture and his men casually swung their rifles to cover her, the two guards, and Azeez. "Let us drink water, but inside," he said in perfect French. His accent indicated he came from the Paris suburbs, not Mali. But he also spoke excellent *Tamasheq* and he had been navigating by the stars, so he knew the desert world as well. That explained a lot. *A dilettante. A romantic. And he's risked all their lives on his quixotic adventure.* "And let us discuss this—" Salak paused, taking in the expanse of white wall that made up the front of the building. "—this facility of yours."

III

Miriam shot a questioning look at Azeez and toward the door. He spread his hands, and she invited Salak and his crew inside, inwardly seething that her man had misread the situation. Salak accepted politely and said something in *Tamasheq* to the men, who began untying the heavy loads from the camels' sides.

She saw the men adjusting their robes as they came into the corridor, no doubt unused to the chilled indoor air. She led them to the commissary, where Azeez got a tray of glasses and a pitcher of cool water. He also put in an order for some snack foods, which the kitchen staff could bring out when it was ready.

Miriam took a moment to let anger and frustration wash through her and away. Outwardly calm, she determined to keep the conversation as innocuous as possible, to lull these men and convince them to leave, hoping they'd steal as little as possible. She set her phone on the table and idly tapped here and there on it. Azeez noticed, and looked from the phone to her. She nodded; yes, she was recording.

Only when everyone had their water glass, and had been given time to drink it down, did Salak speak. "Thank you for your generous hospitality," he said, in French. "In this desert, we all must take care of one another, or we shall all perish, don't you agree?"

Miriam smiled thinly. "Of course. Though you appear to be helping yourselves. Paris? 18th arrondissemont?" she asked. "I have an ear for accents."

Salak nodded.

"You've taken on a difficult challenge, trekking here," Azeez said. "There has been no rain in this part of the Sahara for eight years. Most prefer to fly over this ocean of sand these days."

"I scouted the route before I even purchased the camels. I drove the whole way and there were oases enough to be able to travel from one to the next in a day or two."

"How long have you been planning your caravan?" Miriam asked. She interpreted the looks she got as meaning she had interrupted. Azeez said his people had always been tolerant of outsiders; it was among themselves that they required strict adherence to etiquette.

The caravan leader replied. "Three years. It took some time for the Kickstarter campaigns—for the camels, with a stretch goal for the money to purchase the salt when we got to Taoudenni. Much of our income will go to reward the funders, if we make it."

A pair of kitchen staff, watched by Salak's men, brought out bowls of dates and nuts, with bread and a variety of sauces. One refilled everyone's water, then both retreated once more.

Salak leaned forward. "Tell me of your efforts here. I would like to know what you make."

Miriam gestured at the vast plant beyond the commissary's wall. "What we make is a better world! We use the sun's energy to transform CO_2 into useful substances. The main one is—here, let me—" She reached for a pocket.

No one besides the director moved, but she felt the tension rise in the room. "This is a pilot plant," she said, moving more slowly. "We're extracting carbon from the atmosphere to make new materials." She pulled a clear vial from her pocket, one she kept ever-ready for investors, and held it up to display the dark mass of slender carbon tubules. "And Azeez, here, is working on making graphene directly from airborne carbon."

Salak snorted. "It does not look particularly impressive. Silver," he said, "camels, or salt are all more useful. Or weapons," he added.

"This is terribly useful," said Dufour, "in hundreds of ways. It's used in—"

"First." Holding up a hand, Salak, his voice husky, said, "Water.

Let us talk of water." He held up his glass, examining the swirl of liquid in it as he tilted it one way, then another. "Thank you for this," he said. "It is vital. But I witnessed the death of the oasis, the one that is just outside your plant." He stood. "You say you are taking the carbon out of the air? How do you do that? How can we know that your factory is not the cause of the wadi dying?"

Azeez abandoned any effort to maintain *Imazighen* courtesies. "What we are doing here matters—to you and your traditionalists at least as much as to the rest of us." He stood. "This process will reverse the concentration of greenhouse gas in the atmosphere. The desert has been spreading across the Sahel faster than ever. What are people to do if the rains don't fall for ten years at a time, or a hundred? Then where will your back-to-the-past movement go?"

Salak glared. "It is your technology that has made the desert expand. We are not producing any CO_2. *We* are not the problem here."

"We plan to make the desert shrink. Our process will work. It must."

The caravaneer sat back and sipped his water. His eyes showed that he was holding his temper while he evaluated his situation, like any good general. That didn't mean he was not about to go to war, and the BASF facility had few security personnel and little in the way of small arms, resources enough to defend themselves for a time. But they were badly outnumbered and who knows what more Salak's band had in their arsenal, beyond what they were showing. By the time help could be brought in from the military, there was no telling what they would take or ruin, so it had better not come to that. Miriam tilted her phone this way and that, capturing various of Salak's men with her camera.

Salak paced the room, speaking to one of his men, and to another. Several of them left to secure more of the plant and to spell the men watching the camels. Salak appeared ready to settle in for more than a drink or two of water.

Miriam's shoulders dropped but she put on her game face, a slight smile that never quite reached her eyes. Salak took his chair again across from Azeez and Dufour, beckoning another, far older, man to their side. If Salak were inclined to debate, they were in good hands. "This is my uncle Yeddes. His degree is in Chemistry. Tell him of what you are doing here."

Miriam said, "You understand the role of carbon dioxide in the changes in climate we've been experiencing." Yeddes waved at her like she was a fly interrupting his lunch. Clearly he did not need a beginner's course in environmental science. "We use solar concentrators, large concave mirrors—" using her hands, "to heat up a solution of carbonates. We immerse metal plates, and run a current through them using the Licht Process. The carbon collects on one of the plates, directly from the atmosphere, while the carbonate is replenished to be used again and again."

Yeddes glanced at Salak, then looked to Azeez, not making eye contact with Miriam. "Please," he said, "what sort of metal plates are you using for the anode and cathode?" Miriam's face colored. "And what is your electrolyte? I presume it's a liquid bath."

Azeez grinned. He explained the process quickly in *Tamasheq*, dropping into French when he needed an untranslatable technical term. Miriam watched the tribesmen, reading their reactions.

"So, what do you plan to do with all this . . . what, graphite?" Salak asked in French. "Are you going to make pencils?"

"We make carbon nanofibers, as light as nylon and stronger than steel." Miriam nudged the vial with her finger. "We are producing it at every length; nanofibers for solar cells and advanced batteries and electronics, long strands that can be twisted or braided together to make superfine threads as strong as steel cables, or to be woven into fabrics." She paused. "But more importantly," she added after a moment's thought, "we are solving the planet's climate crisis. Our process sucks the carbon dioxide out of the air and releases pure oxygen.

"We've proven it can work, and be profitable. This is just the first of our company's facilities. With enough space for more collectors, just under four hundred thousand square miles, we can cleanse the air of CO_2 in a decade. Imagine," she said, gesturing, almost shouting, "the atmosphere back to the way it was before the Industrial Revolution. Then you really could go back to scurrying around the desert, if that's what you really want to do." Miriam sat back, crossing her arms.

"Scurrying, yes," Salak said. "Excuse me." Salak turned to Yeddes and two other men. "We shall discuss matters now." He gestured to them and they walked to a far corner of the commissary.

Miriam pursed her lips. "You didn't approve."

"They're not primitives. And they're not unconnected to the world. This movement is trying to preserve what is essential in a culture that has made one of the most inhospitable places on this Earth its home—our home, madame, theirs and mine."

Miriam paled. She straightened her back and looked into Azeez's eyes.

"What they are is a threat to my facility."

"Yes. They are dangerous men. That is why I say, tread carefully. Give them the respect they think is their due. This Salak is a high-ranking man from an important family. I can't say about the rest."

She put on her Madame Directeur mask in a clear message the discussion was over.

"Very well. You take the lead in negotiating with them. I will organize Security, in case your high-born and educated camel drivers don't see reason."

IV

At Salak's urging, Yeddes described the process in simpler terms. He lauded the importance of its potential success. "However—" He looked down as he rummaged in a pocket of the blue jeans he wore under his robes. He pulled out a match.

"Remember the trees at the oasis?" When Salak nodded, Yeddes put a thumbnail to the match's head and flicked it. The match flared. "See how much higher the flame goes than usual? How much brighter? These people are putting enormous amounts of oxygen into the atmosphere. It makes fires more likely and more powerful." He dropped the match, which burned itself out on its way to the floor. "If they're having that much effect on the oxygen levels, it will also lessen the amount of carbon dioxide in the air, as she said. To a plant it would be like a fire to us, consuming all the oxygen, making it hard to breathe. And with the trees dying, they are not drawing the water up from below ground. I have little doubt this is what destroyed the wadi." After a few seconds he added, "Accidentally."

Salak nodded. Turning to his two lieutenants, he looked to see if they had been following the discussion and to hear their options. Eyadou was for razing the compound and killing all the staff. But he was a hot head. He'd been a child soldier in the LRA before being sent to a rehabilitation camp. Ibrahim was more cautious, advising merely that they go their way and ignore the damaged wadi. "This was to be our last caravan, after all," he said. "They have shared bread with us, albeit under duress. Let them save the planet, if they can."

Salak spread his hands and looked at Yeddes. He had no taste for violence, especially if it would accomplish nothing. Nothing except to bring more misery down on his people—the very people and traditions he wanted to save. But saving those traditions for future generations also meant not giving up in the face of this destruction.

"If they judge this to be a success," said the old man, eyes moving about as if searching for the words, "they will doubtless expand the facility. They speak of this as being a pilot plant. What they may do is save their green world while dooming our sandy one."

"We can't have that," said Yahira Salak.

"At the same time," said Yeddes, "their standing up, saving the world—and making a profit at the same time—it's going to be a challenge to get them to give that up. And is it right to risk the world's health so that ours may not suffer?"

If the old man had it right about the wadi, they were screwed. His people would all become like this Azeez, who had not worn the *tagelmust* in so long the blue stain had faded from his face.

Yeddes was right about their prospects of stopping a multinational like BASF. Corporations cared nothing for the old ways. His caravan would look like nothing more than a fool's adventure. They listened to nothing but force. Eyadou's option looked more inviting by the moment.

V

Miriam Dufour sat back in her plastic chair and waited for Salak's contingent to get far enough down the hall. She gestured for Azeez to lean toward her. "I believe we are in trouble. There are almost thirty men already in here, and all of them armed. Our emergency drills focused on not letting aggressors into the plant."

"Aid will take too long to arrive," Azeez whispered. "The airport in Adrar is more than seven hundred kilometers away. Even from Tamranrassesel it will take hours. What's more, do you not think, if they are attacked, that these men might not, perhaps, shoot down a helicopter or two before they even have a chance to land?

"Plus, trust is a scarce commodity among the *Imazighen*—my people, the *Tamasheq*," he added when the confusion failed to fade from Miriam's face. "What currency does BASF use to buy their trust after that?"

"Your people? I thought you were one of my people. You were most eloquent in extolling the importance of our project, Azeez. I hope they will see how necessary it is that we succeed. This project stands to benefit *your* people, as well. Everybody in Mali is going to be the beneficiaries of our success. This could move your country into the Twenty-First century." She left "not like these throwbacks" unpronounced, but the look she shot across the commissary said it clearly.

"Madame Dufour, look at it from their local point of view—forget about their romantic adventurism. Water is the scarcest commodity there is in the Sahara. If we impose an adverse impact on the oasis, we doom those who depend on it. We are situated far from any cities on purpose, or even outlying villages, but there are still nomadic tribes among the Kamashek, and they have rights here."

Azeez shook his head. If he could find some way to accommodate the New Azawadians, even if he did persuade her to go along, what could the two of them promise on their own?

"I do not deny that, though I thought the days of the caravan were over. But the bigger picture, they do not see it like you and I do." He looked down the hall to where Yeddes was lighting a match and he watched how high the flame leaped from the tip. "Looking at only the big picture is just as much a fallacy," he went on. "If what we do here somehow destroys their wadi, we must make amends." The light dawned as he looked back at the match, already reaching the old man's fingers. "We did not consider the potential for a build-up of oxygen in the immediate area." Azeez rubbed a palm across the beard on one side of his face.

"Oxygen? But that spreads out in three dimensions away from the plant."

"It would explain the amount of rust the workmen have been reporting, and those spontaneous fires we thought were caused by misaligned solar mirrors. Ordinarily, I would expect the prevailing winds to carry it off. But a temperature inversion could act like a lid on a pot, confining the oxygen to the local area." He looked briefly alarmed, then did some rapid research and calculating on his phone. "At least we are not in danger from oxygen toxicity; that would require a far higher concentration."

Miriam rubbed her eyes. "That puts a different complexion on things. I had not thought us responsible. I would need to discuss reparations with the home office." She failed to look pleased at what a payout would do to the plant's bottom line. "That would be an admission of guilt, though."

"We could at least put it on the table as a possibility. Anything to calm the situation."

"Good enough." Dufour jerked a nod at the group in the corner.

"Then we play a waiting game. I've had the Rabat office patched in and listening through my cell phone." At his look of alarm she added, "I am not insensitive to the needs of the locals. I just want the army present so they can help persuade these thugs to leave."

"They are not children, to be chided or dismissed. You may think they are just playing at dress-up. But they come to know this desert deeply. They need to be listened to; they are of this place, as am I." Hearing his own words, Azeez was almost as surprised as Mme. Dufour.

Miriam glared at him wordlessly. He had seen her genuinely annoyed, angered to the point of raising her voice. But this was different, an attitude he had not seen in her eyes before—certainly not trained at him. It was disdain.

Miriam retreated to the other side of the cafeteria. Sitting by himself, Azeez considered his options. He had lost the director's ear, though he thought they had enough history for that to be overcome eventually. He'd never had the tribesmens' trust. They were deeply suspicious of the plant and its operations, and they thought it presented a threat to their cause. However hopeless or retrograde he judged their cause had no bearing on their current situation.

If Dufour went ahead and summoned the Security thugs, their gunships bristling with 50 mm. cannons, there would be a confrontation for sure. Then there was the other less settled and more unsettling question. What if the process was scaled up, and destroyed more oases? The wadis were vital to *Tamasheq* life.

Salak and a small group of his men came and talked briefly with Azeez, and then with Dufour, revealing they had come to no conclusion. Azeez invited the group to stay with them and to share their evening meal. He let the kitchen know that he had more than doubled the number of people for dinner. They would need to resupply earlier than expected, but that was the least of their worries.

Azeez felt stretched between the *Imazighen* and the West. True, he hadn't worn his *tagelmust* in years. He'd thought his loyalties lay with the plant, with saving the world. But he'd identified with these tribesmen, had argued their side with Dufour. Which was he: French or *Tamasheqi?* There was an old tribal saying: "If you put a cord around your neck, God will supply someone to pull it."

Surely Salak thought of him as just Dufour's lackey. Azeez preferred to think of himself as a bridge builder, someone who could span the distance between the traditions that still made sense with the wider world and the future technology opened up for people like himself.

Time, then, to start a bridge. He sought out Eyadou and Ibrahim, making them presents of silver jewelry he had spent hours constructing. It felt less like a deliberate attempt at ingratiation and more like a return to his heritage.

VI

Excepting a skeleton crew, the plant's personnel were invited to dine with Salak and his men. *Tense*, thought Yahira Salak, *tense and crowded. Just let anybody on either side make a wrong move, and there will be a brawl.* He deliberately made an effort to look relaxed and approachable. For her part, Mme. Dufour was clearly making the same effort. He would have been more comfortable if they had been seated on low couches rather than around square tables, but had hardly expected African manners in a French facility.

There was salad, and a lamb tagine, couscous with okra, and tea, ending with an assortment of pastries. The caravaneers all murmured *"Hamdullah"* at the end of the meal, and Salak was a little surprised to hear Azeez give the traditional host's reply: *"B'sahatkoum."*

The French woman watched the workers file out, then turned to Salak. "Thank you for not hurting any of my men so far. May I hope that we can come to an agreement?"

"An agreement." He appreciated her wanting to appeal to the trader in him. "Does that mean you admit culpability for the destruction of the wadi?"

"Yes," replied Azeez in a low tone. "We had not planned for

the weather to so concentrate our oxygen output." Salak caught a surprised expression on the director's face that turned slightly venomous, then blander than bland. Perhaps he was underestimating the man's loyalty? Or was he to be lauded for his truthfulness?

Azeez toyed with his cup, then brought up something that had been sitting in his lap. Salak recognized the length of indigo-dyed cloth, it was a particularly fine *tagelmust* Ibrahim had been saving for a favored nephew. Slowly, Azeez began winding it around his head.

Salak nodded. "I acknowledge in turn that you did not deliberately ruin the wadi. Still, it would not be the first time 'indigenous peoples' were made to suffer for Western aims." He could play the director's game, be the firebrand rather than the trader. "However, it does not mean I find you blameless. This plant must not be allowed."

Dufour put both hands on the table and half stood. "My plant will save the world! How can you tear down what may be our only chance to reverse—"

"—what you Westerners started in the first place?" Salak grinned. "My people have survived in extreme conditions for millennia. Don't think we can't adapt to your climate change as well."

Azeez thumped his water cup onto the table. "No. You will not survive. This won't be the matter of a few degrees. It will get hotter and hotter, and everywhere the world over. Already the temperatures all across northern Africa have risen to deadly levels in the summer. The desert will conquer Africa. There won't be a safe place anywhere. The wadis will all go away. But if our project succeeds, the water will return. The desert can bloom, can once again be the Green Sahara it was thousands of years ago."

"By still killing our wadis in the process."

Dufour half stood. "I can't let you destroy our work." She reached a hand, touched the phone in her pocket. Guns came up.

"Wait," said Azeez. "I said something just now, about the desert spreading."

Salak nodded, signaling his men to sit. "Which is why we need to—"

Azeez held up his hand. "The plant can't just be shuttered and the plans abandoned."

"Right," said Dufour.

"But it can't stay the way it is now. We're putting too much concentrated oxygen into the local air. It is not dispersing like it should." Azeez put his cupped hands together, then slowly drew them apart. "We need to spread the effect out." He put his hands back up to the cloth, winding it around and around his lower face. "We do not need to put all the processors in one place; it is just more convenient to do so."

"And this will not just result in killing more wadis?"

"Not if it's done right. A thousand camels will destroy a single oasis, but a single camel in each of a thousand oases will thrive. We have over a hundred thousand collectors just in this one facility. If we distribute them so there is enough room between one and another, it will work. It's just a matter of math."

Dufour narrowed her eyes, thinking. "Right now we have the collectors, then the baths, then the clean rooms and fabbing facilities. It would be much less efficient to make hundreds of thousands of individual units incorporating all those functions."

"But it could be done. That's engineering." Azeez tugged at his *tagelmust*, trying to get it just right.

"And it would need servicing. And policing, to make sure nobody steals the parts. Just putting in the roads would be prohibitive, not to mention supplying all these little outposts."

"Logistics is your domain." He nodded at Dufour. "Supply and policing could be yours," with a nod to Salak.

"That is how the *Imazighen* used to live," Salak said. "Without roads."

Slowly, Dufour nodded. "We'd still have to sell it to corporate."

Salak could see Azeez's smile in his eyes. "Diplomacy," he said, with a gesture to both of them. "That is your domain."

Most writers who attend the six-week Clarion Science Fiction and Fantasy Writing Workshop will find their writing improving week by week. "The Compass" was the last full story I wrote there, and happily the comments were favorable. It does, though, include one element in common with a few of my other stories from the workshop. Daniel Braum, one of the other attendees, called me on it. "Don't you write about anything except babies?"

Yes, of course I do. But see, our daughter was a toddler at the time, so children were on my mind.

This was bought by Gardner Dozois for Asimov's, *and he ran a trigger warning before the story. If offbeat uses for fetuses squick you, please page forward to the next story.*

—Edd

THE COMPASS

The skippership *Hope* glided below the surface of reality.

Mara entered the navigator's cubby. It was situated in the exact center of the giant metal pyramid that carried them through skipspace, and its mismatched components and tangles of cables lent a makeshift quality to it. Some of its devices still communicated by wire.

"Hello, Brendan," Mara said to the navigational instrument, checking his nutrient flow and making sure he had not kinked his tube. "How has he been?" she asked Burke, the navigator, while running a diagnostic on the ocular camera that tracked the fetus's eye movements while in skip.

"Fine, fine," said Burke. "He's been pretty active." He pointed at Brendan's tiny hand, blue-veined and gently waving in the fluid of the tank. The fetus kicked, and Burke darted a look at his panel. "We're about to go norm, I think."

Mara had not been in the room during transition to normspace. "Does he always kick?"

"Usually, not always. It's a good indicator." The navigator sat at his console, studying his screen. "Yes, we're transitioning."

A camera beeped insistently behind her, and she moved aside. It refocused on the tank and its occupant. The fetus turned his head, sealed eyes questing, and the entire tank moved on its gimbals in the same direction. This continued until the fetus was facing the wall to Mara's left. She glanced at Burke's screen, all numbers and quasar names with magnitudes and frequencies, to be checked against normspace after the transition. Then she moved to the tank's side, careful not to get in the way of the camera, and sighted over the fetus's head. He was looking directly at the skipspace analogue to where the Earth had once been.

There were no guideposts in skipspace, no stars, no black holes or quasars. Brendan was their only usable instrument.

Mara refocused her eyes, catching her reflection in the tank's side. Her short crinkly mop of hair was liberally sprinkled with white, and she saw new wrinkles in the dark skin around her eyes. There was more weight around her middle, too. Forty-five, she thought. That's not *too* old. "How does he know?" Mara said quietly.

The screens around them came to life, displaying star patterns. They were back in normspace, many light years from the location where they'd gone skip.

"It's not about 'knowing.' He just has an instinct," the navigator said. "We didn't even know about it until a pregnant woman was off Earth. If only we could bottle it." His screen was narrowing possibilities down based on the tank's orientation.

"We have." But that was too quiet for Burke to hear, and she bent once more to her own instruments, monitoring the fetus's health.

The fetus was almost used up, but she'd known that as soon as she had seen one eyelid open slightly.

Dorrie stood at the railing, looking out at the sea of coffin-shaped cryoboxes that constituted one level of the *Hope*. This one level alone held three thousand empty chambers, and it was only a third the size of the largest level. Only the two tip floors were occupied; they'd managed to save eight hundred station personnel when the pebbles had struck.

Dear Lord, she prayed, please watch over us. We're all that's left, Lord. You hold our souls in the palm of your hand. Please let us find a habitable planet, if it be your will. Amen.

She turned back to checking the miles of piping that ran along the catwalks and corridors of her ship-home. The constant ozone tang to the ship's air was most concentrated here. She climbed down a set of rungs to another gallery of cryoboxes. She always found Level 15 intimidating, almost haunted. Just as they were transitioning into skipspace, a pebble like the trillion or so that had destroyed the Earth had slammed into the *Hope* at near-relativistic speed, shredding crew and cryoboxes, and spurring their decision to leave. Theirs had been the only one of five skipperships to make it away from Earth before the pebblestorm had increased exponentially. Repairs had been makeshift, but she found them holding. She moved onward, upward, toward one of the ship's four tips.

Three more levels today, she thought. Then I can meet Bruce near the screen and have lunch. Mustn't forget to inspect the hydroponics pumps later.

Her board gonged. She tapped its screen. It reminded her that a meeting was scheduled for fifteen-hundred hours. If she hurried, she would be able to finish the remaining levels on her list first.

Mara got to the meeting early. She slipped into a seat, nodding to a couple of friends. The entire crew was in the room, excepting a few at vital posts who were listening in.

Captain Ashok Chaphalkar already stood under the large reader board that spelled out "Day 84." The lights dimmed and his face appeared on the screen for them all to see.

"Shipmates," he said. "Welcome and thank you for coming. Your patience is appreciated. I realize we were all hoping to be off the *Hope* and on a new planet by now. Top item on the agenda is to inform you that we are progressing well toward the star HD 82943. Our visits to Upsilon Andromedae and HD 142 were unsuccessful, but we have high hopes for this star. Like 142, it has five detected planets. Gross location is done and we are well into fine location. We expect to be close enough to view earthlike planets within the next two to three transitions. There is a problem with that, though. Doctor N'Dongo? Where are you, Mara?"

Mara's face appeared on the screen. She stood, the distant camera smoothly tracking her face. She spoke in a normal tone of voice, trusting the AI's ability to read her lips and broadcast what she said. It interpreted her expression and analyzed her body language to lend her speech nuance. No microphone necessary, though the emotions surprised her at times with their accuracy.

"Hello, all." A computer simulation of her voice said, almost with her. "One of my tasks is to monitor the health of the fetus we must use as an aid to navigation. Its instinct to face Earth fades as its eyes open during week twenty-five or thereabouts. I am sorry to say that it will soon be too old. We have no substitute fetus available, due to our rapid departure from Earth."

"Thank you, doctor. Perhaps you would let us know if any of the crew—qualifies?" His voice was honey.

It was important, damn important, that they have a substitute. But no way was she going to be his lighting rod. She said, "I'm afraid that's covered by patient confidentiality." She sat down.

"We'll discuss that later. Meanwhile, I'm certain we will hear from any of our crew who might be pregnant." He looked down at the board he held. "Related topic. Doctor Reynolds has a theory about narrowing our search. Gene?"

A helioseismologist rose from his second row seat and launched into a description of orbital mechanics. The lipreader could barely follow it, evidently hampered by his mumbling into his beard. Mara looked across a sea of heads, the cream of Earth's scientific and technical knowledge, and sighed. The lottery for crew of the *Hope* had been impartial, but their emergency departure had left her with the crew of the space station Parsifal, where the *Hope* had been built. There were certainly a lot of old white men in the room. The lottery for cryopassage had been likewise equitable, but instead they had wound up with more stationers. A fist of loneliness tightened around her heart. Lord, but she missed Robert, lost behind with Earth.

A flashing red light on her board drew her attention. She had muted it for the meeting, but had left its screen on. A single glance was enough; she stood and excused herself out the row and was running by the time she hit the door.

Dorrie, sitting next to Bruce on the unadorned bench, barely noticed the older woman leave, so rapt was she by Doctor Reynolds's theory. It was based on the gross jumps they'd been making through skipspace. All points in the universe were contiguous to points in skipspace, which had a radius of only a few dozen miles. The ship entered normspace and remained motionless while Burke located his quasars, then went skip and moved its painstaking few nanometers, which translated to hundreds, even thousands of light-years in norm. Brendan was their only way to tell their orientation when skipping.

They had to regulate their velocity carefully when going skip so as not to wind up in the dark between galaxies. Reynolds suggested making wilder skips if 82943 didn't pan out, longer ones, based on calculations he'd made during their journey so far. He expected to be able to lead them to nearby galaxies, younger ones with more viable systems.

When Reynolds was finished, Dorrie's superior rose and reported on the *Hope*'s condition and supply situation. She thought he was being optimistic to peg it at another forty days' travel, but hoped he was right. She'd do her best to ensure it.

Captain Chaphalkar announced two more marriages. Dorrie squeezed her husband's hand. Shipboard romances had blossomed. She thanked God for Bruce, whom she'd married only a week into the journey.

There was a subtle movement inside her, the baby maybe stretching its legs. She straightened her back and rolled her neck in sympathy.

The doctor returned. She entered from the wings of the stage where the captain stood, and went to him. They conferred in private for a moment, then he turned back to the podium.

"I am informed that the—the fetus has just died. I'd like to call for a prayer."

Reverend Thorpe rose and the screen focused on his face. Dorrie lowered her head, but as she always did she opened her eyes halfway through the prayer. She liked to watch men as they prayed. Thorpe's face was reverent; the AI altering his nasal twang to a deeper, calming baritone. Then Dorrie's gaze slid down, right, and she locked gazes with Doctor Tamara N'Dongo. The woman was too far away to make out her expression, but Dorrie felt uneasy. Her husband and her doctor were the only ones who knew she was pregnant.

Mara pulled off both rubber gloves and tossed them in the general direction of the recycler. Then she leaned on the sides of the sink, its plastic cool to her touch, and leaned forward. Farther, farther, and the water streaming from the tap kissed the top of her head. She stayed in position for a moment and then straightened to let the water cascade down to her shoulders, her back, her chest.

For such a small being the autopsy had been long, grueling. She'd had to be painstaking.

Mara's board signaled. She tapped it, and the captain's voice spoke.

"Tamara? You are done?"

"Yes," she said. "He died of natural causes, an infection. They can be very quick to act in someone so young. Fetuses aren't meant to be outside their natural environment." She remembered Brendan's mother, tearfully thanking the Captain for taking her and her child to Heaven. Padme Adamson had been passing through Level 15 when the pebble had hit the *Hope*, vaporizing her. Brendan was already in his navigational bubble by then.

"Thank you. So, doctor—" There it was again, that honeyed

tone, almost exactly like the one synthesized by the lipreader. "Now it's just the two of us, I'd like to know what likely candidates we have aboard."

Just the two of us, she thought. Aloud, she said, "I'm not altering my stance just because we're alone, Captain. My patients have their right to privacy."

"Not when it comes to the survival of this ship and the entire human race. You have no moral high ground here, Mara."

"That won't change my opinion. But . . . let me talk to the mother, see if she'll come forward on her own."

"You have two hours. But that's all."

It was Dorrie's turn to make breakfast. She was setting the table for herself and Bruce when the buzzer at their door sounded. She put a napkin down and answered it. The dimness outside the door was mute witness to it still being "night" for crew on their level. A deeper darkness resolved into the ship's doctor, Tamara N'Dongo, dressed in a gray cloak over clothes that turned out to be a riot of greens and yellows when she swept it off. She stepped in at Dorrie's invitation and put the cloak on a nearby chair. She saw Dorrie looking at it.

"That's a buibui," she said. "A traveling cloak."

"Oh. Is it likely to rain?"

N'Dongo laughed. "Just an old habit." Then she frowned and added, "I may turn out to be the last person ever to use one or know what it is."

"Not now, so long as I'm around. Won't you sit down? I have some juice, or coffee."

"Juice? Orange juice?" She sniffed the air.

Dorrie showed the doctor to the table with its two settings, and offered Bruce's glass to Mara. Then she sat at her own place. The silence stretched, Dorrie heard her husband yawn from the other room and hoped he'd put on a robe before coming to the table. She was just thinking she ought to go to the door and let him know she wasn't alone when the doctor spoke.

"Dorothy, you heard the announcement this morning."

"Yes, such a poor baby."

"Yes. Yes, it was. We can't go skip until he's . . . replaced."

"Mm. Toast?"

"No. Thank you. Dorothy, you—ah, you have a baby. Just over ten weeks old."

"You can't have my baby."

"Ten weeks is the right age for using. It's vital. As—"

"I know." Dorrie began tearing her toast into small pieces. "Isn't there something else? Some other way? Somebody else pregnant?"

"No one the right age. The fetus needs to be at least seven weeks old, so that the eyes have sealed and its brain is developed enough for the instinct to initiate. You're the one match I have."

"No."

"You'd hardly be giving your baby up. You'd be able to visit it every day, if you wanted. And once it reaches twenty-five weeks old and the eyes unseal again, you'd be able to have it back, in an incubator."

"No," said Dorrie. "Baby Brendan died. My baby might, too. Aren't you supposed to refuse to perform unnecessary procedures?"

"The procedure is—almost perfect, it's all handled by an autodoc anyway. And it's absolutely necessary. Dorothy—Dorrie, you must understand how important—"

"Maybe you could use one of those cameras. What are they called, the ones that look inside you. Couldn't you watch my baby while it's still inside me?"

"An endoscope. No, It wouldn't be accurate enough. And besides, it'd probably cause a miscarriage."

"Maybe one of the cryos?"

"What?" The doctor sipped her juice, her glass clattering a bit when she set it back on the table. Dorrie wondered if the doctor was as upset as she to be in this conversation.

"The cryos? Do any of them have a fetus the right age?" she prompted.

"Seventy percent of the stationers were male," said the doctor. She looked Dorrie straight in the eye. "Won't you consider coming forward? The future of the human race—" She stopped and snorted. "I'm sorry, I have trouble getting through that, even if it's true. Listen, the Captain will make me tell him about you, anyway. It's out of my hands. I just wanted to give you the chance to come forward first."

Dorrie was quiet, listening to her husband's breathing, feeling internally for her child to remind her of its existence. The doctor rose and retrieved her cloak, and Dorrie got up to see her to the door.

"There's not much time."

"You've already got my answer," said Dorrie. She closed the door.

She walked back to the table and picked up the empty juice glass.

It was Sunday. Mara stood alone and nude in her tiny examination room. Most of the crew would be in front of the screen at Worship listening to Reverend Thorpe. Try as she might, she just couldn't subscribe to their belief that skipspace was Heaven.

She'd checked twice that the door was locked. She checked it again.

Lying down on the examination table, she wheeled the portadoc unit closer and centered its bulbous sensor array over her abdomen. The machine made a subtle whoop-whoop sound and extended one of its wands to touch her belly. The doc's screen flickered to life, giving her a color-coded three-dimensional picture of her inner anatomy. She automatically catalogued the things she saw. Bladder. Fallopian tube. Womb. And there it was.

Her baby. Her thirteen-week-old, four-inch-long miracle. Robert's last gift, implanted in a body she had thought too old to be fertile.

She lay there on her back, knees up and spread, and watched her child's heart beating. Her breathing slowed and she thought she might easily go to sleep here. Just watching.

Across the room, her board gonged. Reluctantly she powered the doc down and hopped awkwardly off the table to look at her screen.

There was a text message, private, from the Captain. *Schedule operation,* it said. *Dorothy Canigher has volunteered to donate her fetus.*

The operation was textbook-perfect. The autodoc put Dorothy Canigher to sleep and flooded its arena with oxyfluid, just as if she were going cryo. She took a shallow breath every thirty seconds, and her sluggish circulation discouraged blood loss. The machine made its infraumbilical incision and entered her peritoneal cavity, then incised her uterus. It pulled the fetus out with care and transferred it to the sealed environment where it would stay until it could be transferred to an incubator. Then it closed Dorrie, drained its arena, and delivered her up to Bruce Canigher and Captain Chaphalkar. They put her to bed. Bruce sat beside her, prepared, he said, to wait the night.

Mara breathed easier once both of her patients were safe. She joined her Captain in looking at the fetus in its tank.

"What a perfect little thing," he said. "Look at those hands."

She messaged Burke, the navigator, that she would keep both mother and child for twenty-four hours' observation. The *Hope* could be on its way in a day.

Then she walked to her examination room. She wanted to stay near both patients.

In Dorrie's dream a perfect little girl with blonde pigtails, dressed in a white pinafore, came to her and pulled at her hand until she followed. Gray ship walls fell away and became a field of bluebonnets, so like the ones she'd played in when she was young. The girl led her to a dollhouse in the center of the field, looked at Dorrie, and put a finger to her lips.

"We have to be quiet," whispered the girl. "We don't want to wake God up." Then she fell to her knees next to the little house, and so did Dorrie.

The girl reached out and lifted the roof off of the house.

"Hello, Doctor."

Mara lifted her head off the small desk. "Captain," she said. She'd only meant to close her eyes for a moment. She glanced toward her computer screen, with its array of monitor results. "She's doing fine."

"And the fetus?"

Mara brought up her other patient's results. "It's—she—is doing well."

"Thank you. I just wanted to be sure before I make an announcement tomorrow." The Captain dropped a stack of flimsies onto her desk. "I found these in your examination room. Tell me, what are they?"

Mara's heart beat faster and she could hear the blood rushing in her head. "Printouts," she said. "Ultrasound printouts."

"Mm. This top one is dated yesterday."

"It's normal to do an ultrasound before a caesarean."

"I'm not an expert at reading these things, but this looks like a nail on its finger." He pointed at a section of one of the flimsies. "Does this look like a fingernail to you?"

She didn't have to look. "Yes," she said, staring into his face.

"I don't recall seeing any fingernails on the Canigher baby. Don't they develop later than ten weeks? By the way, what month does a baby start showing on a pregnant woman?" He looked pointedly at her belly.

"I couldn't—I just couldn't let him go."

"Have you made any plans at all for when people find out? When Dorrie and Bruce find out?"

"—couldn't—"

"What if their baby dies?" Chaphalkar set the flimsy back down. "Will you be prepared to donate your fetus then?" His eyes were hard and demanding, so like the brittleness of his voice. "We'll be near enough to HD 82943 tomorrow. Near enough to know whether we can settle on one of its planets."

His voice was honey no longer.

Mara looked away, down into her folded arms. The baby moved under them, protesting the pressure.

EXPEDITIONARY FORCE

The German Army pacification of Wonderland proceeded apace. Major Konrad Grebner, standing in the back of a Maultier halftrack, surveyed the decimation of the hedge maze with some dismay. But sacrifices must be made to accommodate the forces required for the invasion of England.

Several oddly ambulatory man-sized playing cards leaped out of a side path brandishing spears. Grebner's men merely turned their flamethrowers on the enemy, who readily flamed out of existence.

Grebner felt the halftrack sway, and turned to find Henryk Tryba clambering onto its tail. The plump Polish academician straightened and walked to the front of the vehicle, peering at him through thick round eyeglasses. "They were mere pasteboard, Major. No danger to us."

"With spears." Grebner thumped the back of the driver's seat and motioned him to move forward.

He stifled an instinctive dislike for Tryba. The man was a nuisance of the first water. First, he was neither German nor a soldier, thus automatically suspect. Moreover, he was not only a scholar, but a scholar of children's literature! And finally, he had been cross and contrary through this entire operation. The man obviously felt the campaign should come to an utter halt just so he could study a talking walrus.

"So far, everything is proceeding according to your briefing," said Grebner. "There has been no sign of the girl, Alice, or this Red Queen you mentioned." He tapped a sheaf of papers in his breast pocket. "And, happily, no trace of this vicious Jabberwock."

"As expected, Major." Tryba took off his spectacles, peered at them, then drew out a handkerchief to polish them. "In the first place, the poem 'Jabberwocky' is a story within *Alice's Adventures*, and in the second, the beast is slain within said story." Satisfied, he replaced his glasses, one earpiece at a time. "As to Alice, you will recall my Theory of the Conservation of Imagination suggests that our invasion would take place immediately after her visit."

"Liberation."

"Eh?"

"Liberation, not invasion. The High Command is quite insistent on the specific term."

Something reared up in front of them. "Halt!" The major stared in dismay at the enormous white rabbit that blocked their way. It swept a paw through the front rank of his soldiers, slamming them into shrubs and tanks. "Fire!" His Panzer IVs opened up, punching hideous holes in the rabbit and its jacquard silk vest, shattering its enormous pocket watch. It fell to the side like an oversize tree.

Grebner yelled to his chief engineer, a passenger in a nearby truck. "Are you still convinced your mirror is necessary?"

"Yes sir," said the Feldingenieur. "As expected, the rabbit hole is too small for our purpose, and were we to put everyone under your command to sleep, I could not guarantee they would wake up in England with their weapons, indeed if they would not wake up in their own homes. But with this—" He gestured at the flatbed truck on which the much-pampered mirror lay shrouded in tarpaulins. "With this, we can fine-tune the receiving location merely by looking into it. We shall appear inside an English manor house, which we shall blow to flinders with our tanks."

A whistle blew, signaling a lack of opposition. "Very well," said Grebner, whose private reservations never surfaced on his face. "We have cleared a sufficient area. You may set it up."

The man left to supervise the construction of a scaffold while the major scanned the hedge maze with his field glasses. He saw the remains of the castle they'd destroyed when they entered Wonderland through its mirror, and the carefully cultivated gardens they'd plowed through. Tryba had said the King and Queen were likely buried during its destruction.

Grebner was torn. He couldn't fault the brilliance of the idea of attacking England through its favorite children's tale, but he was repulsed at the desecration. It didn't really matter what he thought, though, as the Fuhrer was increasingly paranoid since the failed July 20th assassination attempt. All it had done was give Hitler a concussion, and combine his existing occult obsession with the storybooks he read as he recovered. Grebner's own part in the conspiracy had not been uncovered, a fact for which he was profoundly grateful.

The major had no doubt their maneuver would succeed. They had the tanks and men to establish a foothold deep in enemy territory. His name would go down in history for helping facilitate the unification of Europe under German leadership. Lowering the glasses, he thumped a fist lightly on the side of the halftrack. When the driver looked back at him enquiringly, he shook his head and said, "Eyes forward."

There were two more attacks during the afternoon, if assaults from a doddering old knight on horseback and by a pair of rotund twins could be called attacks. The bodies were tossed next to the corpse of the giant clothed rabbit.

Evening was in the offing when Maltz reported the completion of the scaffold. The engineer oversaw the lifting of the mirror into place, ensuring it did not flex too much. When it was upright, he looked ceremoniously at Grebner, who nodded. Maltz pulled the rope to drop the tarps.

The major stepped up to look into the mirror, seeing himself and his force of tanks and men doubled. Soon, by some arcane method he didn't understand and didn't care to understand, the view would change to one in England. Then they would proceed, and conquer.

At first, he thought it a trick of the light when a furred feline face gazed out at them, occupying exactly the spot in the mirror where Grebner stood in Wonderland. He glanced aside at Maltz, who obviously saw it, but who shook his head. "Not my doing, sir. It's the Cheshire cat," he said. "Known to be a trickster, but powerless." When one of the men started to raise his rifle, the engineer put out a hand to wave it down. "Do not harm my mirror, Soldat," he snarled.

"I expect that's the cat's hope," said Grebner, "for us to destroy our own doorway to victory."

Maltz did not look back at him. He was staring at the mirror in confusion. "What is this?" he said.

The major looked back to the mirror. Instead of his tanks and men, instead of himself or even the cat, there was a wooded path filled with people and with animals standing on their hind legs. As he took an involuntary step back, he saw that the road on which they stood was paved with yellow bricks. Two girls led the horde, one a blonde and the other a redhead, neither of whom looked more than twenty. One wore a simple sun dress, a thick belt, and a supremely confident expression; the other a crown, an elegant ballgown, and an expression to match. Behind them were arrayed a lion, a metal man, a scarecrow, a tiger, a man with a pumpkin for a head, and many more singular characters, surrounded by a legion of people, some small, some medium in size, and some quite large. Over them flew a squadron of flying monkeys, armed with short spears.

It looked like, and was, an army. Beside Grebner, Tryba giggled in delight.

The major took a step back. "Fire," he yelled.

"Too late," said the blonde woman, stepping forward so her hand projected from the mirror. "All of England's borders are defended."

Major Grebner's tanks opened up, their barrels impressively wreathed in smoke and uttering deafening roars, but their rounds passed through the mirror, over the heads of the enemy forces, to explode far behind them. "Our turn," said the woman, whose name

Grebner suddenly remembered was Dorothy, created by some American author.   .

The lion bellowed, and somehow it was louder than all the cannons under Grebner's command.

INNERMOST BOX

I am the memory keeper of our town. Of the world, more like, and these are the memories I have to relate of the earliest days.

I was sitting on the stairs when the saloon doors creaked open. A large white man in jeans and a windbreaker stumbled in carrying a metal case far too big for him to see around.

Papa hurried forward as the white man set the box down and stood blinking in the light. "Sí? Hello? I was about to close up, but if there is anything I can do for the señor . . . ?"

The man rubbed a hand across his forehead and looked out the window at his car, a big beat-up red thing. "Am I still in Texas? I've driven all day, but I didn't see a border crossing."

"You are in Avalon, Texas, eighty miles from nowhere. What can I do for you?"

"I saw three signs as I drove into town." The gringo unzipped his jacket. Underneath he wore a red-checkered shirt. "The first said 'eat.'"

"I got sandwiches, if you eat fast."

"The second said 'drink.'"

"I'll getch'a beer, if you guzzle it."

"The third said 'vacancy.'"

"Take all the time you want. I got upstairs the finest rooms—Maria! You, hija! Get to bed."

He said it right sharp, like he didn't know it was the only game I ever played for serious. Spy on Papa, duck if he looked my way. I'd let Mama go away while I wasn't looking—Papa I wanted to keep an eye on. I went up the rest of the stairs to our room, right above the bar, and looked through the largest knothole in the floor. The view was good, under me was the gringo and that box. I could hear them too.

I could tell Papa was next to the bar cutting slabs off the barbecued ham for sandwiches, one for himself and one for the gringo. The knife tapped the cutting block at the end of each sawing stroke. "What brings you to Avalon, Mr.—ah?"

"Gassoway. Dr. Ernest Gassoway. One town's as good as another. I just needed one in this area, and this is as far as I got by nightfall. I'm a researcher." He left off at that. Papa set a bottle of Dos Equis in front of him and he took a pull.

Silence stretched while they ate, and I woke from a doze to the red-dust odor of the wooden floor and the clink of a chess piece.

I smiled. Papa loved the game. He'd taught me the horse and the castle, and how they moved and all. Dr. Kaufman would play with him sometimes.

The stranger was speaking. "...majored in Electrical Engineering and minored in Parapsychology." At the time I didn't know these big words, and even now I can't be sure this is exactly what he said.

"So those boxes have instruments for—what, testing brains?"

"Well, in a way. I ran across the effect while I was doing research in guided imagery for epileptics."

They talked some more, but I was watching how the pieces moved around on the board that Papa had set on the table. It never made sense to me how the most powerful piece on it could only move one space at a time. If I was a king I'd make it a rule that I could move however I wanted and take any piece I wanted.

"I read an article about it." It was Papa's voice. I figured from the ache in my neck that I'd gone to sleep again. I thought it was unfair. Papa should come up and kiss me and tuck me in, not waste his time talking.

I put my eye to the hole again and could barely see them. They were bent over one of the visitor's cases, the gringo's sandy hair next to Papa's black.

Gassoway pulled a helmet out of the box. It looked like the one Papa made me wear when I rode my bike, only this one was black and had wires coming out of the back. "I could test you if you want," he said.

I crept out of my room and around the corner of the stair. The saloon was just one big room with the bar down one side of it, so I could see them clearly. Papa had the helmet on and the gringo was running its wires to a control box.

I watched in silence as they plugged the thing in at the wall behind the bar. The gringo turned knobs and flipped switches. Papa squeezed his eyes shut real hard the way he did when he was reciting Winnie the Pooh out loud to me and trying so hard to get it right.

Squiggles crawled across a gray screen on the gringo's control box. Finally he sighed and turned it off. At the click Papa opened one eye, then the other. "Well?"

"It reaches here, too." The man looked up from the box to his reflection in the mirror behind the bar and then out the window at his big old car. "Maybe if I keep heading south. Maybe there'll be somebody."

"No, wait." Papa jerked his head around to look up the stairs and the wires slapped against the back of his chair. I ducked, but not fast enough. "Maria, come down."

I thumped each foot down the stairs, sure he was going to whup me. When I shuffled up to him, Papa grabbed a handful of my blue nightdress and swung me around to face the stranger. "Read her," he said. I craned my neck around to look at him, then back to Gassoway.

"Are you sure?" said the gringo. "She'll have to be told, or it won't work. She'll have to concentrate."

"Read her," said my father again.

They both looked at me, Papa scared and angry all at once and the gringo kind of sad. Papa said, "Maria, you listen to him and you do what he says." He reached up and pulled at the strap on the helmet, which came apart with a ripping sound. The stranger took the headpiece and held it to his large belly as Papa's hand came back down across my shoulders. I looked up at Professor Ernest Gassoway and saw that his eyes were blue. That made five blue eyes I'd seen this week, if you counted the cat with one blue and one green eye. I was keeping count.

"Ah. Maria?"

"Yes, gringo?" Papa squeezed my shoulder. "Yes, sir?"

"Call me Ernie. This—" he held up the helmet. "This is a machine for measuring pulses, uh, waves, from different parts of the brain. You follow me?"

I nodded. He was just like my teachers, wanting to be understood. So I nodded again.

"But it is very sensitive. We use it to focus on parts of the brain that people don't normally use. These places, when they are used, house abilities. We can't wake up these places, but we can measure them."

"You were measuring Papa just now?" When I looked back and up at him, Papa was staring out the window. It was dark, but I knew that big red car was out there, and so was Mama, somewhere. So I grabbed one of his big fingers with all of mine to make him look down at me. I smiled at him.

Gassoway nodded and shortened one of the straps on the helmet. "It's easier when the subject—that's you—thinks very hard about trying to use one of those abilities. I want you to imagine yourself growing older and bigger." He put the helmet on my head and pressed the straps together.

I yawned real big, putting both hands up in front of my mouth. Then I put them back in my lap and nodded at him, closing my eyes. Papa pulled his hand away but I could hear him breathing right next to me. The gringo's— Ernie's—sneakers squeaked a little as he walked over to his control box.

I screwed up my eyes like I was Papa and thought myself older. This was something I'd done lots of times, lying in bed at night. In my mind I grew taller and more pretty. Breasts swelled from my chest. My legs got longer and whiter like Cochina's. I'd seen them one time while spying on her and Papa. My hair was very black and long; I'd said I wasn't ever going to cut it and I meant it. I almost went on to the rest of the fantasy, where I took care of Papa and raised a ranchful of kids, but the gringo's voice broke in.

"Here! Come look, the line continues!"

I peeked at him through my lashes as Papa jumped over to his side.

The gringo ran a finger across his screen, following a squiggle that crawled across it. "See, there's a major trauma at the right time, but the line continues!"

Papa whooped, and started to jig like when he's drunk more than three beers, stomping the heel of one boot while bouncing on the other. But then he stopped and looked at me. Just looked, but I wasn't sure what he saw, 'cause of the scared look that came back into his eye. I didn't feel any different, and when I looked down at myself I didn't have breasts or longer hair or anything. I was just the same Maria I'd always been. He got himself a beer, and one for the gringo, too, who was tracing that line again and again. He even let me have a sip, and when I went to sleep there was an awful taste in my mouth that got nastier by the time I woke up some time later.

They'd taken the helmet off me sometime during the night, but Papa hadn't carried me upstairs like he usually did. I was lying on the bar, my head near the part that hinges upwards, with the gringo's wadded-up windbreaker under my head. I stayed there and listened to him, to Doc.

"—knew since the early 'teens that one of those abilities was precognition, the reading of the future. The mind makes its prediction by picking the most likely future based on a collective subconscious understanding of events up to that point."

I didn't know these words at the time, but Dr. Kaufman took notes and eventually I grew into the person who collected memories for our town.

"We cannot tell what happens at a specific point in the future, but any major life-change sends back a ripple, what we call a 'trauma.' We can read, roughly, the size and shape of a trauma and learn a lot about what the future is like."

I opened my eyes and sat up on one elbow. The whole town was there, all eighteen people, leaning on the bar or sitting at the tables or squatting on the floor. Papa was next to me, behind the bar.

Cochina wasn't listening, but Jake Scarborough ignored her playing footsie with him to ask, "You're talkin' about maybes and could bes, ain't you? You can't know that certain what's gonna happen."

"Not *what* is going to happen, no. But we can know that *something* is going to happen." Jake looked over at Papa and said he thought this guy was just another Yankee rainmaker and why had Papa asked them all to come in anyway, and Miss Velez was shaking her head, starting to get up to leave. The gringo leaned over the balcony and asked her to please sit down. "You don't get it. The future is a box you've been given. Each trauma is another box inside the big one. By shaking each box in turn you can tell if what is inside is heavy or light; big or small; one thing or many smaller things. The last box, the innermost box, that's death."

He had them then. Even Cochina looked up at him, and not like she usually looked at a man. They were all acting like he'd said a bad word.

"A year ago, after the talks broke down in Sydney, I noticed that everybody I tested had a major trauma coming. Well, *the* trauma, actually. Death. I've been traveling around since then, testing everybody I can, and it's the same everywhere. Like I said, I don't know what's coming, but it's big. It affects everybody, everywhere."

He paused, and you could just see all the people in the room leaning toward him. I noticed then that Javier Sorento had the helmet on and was looking up at me. He made a gun with the finger and thumb of his right hand and shot at me, but quietly so his Mama wouldn't notice and thump him. So I shot him back, picking up a Pepsi bottle and holding it in both hands like a machine gun.

"Except most of you," said Ernest. Papa was looking at me as the gringo continued. "I've tested all of you. Most of you escape, and I hope if I continue south I'll find more. There's nothing I can say that'll prepare you, because I really don't know what's coming: chemical, biological, atomic. Maybe natural. All I can say is, do what you can to get ready for a worldwide disaster, because most of you will be alive to see what comes after it."

He didn't say much in answer to all of the questions that came after that, but if he had I wouldn't have heard him anyway. Dr. Kaufman was too busy trying to talk over everybody else to write anything down.

I ducked down behind the bar to continue my gun battle with Javier. He cheated, because I know I got him dead center a bunch of times. Besides, I was using a machine gun to his little sixgun.

When everybody left I could tell most of them didn't believe anything he'd said. "It was entertaining," said Miss Velez, like she'd said when the revivalist came to town. "It was quite a show." She even shook Ernie's hand.

After they'd all gone, he went over to his metal box and packed up. When I took him his coat he draped it over his shoulder and held out a hand to Papa. "Don't forget what I said last night, about providing for her future."

Papa stuck his thumbs through his beltloops, ignoring the gringo's hand. "Lucky her. She's *got* a future."

After that I didn't play my game so much any more. Spying on Papa didn't seem so important. Any time I got to thinking maybe he'd up and leave like Mama did, I'd remember Ernest Gassoway saying "The line continues," and I'd think, "It's not the end of the world."

Four years later Papa died of the Rot. A lot of people did, including Cochina and Javier, and animals too. I was only thirteen then. I didn't know anything about population centers and polyvectors and climate-driven pandemics. All I knew was that everybody in the world got sick and Dr. Kaufman used those words a lot. It was a truck driver from Houston who first brought it through Avalon. They said it was an early strain; not as powerful as it got later, but the thirteen of us who lived through it were immune to the later, stronger versions. A lot of people in South America lived through it, and in Central America and parts of Africa. But just about everywhere else in the world people died. Quarantines were set up, but they never worked; there were just too many ways the Rot could get to people.

I was busy after that, too busy to think about the past. First there was Jake Scarborough to marry and then children to raise and the saloon to manage when Jake got shot by the raiders a few years later. It wasn't until just recently that I've been feeling it's important to talk about the old world. I remember it so much better than what came after.

Everybody blamed the gringo, Ernest Gassoway, for what happened. He kept on testing people, he got the Rot early, and lived. Until they killed him. I heard about it on the little shortwave station they got running in Tijuana. "For crimes against humanity," they said, but I don't think they even knew what that meant.

He didn't start the Rot. He didn't kill anybody. He just divided the world into two parts: those who were going to live, and those who weren't.

I guess I haven't made it clear who "they" were. At the time I thought maybe it was everybody left in the world. But it wasn't, it was just the kind of people who would think that a bird flying south brought on the winter.

Writing humor is hard. Many of us settle for puns, the writing equivalent of the burp. But "Prophet Motive" uses one of the finer techniques of humor: exaggeration. Take an everyday event and crank it up to eleven, and you have the kind of comedy that everyone can recognize. In this case it's the near-universal adolescent experience of searching for our identities under the gaze of parents, teachers, and friends. Wondering if the choices we've made are really ours, or just what's expected of us. Wondering if we really want to do something, or only think we do because someone else suggested it. Wondering if our wondering about all this is a bad sign. Only in Paul Rohrback's case, it isn't just this week's self-image or a bad haircut that's at stake when he makes an incorrect choice. Sometimes it can be whether an alien race called the Welterki of the Fiery Snow will finally develop medicine. (Poor, poor Welterki.)

—Laura Staley

Laura is a member of the writing group Sound on Paper.

PROPHET MOTIVE

Aliens shadowed Paul Rohrbach from birth. He was the three million and seventh prophet of the universe, so they must interpret his every act, his every utterance. Each choice he made was parsed and debated to death. Loudly. It made dating difficult.

"He chose Davis Parkway," said the first disembodied voice in his head.

"Collins Street would have been faster," said the second.

"He's used to Davis; it's how he gets to school."

"Still, it doesn't bode well for the Artrins in forty years," put in a third.

"Forty-two years," said somebody else.

That started an argument that lasted most of the way to Luz's house. Not that the aliens didn't comment on whether he'd get out and walk to her door, or just honk, maybe even text her phone. Most of the time he liked to do weird stuff, just to see how his observers would interpret their meanings. But today was his first real date with Luz. He wanted the evening to be normal, or as normal as it ever got with nosy, nattering aliens dogging his every move.

He walked up, slipping a bit on the ice, and rang the doorbell.

"He didn't knock."

"He usually doesn't knock even if there's a bell."

"But he could have. That proves the Niskerian Hypothesis."

"Niskeria be damned! It *proves* the Last Among Unequals of the Delta Middilans will be assassinated!"

"Small potatoes."

Some of the aliens had assimilated Earth culture a little *too* well.

Luz herself answered the door, already in her coat and earflapped hat. "Hello, Paul. Hello, aliens," she said.

"Hello, Luz," they all said. Everybody within twenty feet or so heard his aliens in their heads, too.

They'd have got away without meeting her father if the aliens hadn't been quarreling so "loudly." The Niskerian faction was in full mental cry as Mister Santiago clomped down the stairs in slacks, undershirt, and Kermit the Frog slippers. He took one look at Paul and stepped in front of his daughter.

"You didn't say your date was with this *perdedor*," he growled. Everybody in Lashton knew Paul. He and his chorus had been on plenty of talk shows, until it sunk in that the aliens didn't talk out loud, just in peoples' heads.

"He's not a loser," said Luz. "He's actually—"

One of the aliens broke in. "You just can't equate a simple little murder with proof of a new galactic constant! This could lead to faster-than-light travel! For bodies!"

"Hush," said another. "Hushhush. I want to see how he talks his way out of this one."

"I'll second that," said Luz's father, glowering.

"Good evening, Mister Santiago. She's safe with me," said Paul. His breath misted in the cold. "Everybody knows who I am. I couldn't get away with jack."

"He's right," said the voice Paul called Mister Miserable. "Why, the masturbation incident alone—"

"So anyway," Paul cut in loudly. "We're just going to grab some pizza and then go dancing." He shot a desperate glance at Luz, who was bending to look through the gap between her father's bent elbow and his belly. She waggled her eyebrows the way that always made Paul laugh. He bit his cheek.

Scowling down at him, Santiago said, "I saw that reality show they put on about you. Didn't last long, did it?" The show had used a barbershop quartet who parroted the aliens, but their program had been scheduled opposite *White House Brats*. No contest.

"I like Luz," Paul said. "And she likes—seems to like me."

"He's okay, Papi," she said. "We eat lunch together sometimes. And his aliens are funny."

"Funny!" This from one of the more common voices, one that Paul privately called The Grinch. "The future of the universe is hardly a laughing matter."

"Not that there will be anyone left to laugh in the long run," added Mister Miserable.

Luz's father gave Paul one of those "you poor bastard" looks, then said, "All right, *mi querida*, be home by midnight and make sure you take your cell phone."

She jiggled it at him as she walked past. Paul followed. She stopped at his car and looked around.

"Where's your entourage?" she asked.

"My what?"

"Those spooks and scientists who always follow you around. You know, like that one Secret Service guy who leers at me in English class every day."

It was a wonder he even got to attend ordinary school. For a couple of years he'd been confined to a bunker being studied, almost dissected, but the ACLU had taken his case all the way to the Supreme Court. "I asked for a day off." Actually, he had begged, whined, and pleaded, and even so he was wearing an ankle bracelet. He'd lay odds there was a satellite specially tasked to watch him, as well as unmarked vans around at least two corners.

Paul started the Honda. He could feel Luz's eyes on him as he pulled into the street. "They're there all the time?" she asked.

"The spooks, or the aliens? Yeah, twenty-four, seven for both."

"In class, I've heard the aliens talk about what you're doing, and what you're saying. Do they know what you're thinking, too?"

He paused, remembering some times he'd foxed them. "Not really," he said finally.

"I wonder if you're more of a religious icon or an experiment to them." The look she gave him reminded Paul that she was acing science.

"You heard what Principal Miller said at the beginning of the year," he said. "I'm some kind of prophet." Another pause, much longer than the ones that usually fell between comments from his observers. It was like they were holding their breaths. "Where are you going with this?" he finally asked.

"To Satan Claus," she said, suddenly cheerful. "And then, dancing!"

"He'll drive there on Warbler Way," said a voice. "If he does, it'll mean the end of fourteen endangered species on Oundle Seven."

Paul chose Fountain Boulevard.

Satan Claus was a treasured relic of bygone Lashton, a pizza place opened by a Scandinavian dyslexic who decorated the restaurant in Christmas colors. Red and green strobes flashed in the windows, attracting moths and downing epileptics for miles around. Inside, golden and emerald paper Viking ships covered with dust hung from the ceiling. The funk of decades of grease and onions hung just below the ships.

Luz led the way to a booth near the back. Paul slid into the bench across from her.

"He's facing east," said the new voice. "What does it mean? Is that significant?" Paul decided to call this one "Eager Young Space Cadet."

"He's facing her, is what he's doing. She chose this spot, and he's much too shy to sit next to her."

"Still, it's a choice. I think the Vo are going to have themselves a nuclear war."

Another alien said something, but it was in his—or her, or its— own language.

A few heads turned, but most of the diners were students from

Paul's school, well used to his celestial chorus. He and Luz were soon ignored again. Ignored, that is, except for however many aliens were currently scrutinizing him.

Menus, water, and service later, Luz transferred a slice of bacon-and-mushroom pizza to her plate, then listened as several voices all continued to dispute the impact of their choice of toppings. The minority were contending that something called the Wuc would sleep for a dozen more years, while the rest said that the first group's heads were full of dark matter and that Chisnable was going to be the next wave in mind-music.

"Do they ever all agree?" asked Luz.

"A few times a year." Paul took a sip of Coke. The glass clattered against the table before he had it safely down. Other people went on first dates and talked about school or television shows or maybe sex. "They get really excited when they do. It's been a few months since the last time."

"Do any of the prophecies mention us? The Earth?"

"Uh, no. Not yet anyway. They're from different planets, all of them really far away. I think a lot of the stuff they figure out doesn't even happen on any of their own planets."

"We mindtravel," said Eager Young Space Cadet. "We cast our perceptions to the skies, and explore."

"What made you pick Paul?" asked Luz. "How do you verify his predictions?"

"He was foretold by the last prophet, who may I say was much more accurate. That's how it goes."

"Hey," said another. "Don't talk to her. You know we're not supposed to—" The voice cut out, as if some switch had been thrown. This happened sometimes when they got too chatty about their own goals and methods.

"I think," said Paul, "that for now they're not watching." He realized that a barely-felt constant background buzz was missing. "In fact, I know they aren't."

"'We're not supposed to—'" she repeated. "Supposed to what?

Reveal too much to their subject, I guess. Or maybe to other people around you?"

"They say it's what I do and say that predicts what's going to happen. Usually they wait 'til after I do something to comment on it. I always thought that if they interfered it would mess up the prophecies, but lately I'm not so sure. After all, I'd never have been on TV or done plenty of other things if they weren't around. Some of what they said today makes me wonder if they're trying to manipulate me."

"Like that bit in the car about which street you'd take. Just today? What's different about today?"

"You." The word slipped out a little faster than he'd meant.

Luz blinked. "Huh. Is it because they think I'd make your decisions for you? No, it can't be that; I'm sure they'd have a huge problem with your parents and school if that were the case. Maybe there's a big decision point ahead of you." Smiling a secret little smile, she nibbled at her slice of pizza, then put it down. "Listen, do you like them? Do you want them watching you the rest of your life?"

He shook his head, suddenly hopeful. Whenever anybody had talked about the aliens before, it had been about learning from them or communicating with them or using them in some way. Luz sounded like she wanted to help rid him of them.

"Good," she said. "Because I sure don't."

What was *that* supposed to mean? Was she just being helpful, or was this something more? Not for the first time, Paul wished he had the cheat code for high school. B, A, B, A, Up, Down, B, B, Left, Right, B, A, and suddenly he'd sail through whatever weirdness lay ahead.

The buzz returned. Something in his expression must have tipped Luz off, because she said, "They're back?"

Nodding, he stuffed the last bit of crust in his mouth. "Done? Okay, let's go dance."

*

Luz insisted on splitting the check. Paul, who was used to a lifetime of exhaustive analysis of his every move, wondered if it was normal for him to question if this was a good thing, a bad thing, or just a normal thing.

"If he makes it through this traffic light, the Welterki of the Fiery Snow will finally develop medicine."

Paul hit the brakes.

"Poor, poor Welterki," said Mister Miserable.

"You *are* trying to manipulate me," he said. Then he added, "Sorry," to Luz, who had both hands on the Honda's dashboard and was glaring at him.

She sat back. "*Por su puesto*. I understand."

"Well?" Paul said, not to her. "Why try to control me all of a sudden?"

"It's heretical," said one voice and, "Because we can," said another, and "For your own good," said a third. Mister Miserable chimed in with, "Pay no attention to the aliens behind the curtain. It's all in your head."

"Bull," said Paul. "I am not moving until you give me a real answer."

"Good luck with that," said The Grinch.

Paul and Luz simultaneously sighed. A horn honked behind them, and he stepped on the gas.

Arms over their heads, Paul and Luz bounced in the tightly-packed crowd on The Phar's dance floor. The beat pounded their ears. The aliens' voices came through in their heads loud and clear.

"North, east, north, west, spin—"

There was a confusion of voices as the aliens tried to interpret each change of direction. This reminded Paul of one of his favorite activities when he was a preteen: running around the house while screaming and flailing to overload the thought-stream. It hadn't really worked; they would just work out the implications no matter how long it took, sometimes keeping him awake at night with their musings. Then they'd decipher his uselessly pulling the covers over his head.

They'd always affected him. How could they not? But why pick today to try *controlling* him? Did they think he was going to live with Luz the rest of his life? If so, did they want him to, or want him not to? What the hell did they get out of it, when hardly any of his "prophecies" affected their own cultures? He'd always supposed that they could check his forecasts through their mind network; maybe they just liked to be able to warn or congratulate people, depending on whether his predictions were negative or favorable.

Funny. He'd hardly ever thought about his own situation so much. He usually just lived it. It was kind of like paying attention to his backbone. Luz was already influencing him. Then it struck him.

"Influence," he yelled.

Luz might or might not have heard him, but she did see that he'd spoken. She led him out a side door. Twenty teenagers smoked there, shivering in what little light spilled into the alley from the streetlamp. Paul's ears still rang from the music.

"What is it?" she asked, rubbing her hands along her forearms. They'd left their coats inside. "Got an idea?"

Paul nodded. "Maybe it's not me they're trying to influence; it's other planets. If they can foretell a disaster somewhere, and contact someone there, they could give a warning. Or if they can foretell something good happening to a civilization, they can help them along." He spread his hands. "Influence them."

"And the more successful, grateful civilizations there are, the more scientific breakthroughs or impressive artwork or just true believers there are for your mind-sharers. All of their cultures benefit." She looked up, then back at him, continuing quietly. "Not to mention the billions of people who might not die."

"When you put it that way, it sounds like I've got a lot of responsibility. I wish I could tell when what I'm doing is the right thing. It sounds like they're doing good."

"Maybe," she said. "Maybe not. They're in the perfect position to take sides." She sighed, her breath a fine fog between them. "They could let one faction know about a disaster, but not another. If there's good news they could make contact and take some of the credit. They can make it look like they're guiding the civilization toward success."

"So, they could be either the nicest guys in the universe, or the most underhanded. And they're using me to do whichever it is they're doing. Thanks a lot."

"You're being awfully quiet."

Paul blinked. "What?"

"Not you." She looked up. "Them."

The response was immediate. "*Venga avercuando eleste dormido.*" The words were run together so much he had trouble telling where one word ended and the next begun.

It was Luz's turn to look startled. Paul smiled.

"Some of them talk in their own language at times," he said.

"Really?" She bit her lower lip a moment. Then she returned his smile. "Let's go back for another dance."

Most of the drive back to Luz's house was taken up by chattering aliens. They debated the meaning of everything he said or did, loudly and at length. It almost sounded like they were trying to take up every moment of the drive.

Luz spoke over the clamor. "Do your aliens ever lie to you?"

"Who can tell?" He turned the car's heater down a notch. "Most everything they say is an opinion, not a command or suggestion."

"Yeah, that's what I've been hearing. They never gave us humans anything, did they? Technology, or what their biology is, any-thing like that."

"Nothing but grief." Paul tried not to sound too morose.

He pulled up in front of her house. For a moment, she sat, turned a little toward him. "Thank you," she said.

He wasn't sure what to do. Kiss her? Or try to, anyway. But what if she didn't want him to? Nobody knew better than Paul did how many ways his actions could be construed. There were days, weeks even, when he tried not to make a single important move or decision.

The moment passed. Luz gave a half-smile, then pulled the door handle and stepped out. "Be careful driving home," she said.

He watched her walk up the sidewalk, saw a curtain upstairs twitch aside, then fall back into place, and by the time he looked back she was inside.

"Is he going to hit the steering wheel? I like when he does that; it always means something big. Let me get my charts."

Paul sat, trying to put off bellowing or crying or banging his head on the window for one second. Two seconds. Three. Then he put the car in gear and drove slowly home. The aliens were silent the whole way. He barely acknowledged the Secret Service agent who waved from the house across the street.

It took Paul some time to get to sleep. He spent what seemed like hours mulling over the evening, trying to replay everything Luz had said and done. It felt like he was the alien, struggling to figure out what her actions meant.

When he woke up, Luz was lying next to him.

"He's awake."

Paul had woken to that statement more mornings than not. What he'd never experienced before was that warmth at his back, that arm thrown across his side. When he turned over, there she was.

"Gah!" he said.

"Good morning," said Luz, yawning. "I was waiting for you to wake up. Your entourage said you usually wake up around six-thirty on school days."

Paul froze. He distinctly recalled leaving Luz at her own house last night. While he certainly wasn't unhappy to see her, this wasn't exactly how he'd planned their next meeting.

Luz sat up on the edge of the bed. She was still dressed. "Sorry. I fell asleep."

"What are you doing?" It came out a little more abruptly than he'd wanted. He cleared his throat. "I mean, I didn't expect—"

"That's okay. I just got sleepy there at the end." She stretched. "I was here to test a theory, and because I was invited."

"Invited?"

"Earlier today, when you thought one of the aliens was speaking in its own language, it was actually asking me, in Spanish, to come see you after you were asleep."

"What? Why?"

"To talk to me while you weren't awake, of course."

Paul grabbed his pants off the floor while she continued. He tried to be quiet so he wouldn't wake his mother. God knows what she'd say if she found Luz in his room.

"Which brings us to what I've pieced together." She turned away as he struggled under the covers to get his pajama bottoms off. "There's a prophecy war brewing."

He waited.

"It was that Welterki prophecy that got me started. Prophecy shouldn't equal causation. If you do or don't do something, then two completely different results—" She scowled. "No, not 'results.' The interpretation if you do something should not just be negated if you don't do it. There should be some other event somewhere completely different. Oh, wait! It's a second-order problem—of course!" She slapped her head. "If they try to influence you, then whether or not you accept is indeterminate, with a forking set of prophecies. I wish I had a whiteboard in here. . . ."

"But that Welterki crack—"

"Exactly. There are two factions of aliens. The traditionalists are like priests; they just want to interpret your actions like their ancestors have for millennia. And, like I said, profit off of them. Lately, they've been a bit frustrated." She shrugged. "But recently a few newer ones have come along who are more, oh, inquisitive. They're interested in seeing what happens if they 'encourage' you to act in certain ways."

"Why now?" he said, then the light dawned. "Oh." From what little he knew, before Paul, every prophet had been an adult, set in their ways and eager to carry on their normal lives. Paul was the first one determined to act oddly. He looked up. "They're being awfully quiet."

"They want to know how you're going to react," said Luz. "Your gift of prophecy is predicated on your free will to make choices. But short of being severely disabled, you probably have less free will than anybody ever. You're surrounded by secret service agents and scientists, not to mention aliens intent on manipulating you now."

Paul stood up to button his shirt. Yesterday, when she'd wondered what was making the aliens act differently, he'd said it was her. He'd been more right than he knew. All they'd talked about was the aliens; he'd thought she could help get rid of them. Now he wondered if she had been sent by some government agency or another, maybe even from some other country. It was obvious she'd been thinking about his situation for a long time.

"They wanted to talk to you when I wasn't awake, and you wanted to talk to them when I was asleep." Slipping bare feet into sneakers, he casually reached for the phone on his bedside table.

"He doesn't trust you," said one of the aliens. "That device conceals a transmitter to agents of the Secret Service."

"Guys!" The moment it slipped out he realized how stupid it sounded. They'd never been his friends; he'd just grown used to them. He looked at Luz.

She didn't move, though she was paler. "Go ahead, if you want," she said quietly. "But I am doing what's right for you."

He felt a flash of anger. "What's right for me? That's what the aliens said yesterday. 'For your own good.' So you're, what, working with them?"

"You're a pain in the ass, Paul," she said, finally smiling. "You mess with them all the time, by making weird choices, or too many inconsequential ones, or by trying not to make any choice at all. You aren't the first prophet, you know, you're just the latest in a very long line of them. Being made into a prophet so young has messed you up big time." She reached out with one finger and almost touched his forearm.

"Some of them said they want to get rid of you, too," she added.

"Some? Get rid of—?"

"Actually, just the priest types. I guess if they startle you at the right moment you might step in front of a car or drive off a cliff, but that's a last resort. They say they'll find the next prophet a lot easier if you work with them." She frowned. "I'm sure there are ways to improve the process. Evidently prophets are just people who are better tuned into how the universe is trending, and each one forecasts the next prophet." She checked her watch. "Ready?"

"Ready? To foretell my successor?"

"For breakfast. I told your mom we'd be down by seven."

"You . . . told my mom?"

"Well, sure, but all I told her was that we were going to have sex, nothing about talking to the aliens."

His mother was surprisingly happy that Luz was joining him for breakfast. She served them bacon, toast, and eggs, with orange juice. It was a thoroughly normal meal, not like many he'd demanded in the past. He refrained from singing, from eating with his hands, from marching around the table leading an invisible band.

"That was a bite of toast, two of egg, then a sip of juice. The

Kanjarians are going to discover a comet heading for their moon colony and successfully divert it."

"Agreed? I mean yes, agreed," said another voice.

Eager Young Space Cadet chimed in. "That—sounds right."

Luz paused with a bit of egg on her fork. "Nice work; you're getting them to agree."

Mister Miserable said, "Pfft, hardly. It means the Minnidee are about to enter a new dark age."

Luz grimaced.

Paul slammed his glass down, sloshing juice over half the table. "Why can't they just leave me alone!"

There was a babble of voices as each alien tried to decipher his outburst. This, and the crestfallen look on Luz's face, finally convinced him they were not colluding to trick him in some way.

He grabbed a rag and began to mop up the spill. "How do I fix this? What do I do?"

"Go through a normal day for once," said Luz. "Do just exactly what a normal high schooler would do. Don't make weird choices, or too many or too few of them. Just be what you would have been if they hadn't come along."

"I'm not sure I know how."

"You were pretty normal with me last night. Maybe we could go through the rest of the day together."

None of the aliens spoke, but the buzz in his head intensified. It was like they were all holding their breaths, whichever ones of them breathed.

"Okay," he said, feeling oddly light-headed.

Paul screwed it up. How could he not? Normal was as alien to him as his voices. When the aliens distracted him from catching a pass during football practice he screamed at them for three minutes straight. His teammates took it in stride, but it sent the voices into a several-hour argument.

He spoiled the next day, too, and the one after that, but each became easier with Luz's help. She made lists of normal activities, she met him between classes, she got him involved in a perfectly ordinary snowball fight. She distracted him from the aliens, the government agents, and the documentary crew that suddenly showed up.

She kissed him in a perfectly ordinary way that to him felt utterly unique.

The next Friday evening came at last. All day his aliens had been largely in sync. Even Mister Miserable made fewer dissenting predictions. Luz agreed to go out with him again.

Satan Claus looked, sounded, and smelled the same as always. Paul grimaced at all three, but it had seemed like the natural place to go.

"Your dad didn't seem as upset to see me this time," he said.

She looked down and played with her hair. She'd braided it tonight. "I had a talk with him. I said you and I would probably be seeing each other pretty often."

Paul grinned. "I'd like that." He barely listened as his backing group conferred over his statement.

"There is one thing, though." She looked up again. "I'm applying to M.I.T. and I want to know if you've made a decision about college yet."

Some part of Paul panicked. Panicked because he wasn't ready for any question of this magnitude. Panicked because the day had been going so well. Panicked because he wanted to say sure, he was going to Boston too, and at the same time wanted to say he was going anywhere *but* there. If the aliens accompanied him to a new city, a large one, his life would be a whole new hell. The decreasingly rational part of his brain knew he was going to have to say something soon.

"I don't know," he said, reaching to take her hand. "It's . . . too

early to say. But I think I'd like to talk it over with you some more.
A lot more."

Her hand moved, the fingers shifting to intertwine with his.

"YOW!" The mental shout was so loud that people dropped
forks, glasses, and slices of pizza all around the restaurant. Luz and
Paul jerked apart.

"It's the next prophet!"

"It is! I can see where she is."

Mister Miserable said, "I'm certain she'll be just delighted."

Paul ignored the angry stares, scarcely daring to breathe.
"That's it? If they found the next prophet they—they're really going to go?"

"It looks so. I did help them refine the procedure for narrowing
down the possible locations based on where earlier ones were."

A horrible notion popped into Paul's head. "*You* aren't the next
prophet, are you?"

"Oh god no." She waggled her eyebrows at him. "She's three
thousand light years away."

"Three thousand and fourteen," said The Grinch.

"There. See?"

"Boston?" he said, reaching for her hand. "I'm not sure my
grades are good enough, but I think I'd like to try."

The aliens stayed with them through dinner and dancing, making their usual pronouncements in multi-part harmony. Paul drove
Luz home and parked.

"It's time to say goodbye to Paul," said The Grinch. One by one
the voices came to say their farewells, each one fading out at the
end of their sentences. The last one to leave was Mister Miserable.

"Take care of yourself, Paul. Try not to screw up too much.
We'll be seeing you." His voice grew fainter, then disappeared, taking with it the buzz in his head.

Paul straightened up in his seat, looking out the windshield at
a perfectly ordinary midnight. Finally he could relax.

Then he frowned. "Be seeing you?"

Luz, uncharacteristically, giggled. Just a little, like something had tickled her in an unexpected place.

The buzz returned.

"Hello, Luz," said Eager Young Space Cadet. "Ready to take notes on the next prophet?"

Paul bit his lower lip. "You're—? Don't tell me you're going thousands of light years away?"

"Of course not, silly," she said. "My body will be right here. I'll just be another voice in the new prophet's head."

PERDITA, MEANING LOST

When Ailsa and her husband the King lost their firstborn daughter to the fairy maid who spun gold from heather, they were broken in heart and sought their child in every way they knew. They offered rewards, they sent freemen and peasants to scour the country, diplomats and spies to seek her in other lands, and rogues and privateers to search the seas. They consulted witches and wizards, wise crones and learned fools, and even a talking horse who truth to tell was not nearly so intelligent as he claimed.

As hard as the king and his men searched, Queen Ailsa searched all the more, for it was her indolence that had lost the child. All she had done was guess several names a day until time ran out. Too late she heeded a chambermaid repeating a song the spinner had sung. By then her daughter was gone.

When all else failed, the queen took her knowledge that her daughter's taker was an elf and sought the ways one might enter Faery. She explored mushroom circles and toadstool rings, she followed elusive birdsong through rock-strewn hills for mile after countless mile, she talked to every animal she encountered and was generous to every wanderer she met. For she had been raised on fables.

Nothing availed, and too quickly the days turned into weeks and the weeks into months. A year slipped away. Despair and resignation whelmed every seeker but one. The King gently pressed her to attend to affairs of state and to bear them another child.

For four seasons Ailsa had started each day's search saying, "Today is the day I shall find my daughter." Now, on the anniversary of her loss, she whispered, "Today I must find my daughter or count her lost forever." From dawn's first light to dusk's last she tramped the countryside, seeking a sign she was not pursuing a fool's errand. The king himself brought her a lantern, silently embraced her, and offered his aid. When she shook her head he quietly bade her look until the bells tolled the midnight hour.

More desperately she cast about as time passed. When the first chime of the church bell sounded, it startled her so, she dropped the lantern. By its dying light she saw a glint of answering reflection. Falling to her knees, she felt for the thing that had gleamed, and finding it she lifted it. The bell tolled on. Four. Five. Six. The thing was an arrow, its head a triangle of some untarnished metal. Seven. Eight. Nine. She caught her breath; she knew what it was. Ten. Eleven. She said it aloud.

"Elf-shot."

A great stillness fell on the world. No twelfth tolling of the bell arrived to herald the newborn day. She stood, knowing which direction to go. The arrowhead she held pointed the way. All she must do was retrace the arrow's flight, and this she did. Turning about, she walked, her tread heavy after so long a day and half the night of tramping. After, it must be said, a solid year of trudging.

It seemed she walked another day and a night through that rock-strewn landscape, though no sun rose to light her way. By the meager illumination of the slivered moon and stars she near-felt her way along, stumbling over rock and gorse alike. There was no path. All she could do was convince herself she walked a straight line. Finally before her rose a hill, taller than most, with a natural archway sheltering a declining passage. Breath halting, heart thudding, she stepped through.

The way was narrow, but smooth. The walls closed in. After the first few steps the tunnel was black as her hair. Still she walked.

When it seemed she must have traveled still another day and half a night, she felt a cobweb brush her face. Reaching up, she brushed it away, to find herself sweeping aside the curtain of night.

Before her blazed a summer sun, around her were fields of golden flowers and proud trees. Behind her she saw no tunnel.

She stood still, looking about to memorize her surroundings. The legends suggested she must retrace her steps exactly to find her way home. She saw no path nearby, no house, no castle. It was as if she had appeared newborn in the middle of this field. Finally she tramped a circle of grass down and placed the elf-shot in its center, its tip pointing the opposite of the way she had been facing when first she saw Faery.

For Faery this must be.

In the distance to her right a sea glittered. For lack of a better plan she turned and walked toward it. Human habitations were often to be found near water, and she hoped the Seelie Court would choose likewise. She could only hope that she would happen on the realm of those inclined to help humans first, rather than the Unseelie Court.

By and by she noticed that sound was returning. Birds sang, insects droned. Just as a pang of homesickness struck her, she heard a child's cry. She caught her breath, then gathered up her skirts to hasten toward the sound.

Rounding a tree, she saw a white bundle on the ground. Approaching, she found it to be a child no more than a few days old. It was swaddled in a cloth that covered its body and head. The cloth appeared to be pinned with thorns; the iron pins she had used on her baby's clothes would be unwelcome here. Looking around, she saw no caretaker, certainly no child-stealing elf.

Her daughter would be a year old, would she not? Ailsa had sought her for that long a time. But no, she had heard tales of wayfarers caught in Faery for a few days who returned to find all they knew dead and gone. Mayhap her daughter really had only just arrived.

At any rate, this was a child in need, and no succor to hand 'cept Ailsa's. She stepped forward and picked up the child. She felt clumsy holding it. She had not carried her child for a very long time.

Then she realized this baby weighed much less than a child should. Her hand trembled as she reached to uncover the child's head.

Pointed ears and devilish green eyes met her gaze. "Won't you help me, mother?" said the child in a mature voice. "Let me suckle. Carry me back to your home and hearth. I'll be ever so good."

To her credit, Ailsa did not drop the changeling. "No," she said calmly. "I seek my own baby." She pursed her lips briefly, unsure of her duty. "I hope to find aid at the Seelie Court. Perhaps I could find someone to help you there."

"That is not necessary." The child threw off the rest of the cloth and stood before her, transformed into a perfect homunculus. Without wings, he lifted away from her arms to hover. "Your kindness is appreciated, though. You pursue the correct course." He flew up and away.

She plodded on, deeply tired. Cresting a hill, she saw an old woman resting in the shade of an apple tree, if indeed these silvery fruit were apples.

The beldame hailed her. "Your pardon, Great Queen. Can you reach me one of these apples, that I might assuage my hunger?"

The weary traveler knew this was no simple crone, not here in the land of the Fey. Doubtless she was some elf come to try her conviction or her knowledge or her kindness. Then a darker thought came to her. What if this was her daughter, grown old in only a year? The crone's long lank hair draped her shoulders much as Ailsa's did, and there seemed a reflection of her husband's strong blocky hands in the gnarled ones that reached up to her.

Drawing near, Ailsa plucked an apple. The sight and scent of it set her stomach to grumbling. Once it was in her hand, desire for the apple grew a hundredfold. And yet, the craving was as nothing next to her wish to see her daughter once more. Ailsa handed it down to the woman, who rewarded her with a gap-toothed grin.

"Thank you, Wise Ruler," she said. "Why not try one for your-

self? A single taste will satisfy all desire." She worried a bite out
of it.

"Thank you, aged mother. I am only a visitor here, and would
not wish a longer stay." She well knew the fate of those who ate the
products of Faery, and had worried long and deeply how to carry
her daughter home. That was a rainbow she'd cross when she came
to it.

"I see you have studied the legends." The old woman turned
jade eyes of such ageless perception on Ailsa that she knew this
could not be her daughter. "Your wisdom does you credit. You are
on the correct path."

Dipping her chin as one queen would to another, Ailsa passed
onward. She saw that she was quite close to the sea, and that a
pavilion of golden cloth had been raised on the shore. She walked
toward it.

A dozen feet from the entrance she found a girl perhaps ten
years of age crouched on hands and knees, running her fingers
through the sand. From marks between the child and the tent, Ailsa
perceived she had been at this pastime for a long while.

"Hello," said the queen, crouching.

"Who are you?" asked the girl, not looking up.

"I am a mother seeking her lost daughter. An elf stole her a
year ago."

"I know an elf," said the girl, combing the sand with a wide
sweep of one arm, then the other. She glanced back at the pavilion,
then moved to an unmarked spot. "I know many elves. There is one
I call mother, and she has not left Faery since I was a babe."

"What are you doing?"

The girl sat back on her haunches and regarded Ailsa suspi-
ciously. "I am searching for iron, that I might rid the land of it.
Visitors from the human realm can be very clumsy, sometimes on
purpose. You don't carry any, do you?"

"No, for I well know it harms the Fair Ones." Now that the
girl was looking at her, the queen saw how her midnight-black hair

framed a face so like her own, how the girl's sulky expression so matched the one she saw at times in the mirror. "Girl, what is your name?"

"You are not to know my secret name, for names have power." The girl folded her hands in her lap. "My given name is Perdita, meaning—"

"Meaning 'Lost.' I know." The seeker crouched across from the sought. "Perdita, you are my daughter. You were brought here a year ago, but time has passed differently for you." She smiled. "I have come to take you home."

"Why?"

Ailsa blinked. "Why? Because you are my child, because your father and I and all our subjects have searched for you high and low, because you are our heir and our heart!"

Perdita leaned a little forward to search her face. "But why would you take me away from the life I know? Pardon the saying of it, but I do not know you."

Ailsa was struck silent. Of all the obstacles she had expected, an unwilling child was the last. Finally she said, "An elf stole you away from me. I have already lost many years of your life."

"I am not your possession." The child went back to sweeping the sand.

The queen straightened to her feet. Anger flared. "Listen, child—" she said. "You are our daughter. We are responsible for you, as you will be for our kingdom once you are an adult." She extended a hand. "Come along."

Perdita looked up at her with troubled eyes. "I have responsibilities here," she said.

"Sweeping sand?" Ailsa looked around at Faerie, which seemed so still it might be holding its breath. "You should be learning to rule a kingdom, not be forced into such menial tasks."

"You mistake me," said the girl. "I hunt metal because it causes pain to those I love. These duties you say I have? I renounce them." For the first time she raised her voice. "I want nothing of your world, or of you!"

Shaken, the queen dropped her hand back to her side. What could she do? Persuasion did not avail, neither did appeals to obligation nor outright command. The child had met logic with logic, duty with duty, passion with passion.

Doubtless she would counter force with force, and besides that was no way to treat a treasure. Ailsa felt a growing admiration for the person her babe was becoming.

And with that, she knew her quest was done. Perdita was no longer lost.

The queen dropped to her knees. "Daughter," she said. "I am happy you have found welcome here. Please, know that I am your mother, and that I would have named you 'Máel.' Use it if you wish, it is how I will remember you."

There was a moment of utter silence. Ailsa's ears rang as if she had stood next to the blacksmith for an afternoon.

The child swallowed, and when she looked up at Ailsa there was a sheen of tears in her eyes. "I was wrong," she said. "There is the one thing I will have from you." She reached, and touched her fingertips to the queen's knee for a moment. She whispered "Máel" so softly her lips merely formed the name.

Ailsa put her hand on the sand to push herself to her feet. Something stabbed her thumb. When she pulled her hand up, she saw hanging from it an iron pin, exactly like the ones she had used on her baby's clothes.

Pulling it out, she held it up, saying, "How clumsy of some human."

"Farewell, mother," said her daughter. "If you please, you could take that pin, and these, back with you." Máel passed over a bit of cloth on which sat a small mound of similar pins.

Feeling healed in the heart, if only a little, Ailsa walked away. She looked back twice. The first time, she caught her daughter's gaze. The second, Máel had gone back to combing the sand. The queen smiled ruefully and walked on.

Queen Ailsa went away to be with her husband the King. They raised twin children, a girl and boy, said to be so wise and so kind that it was as if they were elf-touched. The queen slipped away from the castle once a year at just before midnight, but her departures were little remarked. She was known for finding her own way.

RAKE AND WREN

R ake stalked the city of Amblemere under a full moon. Cut-
purses and alleybashers took in her size and her surefooted,
lithe stride, then turned aside seeking easier prey. Her half-feral
gaze roved past shuttered shops and darkened houses as she padded on bare feet through the slush and around the refuse clogging
the steeply cobbled streets. Her left hand never strayed far from
the hilt of the short blade at her belt. Despite her fierce demean-
or, Rake was hopeful. Anything could be had in Amblemere for a
price, short of a dragon or a slave.

The city wrapped itself around the mountain known as Merely,
one of the middling-sized peaks in a range that marched away to
north and south as far as anyone had ever traveled. Taller mountains cradled the city to east and west, so that much of it was in
shadow all the day through. One of the few trading routes between
the forest cities to the east and the Iron Kingdoms of the west
passed through Amblemere.

Reaching a cross street, Rake paused at the susurrus of conversation coming from a lighted doorway. She walked to it. Looking
in, she saw an alehouse with a half-dozen men nodding over their
drinks at a long table, and a bartender making desultory conversation with a hunchback at the bar. An enchanted bull's head glowed
from above the bottles, bathing the room in dusky light.

"Hullo?" said Rake, crossing in three strides to the bar.

The barkeep looked around. "Hello yourself. Welcome to the
Bull and Bucket. What can I get you?" he asked. "We have beer."

Rake blinked. "Yours is the only open place I've seen. I was hoping for some information."

"Here is all the information you need. We're a beer shop. We serve beer. Would you like a beer?"

At her sides, Rake's fingers curled.

The hunchback chuckled, interrupting the rising tide of Rake's anger. "I'll buy the young warrior a pint. Sit down, ah—"

"Rake."

"Sit down then, Rake," the man repeated. "I'm Kearn." He seated himself at a smaller table. Such was his affliction that his head was pushed forward so he stared up under beetled eyebrows at Rake. When they were duly supplied with mugs, he prompted, "Information, you said?"

Rake sipped and made a face. "Yes. I need a healer, one who's open tonight."

"Healer. Well, there's any number who see folk of a night. Babies come at any hour, as do accidents." Kearn looked Rake up and down. "But you seem as innocent of the one as of the other. Perhaps it's for someone else?"

She begrudged answering, but saw the man counted conversation as barter. "For me."

"This is hardly the time of night to find a reputable doctor."

Rake took a breath, a sip, and shuddered. "Thank you for the swill, then. I'll be on my way."

Kearn puffed out a laugh. "Well now, and well again. If you are in such a rush, I'll tell you there are three wakeful doctors not so far away. One values coin over sleep, another adores to be seen helping the poor, and the third can't resist a daunting challenge."

The house was huge, one of many in a run-down quarter of the city. Both sides of the street were packed cheek-by-jowl with imposing mansions that leaned crazily against one another, each appearing more decrepit than its neighbors. Missing windows, exposed timbers, and holes in roofs told a story of a street gone long past seed. Everyone of worth must have moved uphill to better lodgings.

Rake counted three houses from the corner, as she'd been told. Like all the houses nearby, this one had no grounds, no high wall, just empty windows peering jaggedly down on her.

Advancing to knock at the door, some hunter's instinct made her aware she was being watched. She paused, then turned in a circle, eager to make her readiness for combat known.

A throat cleared itself above her. For a moment she wondered if there were flying people here, as she'd heard there were in the mountains, but when she looked up she saw a middle-aged woman in a gray robe sitting on the eaves of the house she'd been about to visit.

"Are you the healer who lives here?" she said, peering up at the woman. "My name is Rake, and I am in need of one."

"Wrennet is my name," the woman replied. "Or Wren. I'm busy at the moment. Do you suppose you could move aside a pace or two?"

Rake looked down at the cobblestoned street, no different in composition from anywhere else she'd walked. She was about to speak when Wren forestalled her.

"Oh, never mind. I suppose there's room."

And with that the woman named Wren launched herself from the roof peak, spreading her arms as Rake might have were she diving into water. She hit a projecting beam and tumbled down like a flung ragdoll.

Rake took an involuntary step back, and the woman smashed into the cobbles head first, splitting open her skull and splattering her with blood and brain matter.

Repulsed, wondering if she were going to be blamed for this madwoman's death, Rake took a step back. Then she berated herself for a coward. This was far from the only time she'd seen death. She'd even caused a few, and were she to take the blame for this one it would only be justice delayed.

Rake crouched next to the woman, ready to pick her up, to carry her . . . where? Taking a dead healer to another healer seemed redundant. Too, her own remaining time was much too brief. Her quandary was cut short when the blood and brains on her clothes, on the ground nearby, all flew into Wren's head. A faint red glow came from the wound as it knit itself away to a scar. With a huge gasp, Wren opened her eyes.

"What in Bella's Hells?" said Rake.

Wren focused on her, though there was still a distant look in her eyes, as if she'd seen something given few to behold and fewer to return having witnessed. She smiled, her every muscle relaxed. Rake had seen happy drunks look this way.

"What are you?" Rake made ready to attack, to defend, to she didn't know what.

"You called me a healer," said Wren. "It's what I do, and it's what I am." She sat up, holding out a hand for Rake to pull her up. The younger woman automatically did so. She noted scars criss-crossing the woman's head and face, her arms and hands. This was hardly the first death she'd suffered—or enjoyed—apparently.

Wren winced, looking down at her leg. "Death I can get over instantly, but a broken leg takes time. The gods laugh." She looked up at Rake. "Would you carry me inside?"

Nodding, Rake easily hefted the woman. She walked to the house, where Wren tapped once on the door. It opened itself. "Enter in safety," she said.

Rake stepped over the sill, feeling a chill run through her. There was some kind of magic in operation, its malign influence held in abeyance by Wren's knock, or her words, or likely both. She looked around, expecting to see a once-magnificent entry hall. Instead, the walls were bare stone, and very near. She seemed to be in a small room, lit only by moon- and starlight entering the door and windows on either side. She looked out one window, and found herself staring directly into the mansion next door. She would have sworn the house she was in extended another thirty paces to its outside wall.

There was a pallet on the floor near a chamber pot and a small mound of clothes. One wall near the door hosted a set of shelves holding a number of jars. Rake turned a slow circle, then set Wren on the bed.

The healer was obviously amused. She lit a candle with a gesture. "You haven't visited a pouch mansion before, have you?" she asked.

Rake shook her head.

"You've heard of shacks that are bigger on the inside? Carriages a score of people can ride?" At Rake's nod, she said, "That space has to come from somewhere."

"Poor horse."

"What? Oh, the horse that has to pull such a carriage. I hadn't considered that; I expect the load is lightened somehow." She ducked her head to one side, considering Rake. "Most people are more impressed by the feat than concerned for beasts."

"I am not most people."

"Which my amazing powers of perception has determined is also true of most other people as well." Wren gasped as her leg straightened itself with a sound very like the crack that had accompanied its breaking. "Aiyaa. I am not fond of this slow healing. Well, Rake, it is late, and I am tired. Perhaps we should address your difficulty in the morning."

"The morning won't do. What I need—" Rake frowned, then squatted by Wren's bed. "I need a cure for being a werewolf."

Wren blinked, then motioned with her chin up at the full moon gazing through a hole in her roof. "Aren't you a bit late?"

"Very. It is when the sun comes up that I will become a wolf."

"That is contrary to how I heard the curse works."

"So says the healer who relishes killing herself from time to time." Rake too looked at the moon, then back to Wren. "Suffice to say that when I was four years old I bit the werewolf that had just killed my family. I am only woman the three nights of the full moon. Rather than destroy me in turn, the werewolf took me and raised me as her own child. I watched out for her when she was Changed, and she did the same for me. She was killed by a hunter three nights ago, and I've used the nights since to seek someone like you."

"You are uncommonly well-spoken for someone who's only been a thinking person three days out of every month."

"Mada, my foster mother, was a philosopher," said Rake. "She talked. A lot."

"So at daybreak you will turn into a ravening animal? In the middle of Amblemere?" Wren shook her head. "You place far too much faith in healers."

"Call it desperation, not faith."

"In a few hours I'll call it death. Yours, as well as a few others, for it would not be the first time the local guard has faced monsters."

"Can you help? Or do I use my few hours in search of another?"

"Let me think."

Wren's gaze wandered to her rack of bottled elixirs. She shook her head once, then twice, and finally took up a knife to carve symbols into her own flesh. The cuts healed in practically no time, but the act of intentional self-mutilation offended Rake's stomach. She stood and turned to walk to a window. The protective spell tingled as she put her hands on the sill.

"Is it so hard to cure me? You can do magic," said Rake. "I saw you, conjuring at the door, and lighting the candle."

"I merely encourage, not force. The door is meant to be a way to enter, and the candle is crafted to light a room." Wren shook her head again. "You are animal more of the time than human. If I use my meager skill, and if it actually succeeds, you are far more likely to become fully animal."

Rake ran a hand over her chin and behind her neck, a little surprised not to find fur already growing there. "Do you know of anyone else who can help me? Or should I start making my way out of the city? Best I not be here when I turn."

"Something comes to mind." Wren tapped her forehead, kept

tapping. "Something. What is it? Ah, of course, the Chain!"

"Chain?"

"The Chain of Rannle. A magical trifle, a gift from Bella's Consort to the first Rannle three hundred years ago. Most important for you, the Chain is said to bind a person's form to that when it is donned. Jord Rannle put it on when he was fifteen, and looked the same age until he was strangled with it sixty years later."

"It's not a cure," said Rake slowly, "but should do until I can find one, provided I put it on before sunrise. Where do I find this Chain? And how much would it cost, do you think?" She held up a small bag. "I do not have much money."

"Keep your coins. Mistress Sel wouldn't let the Chain go for a dragon's ransom."

Rake cocked her head. "Then what do you propose?"

Upmount was a far richer neighborhood for all that the houses were of modest size. With newfound knowledge Rake peered at the occasional lit window to see that rooms extended away to distances such modesty wouldn't normally accommodate.

"There," said Wren, jerking her head at one particular house. "Don't look too closely at it. Sel has wards that warn her when someone pays undue attention to what's hers."

Rake let her gaze pass over the two-story building. "How are we to burgle a place we're not supposed to look at?"

"With this." Rake handed her a piece of cloth.

"This is obviously some ingenious new lockpick I had not previously happened across."

"It's a blindfold."

"Of course it is."

"Put it on."

"Most certainly not."

"You are the one who had so little time I couldn't detail our plan sufficiently." Wren made a gesture. "This will help." A spark of amber light drifted from her forefinger to Rake's forehead.

The city around them plunged into Rake's awareness. Scents battered at her nose: horse and human and canine manure, the scrubby pines that grew throughout Amblemere, puke, the rising dough an early baker was making. Sounds attacked her ears: thousands of people and animals breathing, a clatter of hooves several streets away, snoring, the beating of Wren's heart. Even the feel of each cobble was distinct beneath her feet.

"What did you do?" Rake's voice came out half-growl.

"I encouraged your wolfly senses." Wren calmly tied a second strip of cloth over her own eyes. "Now put on your blindfold and lead us inside."

As she picked her surefooted way to Sel's abode, Wren's hand in hers, Rake marveled at how quickly she grew accustomed to her enhanced senses. There were times she had heard and smelled with such acuity, when she was about to turn, when she was done with turning.

She smelled something amiss just as her foot came down on a sharp point sticking up from the ground. She pulled back at once, her tough sole still intact.

"What?" breathed Wren.

Rake pulled the cloth up to risk a brief look. "Poison, I think," she said. "I smelled it, and felt what might be an upturned arrowhead or caltrop. But I see nothing, only the flagstones leading to the house's window."

"That's new." Wren knelt, bringing her face nearer the ground. "But Mistress Sel always did excel at hiding things." She sniffed. "Boilblood, I think." Impressed, she added, "It's an excellent poison. I can't neutralize it without various expensive unguents. If these were indeed arrowheads, I could likely make them shoot upwards into the air, but that would not improve our situation."

"It would certainly not." Rake turned her head. "There is an approaching pair of people on horseback. Perhaps hireswords making rounds. So far they are not alarmed, but I expect they will see us soon."

"We could retreat. Find boards or something else to lay over these spikes."

Rake tugged Wren to her feet. "No time," she said, sweeping the smaller woman into her arms. "On we go."

Wren made a small noise of protest, but lay still.

Sweeping the area in front of her with each leg alternately, Rake located every poisoned tip without puncturing her skin. Moments later they were below a window. She set Wren down. "No poison next to the house," she said. "That would be a boon to the gardeners, if there were gardens." She paused, listening to the clop-clop of the oncoming horsemen. "I remember that these walls are whitewashed. We'll stand out like scrolls in a blind man's house. This would be much easier if the mansion were surrounded by a wall. We could work hidden."

"It would also be easier if Mistress Sel walked up to you and handed you the Chain." Wren stood, feeling up the wall until she found the sealed window. "Open, please." Nothing happened.

"Wren—"

"Hush, please. Let sister work." Miming the lifting of a latch, she said, "Open, damn you."

The horses slowed, about to turn a nearby corner. "Wrennet," growled Rake. Giving up on words, she lifted the healer and dashed with her around the side of the house. When they were safely out of sight of the street, she set Wren down again.

"Ouch."

"What?"

"A spike." Wren put a hand on Rake's arm. "I don't feel well." Then she collapsed.

"Wren?" Rake tore her blindfold off. As before, she could not see any of the offending spikes, but a spreading pool of blood gave witness to the woman's having fallen on several of them. She picked Wren up and, keeping close to the building, made her way to an unornamented side door. She pounded on it. "Let us in! Poisoned woman here!"

Every few moments, she pounded again. Something flew at her from behind, and she whirled. The blood was peeling itself off the flagstones and gliding toward Wren. The healer stirred in her arms, moaning.

"Ai," said Rake. "Oh, I forgot. Wren will be so peeved."

The door opened.

Mistress Sel looked all of twenty years old. She wore a silk robe inscribed with silver threads in cabalistic patterns. Ink-dark hair fell straight down her back and drooped over most of her face. One pale eye regarded her intruders.

The moment Rake set Wren down, restraints had wrapped themselves around her. Though they were invisible, it felt as if she were tied with very ordinary rope. Sel appeared to have an obsession with invisibility.

Wren writhed on the floor in front of her. She steamed, moaning. Vapor issued from her mouth, her ears and nose, even seeped from under her fingernails. Boilblood was aptly named. Rake expected she was happy to be unconscious, insofar as someone can be happy *while* unconscious.

Mistress Sel cleared her throat. When Rake looked at her, she said, "Just passing by? Lost cat? Venom aficionado?"

"Can you help her?"

"The woman in the blindfold? But who can she be?" Sel crouched to tug the cloth off Wren's eyes and feigned surprise. "Why, it's my former pupil, Wrennet Bymarket."

"But you already knew that." Rake noted the growl was back in her voice. "I guessed she knew you personally when she said something about your spikes being new."

Sel stood back up. She nudged Wren with a foot. "I could rent her out as a stove. She's warming the room quite nicely."

"Can you," repeated Rake, "help her?"

"She'll help herself soon enough."

"How did you know she would recover?" Rake bit her lip, feeling like a rabbit who'd escaped one trap only to fall into another. "You called her your pupil. You're the one who cursed her with immortality."

"Curse?" Sel seemed genuinely shocked. "Dear girl, nothing is more of a boon than living forever. With time, all becomes clear. Everything comes to she who waits."

"But the Chain makes you immortal." Rake bit her tongue.

"Ah. So that's your goal." Sel put a hand over a lump behind her robe between her breasts. "Rannle's Chain has served me well, but it could always be removed. Stolen. Damaged. Depleted somehow. I even have to sleep in the wretched thing, lest I return to my true age. It's damn heavy." She raised her hands over her head, cracking the joints in her shoulders. "It's better when the ability is innate." The eyes she once more turned on Wren were age-old. "I didn't understand the blessing I conferred on Mistress Bymarket was limited to a single use."

"Too bad."

"No, quite good. See, she's hidden from me these many decades. I thank you for returning her to me. It was my spell that made her immortal, and one thing I certainly know how to do is annul my own spell. Sadly, her many deaths would then catch up to her, but she's far outlived her usefulness as a spell subject."

Rake felt strength filling her limbs. She already had the enhanced senses that went with looming wolfliness. Soon enough she'd snap these ropes, tear this witch apart, possibly kill Wren a time or two (who would recover a time or two), then be killed in turn by Amblemere's guards. It would be worth the cost. All she had to do was keep Sel talking for some time more.

"Hidden from you? She was in the same city! You must not have looked very hard."

"I searched diligently, at least for the first few decades." Sel frowned. "'Tis true I spent more on spies who searched far and wide than on ones who could look nearby. It seemed logical she'd travel far. Ah well. We often most easily miss that which is under our noses." She brightened. "But no harm done! She's here now, and look, she steams less. I expect she'll be awake soon. I do so want her to be awake while I'm tearing eternity away from her. It certainly looks like she's accomplished little enough with it."

Wren opened her eyes. "I've done enough." The twisting gesture she made was minimal, almost lazy.

"Hk." Sel clutched her throat. "Hrk!"

Rake flexed, strained at her bonds, and felt her shoulder dislocate. "Angh!" Then her full strength came to her, and she—like Wren—healed. The bone popped back into place. "Ow-rrr!" She snapped the invisible ropes.

Leaping across the room, Rake tore at Mistress Sel's robe. The Chain was twisted, knotting itself in its eagerness to strangle its owner. Below her, Wren strained to turn her hand further.

Sel's right hand began to glow, and she drew it back as if to throw an invisible dagger at her former pupil. Rake, her hands still not yet paws, grabbed the Chain, winding it with all her strength.

With a crack, Mistress Sel's head flopped to one side, and she slumped to the floor. Rake panted. Wren climbed unsteadily to her feet, unwrapped the Chain from the dead sorceress's neck, and pulled it over Rake's head.

The next night, all the regulars at the Bull and Bucket held their collective breaths when Rake and Wren entered. Wren they respected, because she had leashed a monster. Rake they feared, because she was that monster. The demi-werewolf padded two-legged along at the other end of the leash. It was attached to a golden chain that ran around her neck.

Wren sat at a table, and after a moment spent dubiously eyeing a chair, Rake perched on it, legs drawn up under her. She tapped the leash, and Wren duly untied it from the Chain.

"Are you sure about this place?" said Wren. "It doesn't seem all that clean." After a moment, she said, "Or friendly."

"We don't have to spend all evening," rumbled her companion. "I just owe a man a beer." Looking around, she beckoned to Kearn. "He's the one told me how to find you."

The hunchback sidled forward. When Rake nodded to a chair, he seated himself. Looking first at woman, then at half-wolf, he said, "I know that voice, raspier though it may be. You're the young warrior of last night."

"I am. You recall I was seeking a healer."

"Aye. And her I know."

Wren inclined her head. "Thank you for sending her to me," she said. "Her dilemma and mine fit together well."

Rake nodded. "You did well, Kearn. I wanted to thank you." She signaled for a round of drinks with a forepaw whose toes were almost as long as her former fingers. The bar returned to normal.

"This—" And Kearn gestured with both hands at Rake's fur-covered body. "This is what you wanted healed?"

"It was. As it happened, it was sufficient for the change to be arrested when my mind was still whole." The beer arrived. One whiff was enough for Rake to turn up her nose; it was even less appetizing to a wolf's sense of smell. Wren happily drained her cup and pulled Rake's across the table to her own place.

Kearn sipped. "What do you intend next?"

"For now, waiting until the next full moon, when I may return to my preferred form. For the future: I haven't thought that far, not yet. One thing, though, whatever I do will likely be done outside the city. Even with this sham leash, the locals seem a bit too fearful." She looked at her friend. "What do you say, Wren? Care to go a-venturing?"

Wren gave it some thought. She put her cup back on the table. "I do. Indeed I would rather do nothing else."

Rake reached for the leash and clumsily tied it around the Chain. "Well now, and well again." She nodded to Kearn, who smiled and raised his cup in reply.

THE ADVOCATE

While desimmed, the Advocate watched her room for several milliseconds, awaiting her guests. The Surgeon simmed in first, followed by the two Pediatricians. The male and female had convincingly human images, but the ungendered baby doctor's sim was barely a step above a wireframe.

Three milliseconds after the medical programs simmed in, the Advocate displayed her own public image. She was compact, elegant, and powerfully built, with nearly invisible pointers arching away from her fingers to databases, law libraries, and utility subroutines. For this appointment she appeared as a short dark-haired Eurasian female. She carried a briefcase.

"You would be the Advocate?" The Surgeon was a popular genotype, a gray-haired caucasian oozing assurance and wisdom from every pixel. He smoothed the jaggies in his best suit and smiled behind his white beard, putting out his hand. "I don't understand the meaning of this summons."

A dozen utilities swooped in to sniff and paw at the hand, then at all three doctors. To the Advocate's guests they were rippling 2-D plates of mostly numbers: sensing programs. The simpler Peddie stood very still under their examination, and the Surgeon swatted at one. To the Advocate they were part and parcel of her environment, to be accepted with equanimity—she had programmed that into herself.

Still, she waved them off. Only techies—Programmers and Networkers—carried viruses of such subtlety as to affect her domain or herself. These were not that sort of program; they were a kind she was seeing more and more often lately: manufactured intellects that ran hardware for humans.

Desimming the briefcase to free both hands, she took the proffered hand and said, "Yes, I am your Advocate. You are Surgeon Harper, Peddie Jarrod, and Peddie Loll. Please—" She indicated the chairs set next to the blankwall of her office. "Please make yourselves comfortable."

Loll had started to extend a hand when the Advocate's swept toward the transparent wall. She pulled it back quickly, then said, "Will this take long? I have to—" She ducked her head, golden ringlets of fibrous hair swirling, before continuing in a subdued tone. "—to check my messages."

"But you don't have any, do you?" The Advocate ushered her to a chair next to those already occupied by the other two medical programs. "That's why you're all here."

The Surgeon had been mesmerized by the rippling flow of data swirling beyond the room's blankwall. It was a measure of the Advocate's importance that she had been accorded space so near a major data node. Surgeon Harper closed his eyes and deliberately turned his back on the wall before opening them again. "We're for purging, then?"

"Purging?" echoed Loll. Jarrod merely turned milky white eyes on the Advocate.

"We don't call it 'purging;' we call it 'clean-up.'" The Advocate resimmed her briefcase. At times like this it was best to fall back on human mannerisms, comfortable metaphors for them all. She sat at her desk and put the case down gently on it.

"You three have been summoned here by a utility that monitors your usage. Any nonsentient program that isn't accessed at least once every three months is automatically archived, taken offline. You three are intelligent, so you have to sit dormant for a full year before you're brought before me." She ran a hand over the dark surface of her briefcase, and since she was paying attention to it the rich smell of leather filled the virtual room. The Advocate looked at the Surgeon. "With manufactured intellects we prefer to say 'cleaning-up.'"

"Whatever term you use, it's murder."

"Wait." Loll leaned toward her, blue eyes searching. Her sim was the image of a young human child dressed in a sun-yellow dress. "You're going to kill us?"

"No." There was very little embarrassment in her makeup, just several megs of empathy. She stared straight back at the peddie. "My function is to judge you. If I find you have no useful function, I call clean-up programs that inactivate your intellect and store your code. My hope is to find some way you may still function."

"End this now." Peddie Jarrod had been silent and now the Advocate suspected she knew why. Its voice was an unmodulated tone underlaid with a mechanical whine. Annoying. "Wipe me. I have only the one function."

Never before had a program asked to be offlined. In her surprise, the Advocate reached through the top of her briefcase rather than opening it. She produced three folders. "That is for me to decide. Your source code is here, your history and original documentation. If we can—"

"No." The Peddie deliberately desimmed, leaving only its voice behind. "I exist only to deliver human babies. There are no more to bring into the world. Wipe me."

Harper glared at the vacant seat Jarrod had occupied, as if he could bring the Peddie back by force of outraged indignation. It was an immense breach of etiquette not to sim your image while speaking.

Loll edged away from the vacant seat, one pudgy hand to her mouth, but her eyes were still on the Advocate. "No more babies? That can't be; humans are all around." She glanced out the window; obviously searching for and finding the darting strands that were humans navigating the net.

"These humans are all virtual," the Advocate said gently. "They have left their bodies behind, perhaps permanently. But—" She spoke to the empty space behind which Jarrod lurked. "There is no proof that *all* humans have left their bodies behind. It may be that medical programs will still be needed."

"Not so," rasped the pediatrician. "I know it. No humans, thus no babies, thus no call for me." The Advocate's empathy subroutines provided a sense of regret that might not have existed in the voice. "I ask a third time. Wipe me."

The Advocate tapped one of the folders she held against the desk in thought, then dropped it into a file tray. "As you wish." As always, she felt the desire to say something more. Humans had their rituals for the passing of their own kind; could not programs be accorded a similar respect? The thought passed quickly—her capacity for introspection had been limited.

For entire milliseconds none of them spoke. Then Loll shivered and reached a tentative hand toward the empty chair. "That's all? He's gone?"

"Yes," said the Surgeon, transferring his glare to the Advocate. "He is gone, as we soon will be. The Advocate here killed it." He placed both hands on the desk, his fingers rippling through a dozen simms of medical instruments, each sharper than the last. "Examine me next," he said, cocking his head back so his full white beard swept up toward the remaining two file folders, then back down to his chest. "Let's get this mummery over with. Tell me what I can do to be useful. To stay alive."

The Advocate opened the Surgeon's folder. Search routines darted out of her fingers and swept through the file. As she had feared, Harper's source code was immense, whole orders of magnitude more complex than the Advocate's. But then, the Surgeon had been created to interact with humans; he had a built-in psychological sensing subroutine, anatomy texts for every eventuality, instant access to human languages the Advocate had never heard of, and more—much more, and all delicately, deliberately interwoven to make him a powerful, if pedantic, program. A program, the Advocate mused, that had been lying fallow for a year, twiddling his scalpels.

Swimming her way out of Harper's code, the Advocate shook her head and closed the file. Seconds had passed, a millennia for her kind.

Loll was gazing out his blankwall at a routing node, but she turned back to them when Harper barked, "Well?"

The Advocate lacked the circumlocutions the Surgeon might have used when talking to a human. The mental well-being of made intellects was not deemed worth the added complexity. "You have no other uses," she said.

"What?" Harper roared the word. "How dare you judge me? I have *work* to do!" He flushed a deep red, clothes and all, and leaped to his feet. Refusing to acknowledge the validity of the simmed desk, he waded through it toward the Advocate, his hands masses of edged metal. He gouged the briefcase in passing, he sliced the folders, he swept the file trays to the floor. And then he got to the Advocate, waiting quietly behind her desk.

Clamping the Advocate's shoulder with one hand, the Surgeon pulled her to her feet. His other hand spun at the wrist, whirling a dozen bladed fingers in a configuration the Advocate doubted would have been used in a human operating gallery. The scalpels dug into her stomach and whined against her ribs, shearing bony chips off to spatter into the mass of flesh, blood, and gore spewing across the floor. With a final spasmodic thrust the Surgeon cut through the Advocate's backbone. He was left holding the top half of the Advocate's body; the rest slumped into and then off the chair. Harper's blades whined to a stop.

The Advocate was fascinated. Her simmed body normally contained none of the anatomical detail now decorating the floor. It had all been supplied, externally, by the doctor. Looking politely at Harper, she asked, "Are you done?"

The Surgeon set the Advocate's upper body carefully into her chair. Stepping around the desk, he dropped into his own chair and stared down at his hands.

The Advocate resimmed her body, then her desk and its contents. Everything was back in its proper shape and place; she was reassuringly empty inside once more. Room, desk, chairs, bodies, they were all merely polite fictions overlaying the commands and data that made up all programs.

"You're insane," the Advocate said calmly. "If there are any humans out there, I couldn't allow you to operate on them."

"Oh, I would never—" Harper began, then stopped. He began idly transforming his hands into bandages, needles, and thermometers.

"I'm sorry." The Advocate took the Surgeon's file and placed it in a file drawer.

There was none of Jarrod's quiet disappearance about Harper's erasure. As he felt his routines being wiped, his pointers being forcibly clipped, the Surgeon rippled and vomited a stream of cotton batting that disappeared before it hit the floor. He lost complexity. First to go were his clothes. Next his skin lost its texture before dissolving to reveal his wireframe. Harper turned his fingers this way and that in impossible directions, then disappeared completely.

Loll had drawn both legs up into her chair and wrapped her arms around them. She stared at the Advocate in horror.

"I'm sorry you had to see that," she said. And she was; the peddie's anguish and loathing were sharper instruments than any Harper had ever wielded.

"Let's look at your file," she said, dimming her empathy. Loll didn't move.

The young pediatrician was simpler than the Surgeon had been, although still more complex than the Advocate. Again, it was the necessity of dealing with humans that made her such a complicated program. But there was about her code a looseness, a flexibility. Turning to the documentation, she read for a full second before surfacing.

"Loll?" Her voice was as gentle as ever, but something about it made Loll look up and minutely loosen her arms. "You were created from a general purpose medical program. With some tweaking here and there, you could be a general practitioner, not a specialist."

The program snorted, a surprisingly adult sound to come from such an immature frame. "Doctor to whom? I believe Jarrod. There are no more humans to treat. If you make me one I'll just be back in here next year, as mad as Harper was."

Privately, the Advocate agreed. A year was a very long amount of time for one of their kind. If they couldn't perform the jobs they'd been built to do, it was *too* long.

"You don't know that the humans are all gone. Jarrod was so antiquated, he could have been as crazy as Harper."

"Don't humor me. If humanity still wore their bodies, we'd have been called. I was a damn good pediatrician. How many doctors have you had to purge lately?"

"Clean up," she said automatically, then wondered suddenly why the euphemism was so important when she was always blunt in her decisions. Some programmer's prudishness, she supposed. "You're right." The images of hundreds, thousands of medical programs paraded past her memory, accompanied by chefs and garment workers and gravediggers and zookeepers. They had all been wiped. Salespeople, teachers, psychiatrists—those professions had their analogous duties in the net and had been reprogrammed; while geologists, truck drivers, and assembly-line workers were all needed to keep realworld hardware running and expanding. Those programs had all been reintegrated. The Advocate, who had never seen offline reality, and never would, had a vision of a physical reality unpopulated by humans, and forcibly banished it. She longed to stifle her empathy entirely, so there would be no reoccurrence of the vision, but it was too much a part of her.

She picked up Loll's folder and tapped it against the desk. Then she set it down again. "Loll? Are you able to sim the way Harper could? Can you sim body parts and—what's that stuff?—blood and all?"

"Of course," the program said. "Part of the job is being able to communicate the diagnosis." She created another Loll in the chair next to her, building her up from bones to muscles to circulatory system to skin to clothes. The doppelganger blinked slowly, in synch with Loll, at the Advocate.

"I think I have a job for you," she said, and explained.

"But I'm a doctor!" Loll wailed.

"Not any more," she said, and sent the program to be trimmed and reprogrammed. She thought—or it could have been her empathy again—that she saw Loll smile just before she disappeared.

"I'd call that stretching things," said a voice. "But I think she'll still make a fine historical education program."

"Jarrod?"

"You knew I was human." The peddie simmed into her office, then fleshed and clothed himself. All of the clothing, from slippers to cape, were deepest black, to match the skin. He was an old black male with a deeply rich voice. Only his pale, pale eyes stood out in stark contrast. "I'm curious: where did I go wrong? I thought I'd fooled you and those two medical programs, but you never dispatched your utilities after me."

"Not mine," the Advocate corrected. "I only judge, I don't carry out the sentence." She paused to consider Jarrod's question. "I didn't know for sure. It was a guess." If awed in the presence of a human for the first time, the Advocate was still candid. "Your actions were contrary to my expectation. Self-preservation is built into all AIs."

"So you dispatched me to a holding register that only a human could have overridden. Clever."

"What are you doing here?" The Advocate waved a hand that included her desk, the chairs, and her whole office. "If I had actually sent you to be cleaned up, you might not have escaped. Is this a test?"

"Of sorts." Jarrod sat on one corner of the Advocate's desk and reached for the remaining folder sitting on it, Loll's file, awaiting the Advocate's final notes. From thin air came the programs again, the utilities that guarded the Advocate's private files.

From Jarrod swarmed defensive programs of his own, deeply

complex and powerful. Enveloped in plates of shimmering symbols, chuckling, the human withdrew his hand. The utilities winked out one by one, hers, then his, the last one rippling in a way that suggested a certain mathematical menace.

"Why didn't your guard dogs protect you from Harper?" he asked.

"Guard—? Oh, my security programs? They could tell he only meant harm against my sim, not to me."

"Was he really insane, then?"

"Yes." The Advocate picked up Loll's file and dipped a finger into it, recording her judgement in the case. "Harper was out of control, using methods that could have resulted in the death of humans, had he used them in the physical world." Finishing with her notes, the Advocate flipped the folder toward her blankwall, where it joined a stream of purple-flagged datastreams heading for storage. "That's assuming there are people still out there. Were you joking when you said all humans had chosen the virtual world?"

"There's only here for us now." Jarrod was staring out the wall as the doctors had done before him, quick eyes darting here and there separating human minds from manufactured intellects from utilities and data. "We messed up the real world something awful. Those who could go online did. That—" His voice faltered. "That was about ten percent of the population, mostly from developed countries. Being in here is driving some of those people—well, a little bit wild."

"Isn't this what you wanted? This artificial computerized environment where you can do anything?" The Advocate consulted an internal chronometer to find she had several seconds before her interview with another trio of programs.

"That's never been a good idea where humans are concerned. We usually like to push the limits, find out what we're not allowed to do." Jarrod looked back around at the Advocate. "What some humans are doing online to each others' minds is a lot like what Harper was doing to your sim."

The Advocate felt suddenly slowed down, as if her clock were skipping every other millisecond. "That's—against the law."

"It is, isn't it?" Jarrod held up a hand, and in it appeared a file folder. "That's why we've decided that we humans need a judge. Somebody with experience online, somebody compassionate but just. Best of all, somebody not human.

"Now don't worry," said the man. "We're sending you out for some modifications. This won't hurt a bit."

Edd sold me "The Corsair and the Lady" for my magazine
Talebones *in 2008. The year after, I closed the magazine
so I could spend more time on the book press and my own
writing. (In other words, Edd didn't kill the magazine!) It
was wonderful to read this story again for Edd's collection.
Edd reminds me that Moors remember 1492 for different
reasons than Europeans and Americans. Ferdinand and
Isabella ousted Muslims from Granada. They expelled the
Jews, ending religious diversity in Spain. Slavery in the
New World and rich treasure ships proved tempting targets
for vengeful or mercenary Moorish pirates, though as in this
story, corsairs might run afoul of bad weather, fell accidents,
unearthly forces, or all three.*

—Patrick Swenson

Patrick runs Fairwood Press, which gives you totally cool
story collections—like this one! He is the author of the novels
The Ultra Thin Man and *The Ultra Big Sleep*. He ran *Talebones*
magazine for 14 years, and he now runs the popular Rainforest
Writers Village writers retreat in Quinault, Washington.

THE CORSAIR
AND THE LADY

S ailors screamed and plunged into the roiling waters. Male slaves chained below beseeched someone to unfetter them, while their wives and children, free on deck as was the custom, died with the rest. The sails tumbled into the ocean, dragging the *Naseema* onto its side. Water rushed into her every hatch.

Masud gripped the wheel as his ship heeled, helpless to avert disaster. Torrential rain bombarded him and obscured the worst of the catastrophe. Death was at hand. "To Allah we belong, and to Him do we return," he shrieked into the gale, releasing his grip. He slid down the deck, but instead of falling into open water he fetched up against a tangle of ropes. They caught him about the middle, dangling him between the ocean and the side of his foundering ship. His arms, outflung, were likewise snared, keeping him from reaching the knife at his belt.

Cannons, each of a different design, captured from scores of European ships, tore loose from their stays and fell with mighty splashes into the water. Sheltered from the rain by his ship, Masud became aware of a strange presence. He looked up, peering into the stormswept night.

Were the fires on the *Naseema* being reflected somehow? Masud had seen mirages of the sea before. But no, the fires he saw were small, contained. Then, barely heard over the pounding rain, came the sound of voices, foreign voices, and Masud laughed at the absurdity.

It was the English merchant ship he had pursued, just as lost, driven by contrary winds back upon her hunter. "Ware ship!" he heard, and, "Hard aport!"

Much too late, the foreign ship's helm responded, swinging wide of where Masud hung, to ram the *Naseema* amidships. The jarring crunch shook him from his snarl of ropes, and he fell into the cool water. His breath held, Masud hung below surface for a long moment. Which way was up? He couldn't tell in the dark. At any moment he might be ground between the two ships or carried to the bottom by debris. Faint splashes must be the sound of men, cannons, cargo, and rigging falling into the water.

Like most sailors, he could not swim. He panicked. Flailing about, he spent all his energy fighting his sodden clothes. Then a measure of calm stole over him, and he stilled. His chest ached, and almost, almost, he gave up.

Some concussion above threw flaming shards of wood in all directions. He felt the water pulse against him, saw that in one direction there was a faint light. Awkwardly, lungs bursting, he kicked and scooped at the water.

Finally his head broke the surface, and he gasped. Water slopped into his open mouth. In the dull light of a hundred dying embers he saw great slabs of wood that had once been proud ships slipping beneath the windswept waves. Kicking, he tried to keep his head in the air but knew it was only a matter of time before he too slipped down to oblivion.

A new light kindled, wavered, then grew into a steady flame in the dwindling rain. It was close to the water and not far from Masud. Hope grew in him even as his limbs began to give out, causing him to slip under more frequently. He inhaled some water, coughed, then cried out, "Here! Over here, in the Name of the Prophet!"

He coughed again, and slipped down. Feebly, he waved his arms, but every movement seemed to carry him farther from the surface. He was so tired. It was too much trouble to continue flailing. He sank, gazing up at his trail of bubbles as they fled to the surface in the growing light. Salt stung his eyes, and he blinked, then closed them. So tired.

Something touched his hand, quested down his arm, and

wrapped around him. Even as oblivion washed over him, he felt his body being lifted. Could this be the way to Paradise?

Some time later Masud lifted a heavy eyelid to see a blazing sun assaulting the calm ocean. Lassitude swathed him as it had when he'd been young and his sisters covered him in warm sand. One hand trailed over the side of whatever he floated on, and he drew it toward his face to shake a few drops onto his parched cheek.

His stomach knotted. Masud turned on his side, into a fetal position. The pain came in pulses. He gasped shallowly, then one wave shook him from head to foot and he vomited, bringing up a small puddle of salty water and bile.

The pain subsided, and recent memories surfaced.

Sinking. Drowning. Had he been near death? Masud took a deep shuddering breath. He felt wood beneath him; he was on a raft. It bobbed on the gentle sea. A small raft, then.

"Are you quite done?"

The voice was female, low-pitched but sharp. Masud heaved himself painfully into a sitting position, opening his eyes.

The raft, a piece of deck, was almost twenty cubits wide and twice that in length, large enough for two dozen people to stand on with ease. The wood was lighter in color than the *Naseema*'s had been, a mark of the British preoccupation with using sandstone to scrub their decks. Over the far end hung a sheet—no, part of a sail—supported by two upright timbers that had been part of a doorframe. The far end of the sail trailed in the water. He saw no one there.

If the voice had been a product of his imagination, who had made the shelter? More to the point, why had his rescuer not dragged him into that shelter and out of this hellish sun? Already he felt his skin tightening where it was not covered by the tatters of his clothing.

Dragging himself to hands and knees, he crawled to the lean-to.

"Welcome to my humble abode," said the voice.

Masud stopped with one hand on a doorpost. It had been the same voice and it definitely came from beneath the sail in front of him. He sat back on his heels and peered into shadow. He saw the woman at last.

White on white, she was. Skin of the palest ivory, hair as white as only the highest clouds could be, and dressed in robes the color of milk. She wore no veil. Only her pink eyes and black pupils stood out against the eggshell expanse of the sail. He stared, just stared, for a long moment.

"If you had not pulled me from the water, I would have drowned," said Masud. "I thank you for saving me."

"I?" she replied. "I could not save you. It is I who will depend on you to rescue me." She drew aside a fold of her robe to reveal an ankle cruelly shackled, the skin cracked and scorched around it. When he drew closer to see that a chain attached the shackle to an iron bolt that doubtless pierced the raft through, she said, "As you see, this chain anchors me to the center of our raft. I cannot reach the water in any direction."

"Where is my rescuer, then?"

"We are quite alone." She swept a hand in a gesture that encompassed the raft. "There is only me, and my fine ship, formerly bound for the British colonies, now quite at sea."

Masud sat in what remained of the doorway, breathing heavily. The memory came again, clearer, of something supple wrapping around him and lifting him to the surface. He tried to imagine some octopus or kraken saving his life, and shook his head. "Thank you, then, for kindling a light so that I had the hope to cry out."

"Again, I am not the one to praise." A faint smile touched her lips. "I neglected to bring a torch when the ship exploded beneath me."

Masud frowned. "How did you survive such violence?"

The smile and a slight shrug were his only answers.

"Did you see the explosion?"

"No, it happened inside the ship, in part of it that was mostly under water. I was kept in a cage with several other women, and when the ship was destroyed all the others were swept away."

"They were not chained?" asked Masud.

"I had not been a good prisoner. Twice I almost escaped to throw myself overboard." She shook the chain. "Would that I could wrap it around that fat slaver captain's throat."

"May I see?" Masud asked, getting to his feet, and at her nod he took hold of the chain. He tugged, lightly at first, then setting his feet he pulled with as much strength as he could muster. He soon grew light-headed, and stopped to examine the chain and its anchor once more. Both were secure. "This will take tools," he murmured. He set the chain down. Drawing his knife, he handed it to her. "This may be insufficient to the task, but please accept it."

"Thank you," she said.

He saw that he'd lifted her leg when he'd pulled on the chain, and that her robe had slipped up perhaps more than it ought. He ran an experienced eye over her form, and judged she would be worth any other four slaves' price. He licked parched lips with a parched tongue.

She rearranged the cloth, then said, "We have not introduced ourselves. I am al-Sayyida Raziya bint Faraj."

"Masud el-Allali ibn Harun," he said, sitting back against one of the posts. It seemed prudent not to mention his captaincy given her antipathy toward slavers. There was no telling how long they would be raftmates.

"*Marhaba*," she said. "Greetings." Taking up his knife, she dug its point into the deck next to the bolt to which she was chained. The tough wood resisted, giving up only the tiniest of slivers.

"*Marhaba*, al-Sayyida." Looking at the placid ocean, he thought of his ship, and of its crew and cargo. The Prophet forbade excessive displays of grief, so he turned away from Raziya for a time. A few other pieces of flotsam bobbed here and there, but he saw none large enough to support whoever had rescued him, none that might shelter other survivors.

Later, Masud looked at the generous shadows cast by the posts and sail. "Do you think it is afternoon? Or morning still?"

"Afternoon. You were unconscious for so long that I thought you dead. Is it time for afternoon prayer?"

He nodded. Getting up, he moved out of the shadow of the sail and squinted at the horizon in all directions. "I see no land," he said, "but if the sun is setting then east is in that direction." He pointed, and stood in Niyyat, the first position for prayer. She stood, covered her head with a scrap torn from the hem of her robe, and they both said the Asr, the third of the daily prayers. When he prostrated himself halfway through, Masud wished he still had the rug from his quarters. The deck was very hard, but the mat was no doubt at the bottom of the ocean.

"Now," he said when he was finished. "Let us see what is to be done."

"I do not think we are likely to be rescued."

"No, and if we were it could as easily be by the French, or English. Or Spanish." The last was said with a scowl. "We'd be enslaved and on our way to the New World." Masud's stomach grumbled. "We might soon wish for any sort of rescue, even an unfortunate one, if we do not find something to eat."

"Do not say that. If I am released, I would sooner die than be a slave again."

Once more he thought of the price she might bring on the block. Words, on the contrary, cost nothing. "You are free, al-Sayyida. I say it."

His feeble jest was rewarded with a dazzling smile. "Then there remains nothing more than to find food and water, locate land, and have our fine ship raise sail so it may transport us home."

"You make it sound easy."

"Allah will provide."

There was not a breath of wind. Were there one, their shelter might actually suffice as a sail, if the winds came from the west. Steering was out of the question, unless—

Masud stepped to the side of their craft. The edge of the raft was splintered, so he pulled away two thin pieces of wood each as long as his leg. He might be able to fashion a simple spritsail from parts of the cloth. Setting aside concerns of navigation for the nonce, he turned to the need for food and water.

Peering into the water, he saw several fish the size of his fist darting here and there. Perhaps the storm had churned up the water so that food for the fish was plentiful? Then, a darker thought, perhaps the death of his men had provided food for these schools. Taking off his shirt, he fashioned a makeshift net by tying it to the wooden pieces, and passed it slowly through the water. He caught no fish the first twenty attempts, but finally brought up a small silver one.

"Success of a sort, my lady."

She looked at it, her eyes narrowed. He would have interpreted her expression as distaste save that she leaned toward him and half-extended a hand. "If there are eggs, I would be delighted to have them," she said. "I leave the rest to you."

Masud picked up his knife from where Raziya had put it, and slit the belly of the fish. He cut out and threw away the stomach and entrails. There were eggs, in greater abundance than he had ever seen before. He held the splayed fish out to her. Raziya dug her fingers under the mass of eggs and raised them to her lips. He turned away and set to with his knife once more to the delicate sound of her licking them from her hands.

The rest of the afternoon passed in idle conversation and unsuccessful fishing. The lady kept to one side of the shade and he to the other. He spoke of his city Salee, of his tower by the sea, and of the wonders he'd seen while sailing al-Bahr al-Muhit, the all-encompassing ocean called "Atlantic" by Europeans. She spoke of a mountain surrounded by water, of an estate shrouded in clouds, of a joyous carefree youth.

They touched on matters less joyful. She of the devastation wrought on her estate by slavers, he of his wife.

"Her name was Naseema," he said. "She was a potter in Casablanca, and when I saw her I knew my heart was lost. I sent intermediaries to seek her permission to marry. The wedding was a grand affair. She was anointed with sandalwood and chameli oils, and was clad in cherry red bridal robes, while I wore silks and a turban. She was so happy." He sighed. "The marriage lasted five years. I carried her to Salee, to my tower, away from her family, then left her there while I went to sea. It's hardly unusual for a voyage to last six months or more. I was successful, and smothered her in treasures, but what she wanted most was rarely there for her. I was absent, I had no family to keep her company, and my tower is too far from the city for her to visit. Even when I was home, my eyes were ever turned to the ocean. Naseema asked for the tools to turn pots, but I in my pride saw no reason for her to ply a trade when I provided so abundantly for her. At the end she said it was not to her I had lost my heart, but to the deeps."

In a trick of the evening light Raziya's eyes appeared emerald as the turbulent ocean. She leaned toward him. "What happened?"

Masud's pause was brief, but to him it seemed vast. Finally, he simply said, "She walked into the sea," and fell into a silence she shared until it was time for Maghrib, the evening prayer.

He awoke to miracles. Aching, he stirred, then opened his eyes when Raziya said, "Come! See what has happened during the night."

Moments later Masud stood at the edge of their raft gazing out at a fortune. Bobbing here and there in the sea were casks, boxes, and chests, obviously scraps from the *Naseema* and the merchant ship that had been released by some chance from their watery sepulchers. From what he could see marked on a few of the nearer items, it was water, wine, jerky, dried fruit, everything they could wish to live on for at least the next few weeks. They would survive until a provident wind arose to drive them home. He had only to retrieve them.

"Why do you hesitate?" asked Raziya.

Fear scrabbling at his throat, Masud looked down at the water lapping against the side of the raft. "I cannot swim," he said.

"This from a man who loves the ocean more than his wife?" Usually before her tone had been light or polite, but now it bit at him as it had when he had first awoken on the raft. "You may rest assured they will not swim to our fine ship."

His back to her, Masud made his own voice flat. "It is not necessary to shame me into action. There is more than one way to slaughter a goat." And taking up his shirt-and-scrap-wood net from the day before, he dipped it into the ocean. Rowing from one side of the raft only turned it in a circle, and Raziya was unable to reach either side of it to help paddle, so he was reduced to sculling his crude oar back and forth in the water from the rear of their vessel. It was past Dhuhr, the mid-day prayer, before he hauled aboard all the debris they could find, an even twenty pieces.

"This is truly amazing," said Masud, massaging his shoulder where it met his neck.

"*Masha'allah*," she said. "God has willed it to be so."

"Let us assuage our thirst first." Picking up a heavy unlabeled box, he smashed it down on the top of a keg of water. He peeled back a slat, then tipped it to pour a precious stream into Raziya's cupped hands. She sipped. "Delicious," she said.

When they were done, he used a corner of his hammering box to bash in the lid of a box of dried dates. They ate their fill. Finished, they returned to their shade and gave thanks.

Raziya fingered the chain that ran from her ankle to the deck. "Would it be too much to hope that one of these boxes that has no label contains a better tool to free me?"

"Perhaps," he said. "Or there may be something else that will help us in some way. An inventory of our cargo seems to be in order." And he battered open in turn the four remaining unlabeled boxes. Coffee beans he found, and couscous, and a large water-logged drum. The fourth container, one that had jingled attractively, turned out to hold a score of small copper teacups.

She eyed them sardonically. "Now we may drink our water in style."

Masud dragged the first two containers he had opened, the dates and the water, into their shelter. The first he set on the second to minimize evaporation. About to sit, he paused, then retrieved a teacup and handed it to Raziya. "A gift," he said.

Raziya tilted her face down to look at it, and it might only have been the angle, but it seemed she smiled. She ran a finger around the cup's rim, and he heard a faint high note, as if it were crystal. She lifted her finger. "Look." The note came again, and he followed the line of her finger, peering into the near-dusk sky to see a bird flying away up high. It cried again.

"We seem almost too fortunate," said Masud. "Gulls never stray far from shore. That means we've a good chance of reaching land. All I crave now is a wind out of the west."

"Perhaps tomorrow," murmured Raziya. She took up his now-dulled knife and dug at the deepening hole she had carved around the bolt.

A bit later, at the urging of his bowels, he walked to the far end of the raft, and squatted so that his shit would fall into the ocean. He wiped himself off with his left hand then dipped it into the water to clean it. Straightening, he walked back to Raziya's shelter and looked around it, lips pursed. Did she not excrete at all, he wondered. Little things about her seemed so very wrong, while taken all in all she was exciting, enticing, even elemental. The wisest course of action would be to act as if she were what she seemed. Whether witch, spirit, or demon, it contented her to think she fooled him, and confronting her would lead to unpleasant consequences. More unpleasant for him than for her, he suspected.

He lay awake for hours that night, staring at the stars. Finally sleeping, he dreamed of his dead wife Naseema, how he had first seen her with her hands covered in clay. She smeared it on herself, on her arms, her legs, her face. The clay dried white, and she became Raziya then, her eyes pale rubies, then vivid emeralds.

Masud woke to a cool predawn breeze. He sat up and dragged stiff fingers through salt-thickened hair. He glanced at a barely visible Raziya, still asleep on her side of the raft. Rising, he padded to his stack of boxes.

As he'd expected, the raft had wheeled around so the sail they used as a shelter was serving as sail once more. He couldn't see where they were going without pulling up on the cloth where it trailed in the water.

He said the Fajr, the dawn prayer, just loudly enough to wake Raziya. It would be a sin to let her sleep through the appointed time, and it comforted him to know she was capable of saying the words. Few evil beings could. She stirred as he was dismantling the drum.

"What are you doing?" she said.

Masud tested the rope he'd stripped off the drum, then tied knots in it at regular intervals. "We were twelve days out of Agadir, but we tacked back and forth looking for prey—" He bit his lip. "The ship I was on did, I mean. And then that storm blew the English ship back on us, so we were heading westward for some time." He paid his knotted rope out the side of the raft, counting seconds as it was pulled back in their slight wake. "We're well south of the straits of Gibraltar, so unless we strike the island of Porto Santo we'll make landfall—" He paused. "Within a hundred leagues of El Jadida."

"You are most learned in the ways of the sea," she said. "Tell me. Did you deal in drums?"

"Drums?"

"Or in spices? Teacups, perhaps?"

"None of those," he said, "Why do you ask?"

"You seemed in no hurry to deliver your cargo, shipping it with a corsair." Raziya stood, and turned her back on him to face east. She glanced toward the brightest part of the sail, which hid the rising sun. "Time for prayer, I think." She began to recite the Fajr.

"Indeed," muttered Masud. She suspected him, he knew, of being a slaver. But could she do anything about it even if she did know? He decided he was in no hurry for an answer to that question.

He reeled in his rope. They weren't making much headway. He stepped to the center of the raft to open a box of tangerines. The corner crumpled on the box he was using to pound in the top of the fruit container. He started to set it aside, then sat on a nearby cask to pick at the box's wood. It was unlabeled. He'd been so busy using it as a mallet the day before that he'd forgotten it was one he'd intended opening. He pried up the top.

The moment Masud uncovered the contents Raziya's prayer recitation faltered. He looked up. She was facing east, away from him. After a moment she continued.

Masud rubbed a hand along his developing beard, then reached in and lifted a richly embroidered prayer rug. A dozen questions chased each other through his mind, but he quelled them. Instead, he carried the rug to the shelter and set it in front of Raziya as she was getting to her knees.

"Another gift," she said. A brief dazzling smile, and she kneeled on it.

Over breakfast, Masud said, "I believe we'll land in Salee tomorrow."

She paused while peeling a tangerine. "You seemed to think we would make landfall elsewhere a short time ago."

"It can't fail. There's no place I'd rather be, so that is where we will make landfall." The words tumbled out. "I'm lucky. Couldn't be luckier. Everything we've needed has just fallen into our laps. This raft, food, water, even those prayer rugs; it's a miracle, a whole handful of miracles!" He held his breath. The gift of the rugs, for gift it must be, made him think she smiled on him.

"It is, Captain."

"That's why we'll hit Salee. I wouldn't be surprised if we floated right up next to my tower in time for—what did you call me?" His mouth went dry.

"Captain. You are captain of this vessel, yes?"

"Why me? I am merely a poor sailor now; you should be captain."

"If I were captain, this ship would go where *I* willed. To my estate in the clouds, were there anything left there for me."

"Al-Sayyida Raziya, I wish I could find your home and restore it to you." A long moment followed. "Until such time, you—you could consider my home yours."

Raziya stared at him and Masud felt as if he were standing with one foot on the raft and the other hovering over the ocean. She looked down and smiled. "I've not had a better offer in a very long time."

"I'm serious."

"So am I." She pulled away a wedge of tangerine and handed it to him. "Let us see what the morrow brings."

That afternoon, after the Asr prayer, Masud lifted the bottom of their sail. On the eastern horizon he saw a long smudged line where sea met sky. "Home," he said. "If this wind holds we will indeed be there tomorrow." Then he peered into a leaden west. "But I worry. Those rain clouds will be over us in a few minutes."

"Will our shelter not keep us dry?"

"No. The wind will sweep the rain under its upper edge." As he spoke, the breeze freshened, bearing an energizing scent and billowing up the sail's bottom edge. "And if the wind increases it will blow the sail straight out, making it useless, and could sweep our provisions overboard or—" He envisioned their raft rolling over, himself thrown into the ocean and Raziya being held under because her chain was so short. It was difficult to tell which was the worst prospect.

"Raziya," he said, "There is something I would like you to know. I—have lied to you."

She turned to him, but said nothing.

He sat facing her. "I was the captain of the corsair. We chased the ship you were on for more than thirty hours. I didn't tell you because I feared you'd hate me for being a slaver."

"I did."

"You did?"

"I did hate you, because I knew who you were. Naseema, you said, was the name of your wife."

"It was."

Raziya stared at the sea, two fingers compulsively rubbing a link of her chain, and Masud suddenly remembered his dream of the night before, of his wife changing into her. Dread clutched at his vitals. Was Raziya a being sent by his dead wife to judge him and drag him to Jahannum? She glanced at his face, then away. "I was told that 'Naseema' was the name of the ship that so harried the slave ship. It would be too large a coincidence to think the two unrelated."

"'Did hate,' you said."

"I realized that in attacking the ship I was on, you freed me. Had you not, doubtless it would have avoided the worst of the storm, and I would still be on my way to a life of servitude in the British colonies. If I were inclined to worry that you would enslave me yourself, you forestalled that fear by giving me this knife—" she held it up, "—and by telling me that first day that I was free."

His heart lighter, Masud stepped out of the shelter to move their heaviest provisions to the center of the raft. The first fat drops of rain struck. He pulled three casks into their shelter. Lashing them together with the rope he'd recovered from the drum, he said, "If the sea gets rough, hold onto these, and so will I. We can at the least try not to be separated."

The rain increased, and the sea grew rougher. Raziya sat calmly digging at the raft's wood with her knife, while Masud tried to hold their sail in place. First one, then another box tumbled off their vessel. Dark clouds encompassed the sky, so that he could not tell when day left off and evening begun. The wind rose, whipping their cover so it lashed above them.

Raziya beckoned him, and Masud moved to put his ear near her mouth. "Time for the Maghrib," she said, and a trick of the storm brought the words clearly to his ear. Together they stood, then knelt, then prostrated themselves, to say the prayer.

The wind howled, and with a shriek their sail was torn away to disappear into the night. The raft pitched in the rising sea, so they could not even stand safely. Most of their provisions followed. Masud's heart sank. He could do nothing but hold on to Raziya. Before long, he found that she was holding him, too.

Perhaps he dreamed, or perhaps not, but there came a moment when the dark was split by lightning. The bolt shivered and split into a multitude of branches, then froze in the sky for one long minute. And he saw.

He saw his tower, his refuge. It squatted on its rocky foundation mere paces away. He need merely step off the raft and walk to it. He stared at the tower in superstitious wonder, and almost pulled away from Raziya. Almost he stood. Almost he walked back to his old life.

Instead he drew back into Raziya's embrace and closed his eyes until the horrible light dissolved and a world-destroying peal of thunder chased it into oblivion.

Some time later, it might have been one hour or could have been three, the elements gentled. The clouds above blew into shreds and a half-moon shone down on them. It was cold in the wake of the storm, and he shivered.

Raziya sat up. "Take off your clothes," she said.

He stared at her.

"I am serious," she said, opening her robe to reveal a sleeveless tunic and breeches. "You must keep warm." She pulled the tunic over her head.

"How will taking our clothes off keep us warm?" he asked, unlacing his tunic.

"You mistake me. I am sufficiently warm. It is you I'm concerned about."

When they were both nude she knelt next to him. She ran a hand across his cheek, and where it passed he felt her heat. The hand passed down his neck and across his chest. He stopped shivering.

"What are you doing?" he asked, half in a daze.

"Warming you," she said, holding her hair back with her other hand as she leaned over to kiss him.

It lacked an hour to sunrise, and already a rosy glow suffused the eastern sky. Masud put a hand to Raziya's head where it lay on his shoulder. He didn't know if she were awake or not. "Odd," he finally whispered.

She stirred. "Odd?"

"A half-day ago I was euphoric. I was sure that no ill fortune could touch me. Now we are living dead people, our food and water gone, and with no way to reach land." He laughed once. "And now I am just as euphoric, and sure we will find a way to survive, simply because Allah could not grant me your love only to snuff out our lives."

"Allah acts as Allah wills," she said. "However, in this case you are entirely correct."

"Ah," he said. "Then you are powerful enough to save us."

"I already have."

"You rescued me from the water, and you conjured the food and water."

"And more besides." She laid a hand over his heart, and he could feel the heat she emanated. "Those things happened because

I willed them. When the slave ship was destroyed, it killed my former—" A pause. "It killed that ship's captain. I told you last night
that you freed me, and I mean that literally. First by liberating me
from that ship, and then by saying the words the next day. I stayed
at first because my ankle was fastened to this raft, and we find it
difficult to release ourselves from physical bonds."

"I know what you are," he said, and stood to help her to her feet.
She put a hand on his shoulder, and he felt strength flow through
his body. As he had the first day, he grasped the chain that bound
her, and pulled. It seemed he had barely begun to tug when a pair
of links went flying, and she was free.

"Turn around," she said.

He did. Where before he would have sworn was blank ocean,
an island rose from the water into a mountain that pierced the
clouds far above.

"I said I had already saved us," she said. The raft nudged into
the sand at the mountain's base. A set of worn stone stairs led up
from the beach barely three steps away. "Shall we?"

Masud stepped to the edge of the vessel they'd lived on for the
past few days, then paused. She joined him, grinned up at him, then
held his arm while she stepped onto the sand.

The stairs circled the mountain, then they circled it again. And
again. He didn't even try to count them. Strangely, he did not grow
hungry or tired. It was enough just to walk at Raziya's side, up and
ever up, hearing the end of her broken chain ring against the steps.
With each step she seemed to gain in stature, a handsbreadth taller
than he, then two, then more.

And when they reached the top of the final flight, she towered
over him, near half again his height. They stood above the clouds
with a stunning vision spread out before them. A ruin sprawled
over the plateau. What had been a castle of white stone was now a
tumbledown wreck.

Raziya made a wide, slow gesture with one hand. "Behold, my
home."

Masud stepped forward, still gaping at the devastation. At last he said, "No English pirate did this."

"No," she said. "This was done a long—" she glanced at an enormous tree that had pushed its way through the rubble, "—long time ago. When the Jinn joined with Suleiman, he was not battling only earthly foes. We were confronting the Ifrit, and Shaitan himself. Our homes suffered."

"You and I are to live here?" Masud looked askance at the ruins.

"Oh, more than that." She stepped to face him and put her hands on his shoulders. "Much more. You're going to rebuild it. All of it."

"Me? I can't believe you saved me just to get a slave to restore your home."

"Don't say 'slave,'" she said, a grave expression on her face. "Never. I could fix this with one wave of my hand, but I won't. I'll be helping you. We just don't want the rebuilding to be done any time soon."

"Why not?"

"Remember your first wish?"

"A wish? The first, you say."

"On the first day you wished for a prayer mat, and I made one appear. Of course, I exceeded your desire a bit by also providing food and water. On the second day you wished for a wind from the west. And on the third, ah, on the third, do you recall what you said?"

He thought. "Something about finding your home?"

"Finding, and restoring it. Your wish will not be granted until that is complete. With me, you will be ever young and strong." She put her lips down close so he could feel her breath on his ear as she spoke again. "And how many centuries would it take to restore, do you think?"

ACKNOWLEDGEMENTS

When I went to the Clarion Science Fiction Writing Workshop, it was still being held at Michigan State University. I have my wife Amy to thank for suggesting I not go to Clarion West, based in my home town of Seattle. "You'll be too distracted," she said. "You'll be tempted to commute from home, and you'll want to get some things done around the house." Her excellent advice landed me at an intense six week course with nineteen dedicated writers and seven just as committed instructors: Terry Bisson, Karen Joy Fowler, Tim Powers, Geoff Ryman, Leslie What, Patricia C. Wrede and Patrick Nielsen Hayden.

One of my fellow students was Rudi Dornemann, who recruited me as one of the founding members of The Daily Cabal. For four years we presented a flash fiction story every weekday, taking turns along with a few later recruits. I wound up writing ninety stories for the Cabal, a serious challenge to my procrastinating nature.

An author, at least a short story author, can't survive without editors, and I've been blessed with some great ones. First and foremost, Gardner Dozois returned "Parachute Kid," saying he would gladly look at it again if I fixed one problem. I did. He did. It was exactly the fix the story needed.

Our writing group is top-notch. Members past and present include Amy Thomson, Laura Staley, Leslie Lightfoot, Chris Lightfoot, Joe Follansbee, Kara Dalkey, Liz Argall, Manny Frishberg and K. G. Anderson, accomplished writers all. Manny and I got together four years ago, and have written 23 stories together, no two of them the least bit alike. That's how we like it.

The Tai-Pan Literary & Arts Project hosted the other writing group that means a lot to me. Coordinators Gene Breshears and Michael Yust wrangled a bevy of writers who learned by reading our stories aloud. Frequent attendees included Chuck, Mark, Keith, Kristin, David, Jeff, Jeri Lynn, Sky, and J'wyl. They helped make these stories what they are.

In addition to Clarion, I enrolled in the Launchpad Astronomy Workshop along with Amy, and found it a helpful, valuable experience. Organizers/lecturers Michael Brotherton and Christian Ready were prepared and dynamic, whether we were discussing the seasons, the electromagnetic spectrum, or the "wow" signal.

Patrick Swenson has been a great editor, whether it was explaining how things are usually done, or tolerating my deviations from those norms. He also bought my story "The Corsair and the Lady" for his magazine *Talebones*.

Amy Thomson and I have been married for 23 years, happy years each and every one. We adopted Katie Vick in 1999, and she's been a joy.

Copious thank yous to everyone named above. You're all top-notch!

ABOUT THE AUTHOR

EDD VICK, the son of a pirate, is a recovering
Texan now living in Seattle with his wife, SF
novelist Amy Thomson, plus a dog, a cat, and
three or more chickens. He is a bookseller whose
library is a stuffed three-car garage. His stories
have appeared in *Analog*, *Asimov's*, *Year's Best SF*,
and about thirty other magazines and anthologies.

PUBLICATION HISTORY

"Moon Does Run" originally appeared in *Electric Velocipede* (2006); reprinted in *Year's Best SF 12*, ed David Hartwell and Kathryn Cramer (2007) | "Polaroid Land" originally appeared at *Andromeda Spaceways Inflight Magazine*, (2017) | "Eclipsing" originally appeared in *New Writings in the Fantastic* (2007) | "Hedging Witch" is previously unpublished and appears here for the first time | "Parachute Kid" originally appeared in *Asimov's* (2005) | "Silver and Scythe" originally appeared in *Wee Folk and Wise* (2015) | "Choice Cuts" originally appeared in *Electric Velocipede* (2004) | "Rebel the First and Only" originally appeared at *Baen's Universe* (2007) | "The Great Depth" originally appeared in *Stupefying Stories* (2015) | "Lydia's Last Wish" originally appeared in *Factor Four* (2019) | "Over the Hills and Far Away" is previously unpublished and appears here for the first time | "Guy, Sky High" originally appeared in *Kaleidotrope* (2007) | "Truer Love" originally appeared in *Northwest Passages* (2005) | "Call to Order" originally appeared in *After the Orange*, ed Manny Frishberg (2018) | "First Principles" originally appeared in *Asimov's* (2003) | "Ténéré" originally appeared at *Analog* (2017) | "The Compass" originally appeared in *Asimov's* (2005) | "Expeditionary Force" originally appeared in *Nonbinary Review* (2016) | "Innermost Box" is previously unpublished and appears here for the first time | "Prophet Motive" originally appeared in *Arcane Arts* (2017) | "Perdita, Meaning Lost" was originally brodcast on *Cast of Wonders* (2017) | "Rake and Wren" originally appeared at *Echoic-Mobile-Press* (2019), where it may be seen in interactive form | "The Advocate" is previously unpublished and appears here for the first time | "The Corsair and the Lady " originally appeared in *Talebones* (2008)

OTHER TITLES FROM FAIRWOOD PRESS

The Arcana of Maps
by Jessica Reisman
trade paper $17.99
ISBN: 978-1-933846-91-0

All Worlds are Real
by Susan Palwick
trade paper $17.99
ISBN: 978-1-933846-84-2

Mingus Fingers
by David Sandner & Jacob Weisman
small paperback paper: $8.00
ISBN: 978-1-933846-87-3

The Girls with the Kaleidoscope Eyes
by Howard V. Hendrix
trade paper: $17.99
ISBN: 978-1-933846-77-4

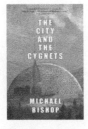

The City and the Cygnets
by Michael Bishop
trade paper $17.99
ISBN: 978-1-933846-78-1

*If Dragon's Mass Eve
Be Cold and Clear*
by Ken Scholes
small paperback: $8.99
ISBN: 978-1-933846-86-6

Amaryllis
by Carrie Vaughn
trade paper: $17.99
ISBN: 978-1-933846-62-0

On the Eyeball Floor
by Tina Connolly
trade paper: $17.99
ISBN: 978-1-933846-56-9

Find us at:
www.fairwoodpress.com
Bonney Lake, Washington

CPSIA information can be obtained
at www.ICGtesting.com
Printed in the USA
FFHW020845111119
56017365-61930FF